To my Family

Table of Contents

Prologue	9
Chapter 1	11
Chapter 2	21
Chapter 3	28
Chapter 4	33
Chapter 5	39
Chapter 6	44
Chapter 7	49
Chapter 8	55
Chapter 9	62
Chapter 10	67
Chapter 11	76
Chapter 12	81
Chapter 13	88
Chapter 14	93
Chapter 15	99
Chapter 16	108
Chapter 17	111

Chapter 18	120
Chapter 19	126
Chapter 20	129
Chapter 21	136
Chapter 22	141
Chapter 23	146
Chapter 24	150
Chapter 25	157
Chapter 26	161
Chapter 27	166
Chapter 28	171
Chapter 29	176
Chapter 30	183
Chapter 31	187
Chapter 32	193
Chapter 33	198
Chapter 34	205
Chapter 35	209
Chapter 36	212
Chapter 37	216
Chapter 38	219

Chapter 39	223
Chapter 40	226
Chapter 41	231
Chapter 42	237
Chapter 43	241
Chapter 44	246

Prologue

The Starry Night
Vincent van Gogh, Museum of Modern Art, New York.

Shame. A man could be ruled by it. It may not be of his making but passed on to him to carry. Or it could be something he has hidden and one day it becomes too much, he cannot hide or carry it any longer.

A sliver of a moon lights the ocean and the flicker of light from Tuskar Rock comes in flashes across the sea, a beacon of hope in the darkened skies. I wonder what other poor souls have the waves taken? Are they at peace now or do they still walk this Wexford Coastline searching for answers? Perhaps they are more like one of these sea shells under my feet, just a memory of a different time, a different place and a different man?

After the tears and the regrets will I just be someone who once was? A brother, a son, or a husband. I wonder how mother will handle the shame? She can't put a twist on this one. Shame, there it is again, my old enemy. I thought I was done with it then. November 1996. But here it is again, twenty years later, back to haunt me.

Sive, my life, my beautiful Sive. My heart is breaking with leaving you. This is not what I promised, will you think I abandoned you?

Maybe if there was a child things would look different. We put too much on hold, Sive. I thought I had it all sorted. The big plan. A child, imagine it, maybe even a little girl. She would look like you, black curls and dark eyes, like a fairy of long ago. When she would smile, she would take your breath away.

The first time I saw you, you took my breath away, like the beautiful Doolin coast that surrounded you. You are my everything. Please remember how we once were. When it's all over, will you go back to your beloved Burren and spend your days painting that rugged land, hating me for leaving? I can't bare to think of you being alone. Forgive me.

I have always loved the smell of the saltwater but now it smells of nothing, it's as if I am here yet not here, already gone. Will this be too much for you to carry Sive? I want you to be able to live your life, learn to love again.

I was here before, I should have told you but I couldn't. I was afraid you would see me differently. Maybe I have misjudged you, have I misjudged us? I should have trusted our marriage. What am I doing? Maybe it's not too late. What the hell am I doing here?

'Where are you God? Where the hell are you? Help me! Give my head some peace.' The howl of the wind is getting stronger now, the waves crashing in. When I am gone and everyone I ever knew is long gone and a new generation lives, will the sea and the wind remain the same? The same as when our forefathers lived? What had it been like for them? Had they had hardship too in their lives? But their lives are over, I am still here, my life to live.

I need to leave here. It is still my time. My life. I must get out of here. I need to talk to you Sive. I need to tell you. Tell you everything.

Chapter 1

Belief, Hope, Love
Anselm Kiefer. Art Gallery of NSW, Sydney, Australia.

A few hours earlier.

Sive loved that each time she played one of her collection of old records it was different than before. The sound of her late mother's turntable was slightly flawed, yet somehow to Sive when she heard the crackle of the vinyl before it played it could not be more perfect. Her art studio at the bottom of the garden was her haven and when it was filled with the haunting music of the past, there was nowhere in the world she would rather be. The glass wall was Dan's idea. It allowed Sive the full view of the wood with its boughs of hawthorn and silver birch that seemed to guard the studio, acting as protectors.

He teased her that she needed to catch up with technology and had given her the latest iPod as a wedding anniversary gift. But it was the sound of her old records that transported her when she was painting.

She had found a sepia photograph of a crumbling old house in a flea market and had decided to paint it. The photo was frayed at the edges, as if it had once been so precious to someone they had kept it with them always, not wanting to forget. Studying the photograph, her artist's eye could see the mirage of colour in the garden, as primroses and wild snowdrops mingled peacefully together bathing in the sunlight.

She longed to spend another while trying to capture it with her paints but reluctantly she started to tidy up, sighing at the thoughts of the evening ahead. She had meant to ring Dan to make sure he would be home early. He had gone to work before she awoke that morning and was in the office until late the evening before. He was working way too hard and Sive was constantly asking him to take some time out.

'I promise, I will cut down the hours soon, I just need to get this deal over the line, don't worry so much Si.' But she did worry. Dan was her everything, she often watched him when he was asleep, his breathing now as familiar to her as her own. She had noticed the worry lines that

had creeped in on his face. How he tended to be restless even in the deepest sleep. But work was his other love and he could become consumed by it.

The sky was full of inky clouds when she stepped outside and hurried into the house. She warmed her hands at the fire in the cosy sitting room surrounded by book shelves. She had also lit another fire in the more formal reception room with its opulent green velvet wallpaper, antique chandeliers and ornate paintings. In the kitchen, the smell of charcoaled food filled the air.

'Oh feck.' Sive lifted the lid and peaked in at the casserole on the hob. Grabbing a bottle of red wine, she flung half the bottle in along with a large bunch of thyme.

'That should fix it.' She was about to put the cork back on when she thought better of it and poured herself a large glass. It would be lovely just to spend the evening with Dan, sit by the fire and watch an old movie. Sive had introduced Dan to an array of films that he had never heard of. Right now, Cary Grant and Audrey Hepburn were much more appealing than cooking for a dinner party. It seemed so long since they had done anything like that, just the two of them. The last thing Sive wanted to do was entertain potential investors of Dan's, but it was all arranged. As she stirred the casserole her mind drifted back to a very different dinner party.

'You can't have chicken casserole without any chicken,' Dan teased.

'Yes, you can, taste it, anyhow it's chasseur not just plain old casserole.'

'Oh, very fancy! Just missing something though, what could it be? A big lump of chicken maybe.' Dan grinned as Sive pretended to be insulted, then he grabbed her and they both fell laughing onto the sofa bed in Sive's little bedsit.

'Marry me, Sive, and make me the happiest man in Wicklow.'

That was twelve years ago.

Sive rang Dan's office and mobile. No answer to both. She went upstairs to get changed. Why had she agreed to this? The hostess was not a role she fitted into comfortably. There was no sign of Dan.

'Where are you?' Sive left yet another message on the phone. Over the last few months it was hard to make plans with Dan, he was forever in the office, or in his office at home. Putting everything else on the back burner. Sometimes she thought they had put too much on hold.

The landline rang. Her mother in law.

'Oh no!' She was not up to chatting to Mrs Gallagher. Sive went to check the table setting in the dining room, willing Dan to arrive in soon and hoping her mother in law would not ring again, just for once. The guests were due within the hour. Her mobile rang this time. Without looking at it she knew who it was. Mrs Gallagher of Thornback Farm was not going to be ignored.

Anyone else would leave a message if the phone went unanswered but not Dan's mother, she would ring both phones persistently so it was easier to answer it and get it over with. She was known to turn up at the door if her call was not dealt with immediately.

A very large woman who loved the sound of her own voice, Dan's mother insisted on being called Mrs. Gallagher to all. Their house and farm spanned generations and Sive knew that she had intended on keeping it that way.

'There is ample land for both sons.' She tended to tell anyone who cared to listen. It may have been an old way of thinking but for Mrs Gallagher it was the only way. An artist with no job as a wife was never going to make the grade.

When they got engaged Sive brought her rather bohemian looking father to Thornback. She could see Mrs Gallagher looking out through the window at him as they stepped out of his old red pick up. She arrived out in a colourful suit, kitten heels, hair set and sprayed to perfection, topped off with her crème powder and some rouge. Her mouth dropped and her eyes were like saucers as she took in Sive's father. Sive watched as her then future mother in law stared at his dark curly hair and shiny earring. He had a twinkle in his eye as he turned to Mrs Gallagher with a basket filled with fresh vegetables, herbs, home made wine and a wind chime. She seemed to lose her balance and opened her mouth to speak but nothing was coming out. At first Sive thought she might be having a stroke but soon realised it was their arrival that was having the strange effect on her. When they went inside to the parlour, Mrs Gallagher had still not found her voice which was most unusual and her husband gave her a glass of rich dark sherry in a small Waterford crystal goblet. She knocked it back in one go and held her hand out for another, while staring at her future in laws. Sive had overheard her hissing at her husband when she did get her voice back and thought that no one was listening.

'Over my dead body is my Daniel marrying into some hippie family from the back of the Burren. Has he lost his reason getting mixed up with this lot? Lord help us but that father looks like he is in some sort of cult. Mary Immaculate I beseech you, look down on us and, if you can, knock some sense into that son of ours.'

The fact that they were vegetarians had gone down like a bomb. Having a farm that specialised in Aberdeen Angus cattle like the Gallagher's, this had not been a good omen. From that day on a very rocky relationship had begun between Sive and Mrs Gallagher.

'I thought you would never answer the phone. Has your dinner party started yet?' Mrs Gallagher asked, clearly annoyed at the phone not being answered at the first ring.

Mrs Gallagher knew all about this business dinner, there was very little she did not know. She had offered to come down and help Sive with the meal. Sive had declined the offer. She knew she was no Nigella and cooking for people she did not know was up there with cooking for Mrs Gallagher and that was saying something, but Dan had looked so stressed out lately she had agreed. He promised her that when things settled down they would take a break, maybe go over to Inishmore on the Aran Islands. They both loved the bleak beauty of the Islands. The rocky fields overlooking the crystal Atlantic.

'I promise Si, we will just roam around the Island and go to that little pub that you love and we will sit and chat and have lots of hot whiskeys by the fire.' That was the thing she loved about Dan, she could bring him anywhere and he would just blend in. He was just as comfortable in a five-star hotel as a thatched pub in the West of Ireland. Wherever they went he seemed to draw people around him. It had amazed many of their friends how different they were. But somehow, they just worked. Like cool vanilla ice cream and warm chocolate sauce. They complemented each other perfectly. His mother was another story however. She wished that she had not heard about the dinner party. Dan had probably told her. It drove Sive mad that she seemed to know so much about them. Her mother in law could get a job with the secret service, she was so good at getting information out of them.

'Hi Mrs Gallagher, no they are not here yet? I am up to my eyes. "It pays to be organised, I am always extremely organised if I am having guests. It's a sign of a good host.

'Look can this wait?'

'No, it cannot. I would never ring unless it was of the utmost urgency, you should know that Sive, I am far too busy for idle chit chat. I rang to check that you are cooking something normal for them and not one of your hippie dishes with typhoid for meat?'

'Tofu!'

'Whatever it's called, I almost had to call the doctor after that last lunch you made. You know me I never make a fuss, but my stomach was not right for days, in fact it's still not one hundred percent, it was that cardboard stuff you pretend is meat.'

'Of course, you never make a fuss.' Sive threw her eyes to heaven.

'Oh, yes and take away those little pots in the window that you smoke or whatever you do with them.' Sive could feel her blood rise.

'I told you before it's wheatgrass, not pot. I don't smoke as I have told you umpteen times. I use it for smoothies.' It was hard to be civil sometimes to her.

'Well whatever they are, get rid of them, grass or no grass, they look very dicey. I am sure you need a license to grow anything like that.'

'They are not DICEY!' Sive was trying to remain calm, she knew how useless it was to get herself into a knot, Mrs Gallagher simply would not notice, she had a skin thicker than a rhinoceros.

'I left a can of Lilly of the Valley air freshener under your sink the last time I was over. Spray it around the room before the dinner guests arrive, it well gets rid of those funny sticks you burn. People talk Sive, you can't be burning funny stuff when anyone is around.' Sive wondered was there another woman on the planet who could be more infuriating. But there was no stopping Mrs Gallagher when she was on a roll.

'Make sure the house is warm. Why you wanted to buy that big old house and pour so much money into it is beyond me, when you could have had a perfectly good site here on the land.' There was no answer to that, but the two miles between the two houses were precious to Sive; if she had to live any closer to Mrs Gallagher her life would not be worth living. It was bad enough as it was.

'I suppose it will give you a chance to show off the house. I hope you have a nice dress to wear and not one of those old-fashioned yokes you bought in some second-hand shop. I really must bring you to Wicklow Town. There are some lovely boutiques and they know how to treat one properly. Not that I would ever be demanding, but I do like to be treated properly when I am shopping for a suit. I am always telling the Ladies Club to use my name when they are shopping in Wicklow and they will be sure to get special treatment. You need to buy some proper clothes Sive.'

'I am perfectly happy with the clothes I have thank you very much, and I love buying something from a charity or vintage shop.' Sive was trying not to rise to Mrs Gallagher, she didn't have the time or energy right now.

'Don't be telling anyone that Sive. It's bad enough where you buy them without letting people know that they are cast-offs.'

I have to go.' Sive replied curtly.

'Remember now, get rid of those little pots, people talk about that sort of stuff. Oh, do not be late on Sunday for lunch, remind Daniel. The parish priest is coming and bringing a missionary priest with him, God knows what I will say about your lack of attendance at mass.' Then she hung up before Sive had any chance to reply. Every phone call they ever had, Mrs Gallagher managed to rattle Sive. She grabbed her wine and downed half the glass. She was tempted to ring her back.

'Maybe I will go to mass on Sunday and set up a stand outside selling pot to all the parishioners on their way in. I will get stoned and wear a big black cape and tell everyone I got it in the bargain basket at St Vincent de Paul. How would you like that? Then I will light my funny sticks and perform a few spells out in the graveyard for all the neighbours to see.'

As for going shopping with Mrs Gallagher, Sive suspected the poor shop assistants needed Valium to cope with her. She thought about having another glass of wine but thought better of it. She could drink a few glasses right now but she knew she would not get the dinner to the table without a clear head. It was going to be hard enough to pass it off as edible without the hostess being out of it. She tried Dan's phone again. Straight to voice mail.

'Dan, wherever you are come home now.' Sive sighed at the idea of showing off the house. She knew she could never be accused of showing off anything. But she did love their house. The first time her eyes fell on it, it had looked so unloved and uncared for. But she knew that someone had loved it even if it was a long time ago. That first-time Dan brought her to see it, her heart was stolen.

It was bathed in a light spring frost with sunlight dappling on the sash windows. Lying derelict for years, it dated back two hundred years and had belonged to the local gentry. Sive had loved that amongst the briers and the wild gorse a magic halo of yellow spread all over the garden. Daffodils of every size mixed with primroses spread out like a carpet fit for angels. It had looked forgotten yet to Sive's eyes it was magical. To the back was a wood with a mist of bluebells and the heavenly scent of honeysuckle. Inside the large hall, the floors were covered in clay and dust. Her back still ached, reminding her of the long hours she had painstakingly sanded and varnished them until the beautiful rich rosewood gleamed in the half light of the stained-glass windows in the hall. She touched the staircase. A staircase she had only ever read about before. Restored now to its former glory, it gave an air of such grandeur to the hall. She had treated the house like a beautiful painting that had fallen into disrepair and only someone who would love it as much as Sive would painstakingly spend the last few years restoring it to what it once was.

She checked the time and went upstairs for a quick shower and to get dressed. She put on a 1920s black dress she had found in a thrift shop in Oxford Street on one of her trips to London. It was a secret passion she had. She loved rooting through markets. Like a magpie, she often found a jewel amongst the clutter. She piled her dark curly hair on top of her head and secured it with a vintage slide. A red lip and a slick of dark liner finished off her look.

There was a car coming up the drive. Looking out she saw it was Dan, and she could feel herself relax already. She could just concentrate on serving the dinner while he used his charm on the guests. She watched as he parked right outside the front door, almost blocking the way in.

'Why on earth would he park there?' She ran down to get him to move it.

She could smell the alcohol as he came in. He shuffled in and shut the front door behind him, catching his jacket in the door. It took him a moment to realise why he was stuck. Sive went over to him and released his coat before slamming the door.

'Jesus leave, le...leave...the hinges on the door for feck sake Si..' Dan put his hand to his head and made his way into the sitting room and fell into the fireside armchair. Sive stood over him taking in his dishevelled look.

'Where on earth have you been?' His face was as grey as his suit. He looked like he had slept in his clothes. She thought back to the night before. He had come home late and was gone so early that she had never even heard him. Surely, he had changed his clothes? But they looked like he had indeed slept in them.

'Have you lost your reason, you have just driven home after drinking?'

'Ah I just had a couple, here sit, beside me...' he said.

'A couple! you are half cut! I can smell the drink from here, what the hell got into you, why did you not ring me?' Sive asked aghast.

Dan sat deeper into the armchair. He reached for a cigarette. Sive tried to grab it, she was constantly trying to get Dan to give up smoking.

'Give me a break, Si'. His hands started shaking as he lit the cigarette. She began to pace the room, wondering what the hell was going on. Since she met Dan he had never come home like this. He needed a shower and a shave and it suddenly hit her how utterly wrecked he looked, like he had not slept for days. He had lost weight and the shadows under his eyes that she had noticed recently had now become dark and hollow. His hair had turned salt and pepper in the last few years. Normally it suited him but this evening he looked a lot older that his thirty-six years.

'I need to talk to you Si, will you sit? I'm dizzy....with you walk ing.. around.' His pallor had a tinge of green about it. He heaved as if he was about to be sick, Sive ran for a basin and made it back just in time for him to throw up. The astringent smell of vomit filled the living room. He heaved again and it spluttered out but this time missed the basin and landed on the rug. She ran for some towels.

'Dan, what the hell were you drinking?' she shrieked.

'Sorry, lov.'

'How did you get into this state, it makes no sense?' She tried to clean up the mess, her own stomach lurching at the smell. Dan put his head in his hands

'Those people are going to be here any minute expecting their dinner? Tell me what l am I supposed to do with them?'

'What people?' Dan asked.

'What people? What people? Are you having a laugh? Your feckin investors.' Sive shrieked.

'Oh, shit I forgot ....' He took the towel Sive handed him.

'You forgot?'

'Oh hell! My head.' Dan put his head in his hands again. Sive wanted to scream at him but knew it was useless. What had got into him? It was not just the fact he was after drinking and driving it was more than that. She looked at the time. They would be here any minute. Only last week he had told her that this dinner was crucial to helping him secure these investors, and now he goes and gets wasted. If she could get coffee into him and a hot shower he could come around. Dan would hate them to see him like this, he was always so professional. She tried to calm herself and take charge.

'Listen to me, you have to get changed. I need to try and clean this up, will you just get up and help me.' But Dan was not listening.

'Dan, you need to get upstairs, they will be here any minute.' Dan didn't move.

'Cancel it. Tell em to shag off.' Dan said as he gave a loud hiccup. Sive could feel herself snap. He was being no help. She grabbed his mobile. 'You cancel it, you tell them to shag off.' Dan looked at her and shook his head.

'Look Dan, I don't know what's going on, but there is obviously something. You are freaking me out.' Dan stared into the fire but made no reply. There was a car in the drive.

'Oh no, it's them already!' Sive wanted to cry. Another two cars came into the drive. She dragged Dan up out of the chair.

'Dan get up.' She tried to think, she would just have to try to get rid of them.

'I have to get the smell of vomit out of the room, I may not be able to get rid of them at the door. Dan, just go! Get a shower.' The doorbell was ringing. Hopefully one of the cars was Beth. Beth was her closest friend and she was coming up for the weekend. They had planned to visit a new exhibition on Saturday. Sive had asked her to come up for the dinner party. Beth was fantastic at anything like that, like Dan she could talk to anyone. She would know what to do now too, maybe she would help her to get rid of them. Sive really wanted to tell them to just leave, but she remembered how important tonight had seemed to Dan. He was slowly making his way upstairs.

Grabbing the rug with the vomit seeping into it, she rolled it up as best she could and threw it out the back. Looking around the kitchen she reached under the sink, searching for something to mask the smell, and saw the can of air freshener.

'I never thought that I would be so glad of Mrs Gallagher's can of toxic air freshener.' She shook the bottle and sprayed it around the room. It made her want to gag. The smell of burnt food with the sickly smell of Lily of the Valley and vomit was not a good mixture.

'Shit the bloody casserole.' She cursed herself for forgetting to take it out. It would be cremated this time. No amount of wine would save it now. She was past caring. She heard the shower on. The doorbell was going again. She wanted to hide and ignore it. Perhaps she could tell them that Dan had some mysterious illness and not let them cross the threshold. Or maybe she could just give them a drink first and then explain that something had come up terribly unexpected. With no idea what she would do, she took a deep breath and went to open the door.

Chapter 2

The Scream
Edvard Munch. The National Gallery, Oslo

Dan just about made it into the en-suite, the bile now leaving an acid taste in his mouth. Slowly he peeled off his clothes. If only he could stop thinking. Stop his mind from tormenting him. The shower slowly started to sober him. Painful reality hit him with a bang. His perfect life. His perfect sham of a life. The pounding of his chest. Stabbing him. Drying himself he shivered in the bedroom, yet beads of perspiration were on his brow. He looked around the room. Sive had painted it in pale blues. Blue was meant to be calming on the mind. It normally worked. It was a restful room with just some books and memories from their back-packing days dotted around it. How simple life was then, hand in hand they had visited parts of the world he had never dreamt of.

Together, with just enough money to get by, they had travelled to places he thought he would only ever read about. Sive had had to drag him to India. His only impression of it up to that was from watching *Slumdog Millionaire*. What an adventure they had had. Trekking through the Himalayas and the dream like cities of Mumbai and New Delhi. Their eyes barely able to take in the cornucopia of colour and their senses alive with the exotic smell of spices.

On the bedroom wall was a seascape in a kaleidoscope of colour that Sive had given to him for their first anniversary. She had painted it as a reminder of one morning they had spent on a Beach in Goa. A morning that was far removed from how he felt now. His eyes took in the painting, as if he had never truly looked at it before.

'Look Dan, this is what life is about.'

'Hold on Sive my eyes are hardly opened. A man needs his sleep,' Dan teased.

'I know but I wanted you to see it, how beautiful it looks. The russets and violets breaking into the ocean, it's breath-taking.' Sive said

'Nobody but you could get me out of bed at this unearthly hour to watch the dawn break, when every sensible person in India is asleep if they can at all. Especially if they are on their holidays I might add. I feel like I am at home and being called from my sleep because a cow is calving or the cattle have broken out. We never got up to see sunrises in Thornback,' he laughed.

'Look at it Dan, maybe this is what heaven is, this beauty, this pure divinity.' Sive looked mesmerised by the sunrise. But he wasn't looking at the sea, he was looking at Sive and he knew then that with Sive in his life everything made sense and he thanked the heavens that he had found her. Being with Sive stilled his mind and brought a peace that he had searched for.

When they came home she had spent hours on the painting trying to capture that beautiful dawn break from some photos. He had never loved a gift so much. He knew the time and love she had put into it. How he had loved to watch her paint back then. She was always so entranced, it was like a ritual of prayer. They could spend hours in the same room, both doing their own thing, just aware that they were together. Unknowingly she calmed the turmoil in his head. But nothing could calm it now, not even Sive. He was here before, he had prayed he never would be again. Sometimes when Sive slept beside him his eyes would flicker open with panic, he would turn to her and hold her and his mind would calm down and eventually sleep would come and his demons would disappear. He lay down on the bed now pulling a cream throw over him, he closed his eyes, willing his mind to calm, but it would not rest.

The sound of the door bell ringing brought him back to reality. He knew Sive would come looking for him as soon as she got a chance. She would hate greeting them on her own. He knew he should go to her, explain everything. But he couldn't. Feelings of shame washed over him, choking him and barely allowing him to breath. He had to get out of here, it was suffocating him. He looked at the painting again, his eyes not blinking as he soaked in the image of the sea. The ocean, he had always loved the ocean. He needed to feel the salt water on his lips now, breathe the sea air, become a part of it. It would bring the peace to his head that he craved. He put on his jeans and a hoodie then left the room and closed the door gently behind him.

Classical music was playing, mixing with the chatter of the guests. Sive was organising some drinks. Without thinking he walked into the reception room. The chatter stopped as he felt them staring at him.

'Dan, you are looking very casual there.' Miranda O Donohoe purred at him. There were three couples. The men dressed in suits drinking beers, the women, glasses of prosecco. Sive's eyes locked on Dan's.

'Sive here has told us that you have had a bit of an emergency,' Miranda O Donohue said in a south Dublin accent.

'I was just telling them that unfortunately we must leave in a hurry Dan, isn't that right? We are so sorry for all this inconvenience.' Sive said apologetically.

'Are you having a laugh?' Miranda's husband Eugene replied, his face half smiling. But Dan just stared back at him. His face was unreadable.

'No, it's not a joke, it's off, sorry to have wasted your time. Please leave my house.' Eugene O Donoghue's smile disappeared.

'Are you serious?' Eugene replied, the smile now a scowl.

'What the hell?' Miranda joined in. Dan raised his voice slightly, so that there was no confusion.

'There is no dinner party, this was a mistake, please leave immediately.' Sive stared at him.

Jennifer Doyle spluttered her prosecco and looked up at Dan.

'Why on earth did you drag us out here, we have cancelled another engagement to be here tonight. If it didn't suit surely you could have rang us earlier?' But Dan wasn't listening. He turned and left them staring after him.

He went into the kitchen and grabbed the keys of the Jeep which was parked out the back. The door opened and Sive arrived in. Dan stared at her, her brown eyes bright with confusion.

'Where are you going?' she asked, aghast.

'Out!'

'What do you mean OUT!'

'I have to get out of here. Now.'

'Wait! What is the big rush for feck sake? Wait until they are gone. What is going on with you? You can't drive anywhere on your own. You have been drinking in case you forgot.'

'I'm fine now.'

'Stop, Dan. Look, if you really need to get out we will but just let me get rid of these.' She went closer to him and put her two hands on his face. He gently pulled her hands away, staring into her face.

'Just wait here, Dan. Wait! Do you hear me? I have no idea what is going on but your frightening me, just wait until I get rid of them, then we can talk.'

'I need to go.' He could feel the walls caving in on him. Underneath his clothes, he was breaking into a cold clammy sweat.

'I am just asking you to hold on for a few minutes. I need to see them out, get their coats, just wait until they are gone.' He made no reply.

'Get some coffee into you, there is a pot made, I will be as quick as I can.' Then she left to go back to them. He could hear them fussing, looking for coats. Sive was apologising as best she could. Another car had just arrived. He recognised it as Beth's. He saw his chance and left through the back door without anyone seeing him. It was too late for explanations. He tried to talk earlier, now it was too late.

He took the Jeep out of gear and pushed it until he felt he was out of earshot. Then he got in and started the engine. He stopped for a moment to look back. The evening was drawing in now. A flight of starlings was gathering in the sky and flying away in unison. They liked to roost in the woods during the day but as dusk approached they swarmed together. Dan watched them as they moved like a vision across the darkening clouds, protecting each other from predators. If only humans did the same. When the storms came would they gather close and protect each other, or would they turn away and just look after their own? How strange life was.

'Enough!' he whispered to himself and slowly drove away.

He drove for miles. The night had turned bad and the rain was slapping on the window. He had no idea where he was going. It was of no importance to him. Eventually he took a turn off the main coast road. He was in Wexford. The roads were becoming very narrow. Eventually he came to a fork in the road. He took the turn which had a sign for the sea. A large pothole threw the Jeep, making it difficult to drive. Suddenly the road came to a dead end into a small car park. The evening sky had turned dark. He got out and took a small torch from the front. It was a short walk to the sea.

He could hear the ocean as he walked along the shore. How had he ended up here? All the people he knew and all the friends he had, he never felt so alone. He thought of Sive. Sive who he loved more than he ever dreamed he was capable of. He could not hide it all any more. It was all too late. It was over. Tears started to flow down his face. The darkness of the night was nothing to the overbearing blackness that was beginning to cloud his mind. The physical pain he felt in his heart. His body was perspiring yet shivering with the icy rain. His heart racing like a greyhound. There was no one here to hide from, nobody, only himself. The saltiness from the sea melting into his mouth and nostrils. He was alone. Totally. This is what alone smelt and tasted of.

The last time he cried was when Sive had agreed to marry him. Tears of pure joy, he was so in love with her. She was so different to him. So different to anyone he knew. He had lots of friends, men and women, but nobody got him like Sive. He knew she was aware of the darkness that clouded him when no one else was aware of it. He had never spoken of it, but somehow, he knew Sive felt it. He had wanted to talk about it, but it was hidden for so long, he did not know how, and he was afraid, afraid he would lose her. He thought back to the first time he had met her.

He had stumbled into a small pub in Connemara with some friends during the last year of college. They had went surfing in Doolin and had decided to drive around the West and stay in some small bed and breakfast that would have them. The pub they had found was exactly what he loved about County Clare. Rustic and full of the locals. There was a sing song going on. Sive was sitting in the background. She had that earthy, slightly wild look to her. They were calling her to sing. She was a Sean-Nos singer, a Gaelic form of singing. She began singing 'The song of Muinis' her long curly hair framing her delicate face. The pub went still and Dan could not take his eyes off her. He knew his heart was stolen as he listened to her haunting voice.

'The surf is fantastic here in Doolin, I am going to stay another few days, can we meet up tomorrow, you can show me the hidden gems in Doolin?' he had asked her.

'I can and I might even bring you over to The Burren…'

For a moment, he thought he could hear the song she had sung that night mixed with the sound of the sea, it comforted him somehow. Suddenly he lost his footing and stumbled forward. He tried to prevent himself falling but failed. There were rocks in his path and his head hit one. Reality ebbed away, it was as if he was in a dream as his eyes closed.

*

He could feel someone push him back, he thought it was Sive, his mind playing tricks on him. Her voice was one with the ocean, her hair part of the waves. But she was different to Sive, like an older Sive. He knew she was trying to protect him, guide him out of the water. It was dark but a light seemed to shine around her, illuminating her. He felt he knew her yet didn't. She reached for his hand and he could feel her lifting him up as if he was as light as a feather, yet he couldn't feel her hand. He couldn't describe her face, yet kindness emanated from it. She was becoming one with the water, she was fading into the darkness. He called her to stay, she smiled and he knew, he knew somehow because of her he was not alone.

When he awoke he could taste the blood on his lips mixed with the salt water. For a few moments, he could not move. For the life of him he could not figure out if he was in a dream or reality. If he was dead or alive. He dragged himself to the water's edge and it lapped over his legs. Like icy waves reaching for him. He shouted into the night as the reality of his situation now dawned on him. His head was aching from the fall.

'What am I doing, do I really want to leave now? This is still my time. My life. Help me God, help me this night. Sive my beautiful Sive, I can't leave you. I just can't.

'I have to go home, back to Sive, this is a mistake, I need to find my way home, back to my life. He walked along the beach, his body getting weaker. His torch was gone and there was only a sliver of a moon to light his way. Eventually he found the gap in the banks that brought him back to the Jeep.

He had left the keys in it. He turned the ignition on, grateful of the warm air. He turned on the light and looked at his head.

'Shit!' He panicked as he realised how deep the cut was, blood was seeping out of it, he tried to stop it, but failed. He searched for his phone but there was no sign of it. He began to drive out of the car park and back up the pot holed road.

'Where the hell am I?' He shouted out to keep himself alert as he drove back down the narrow road. There was no one about, no cars or sign of life. The car struggled with the twists and turns that he had no recollection of travelling down. He could feel the pain in his head and the faint feeling that was coming over him.

'I have to get the fuck out of here! Sive forgive me, I will explain everything, we will be okay, I know we will, my mind is not thinking straight, it will be okay.'

His eyes were getting weaker as he tried to see the sign post. He took what looked like the main road. He could feel his eyes losing focus. It was the main road. He knew he couldn't drive much further, he would have to get help.

'Thank God for that, there has to be someone on this road.' There was. A truck. He heard the roar of brakes. Then there was only darkness.

Chapter 3

The Weeping Woman.
Pablo Picasso. Tate Modern Museum, London

A blonde woman with a tinge of an orange fake tan got into a black Mercedes, closing the door with a bang. Beth drove in and parked beside her.

'I hope you have not come for dinner?' Miranda O Donoghue spat through her opened window as Beth got out of the car.

'Well yes, I have actually. Hi, I'm Beth, a friend of Sive's and Dan's.' Beth held out her hand to introduce herself.

'Well I am afraid you have had a wasted journey, we have just been asked to leave, correction, ordered to leave.' Miranda O Donoghue hissed. She called to her husband Eugene to hurry on. He walked towards the car and looked at Beth appreciatively, taking in her voluptuous curves and her shock of red hair.

'Well hello there, and who have we here?' he asked, his eyes staring at Beth's bust.

'Just get in, will you?' his wife roared at him. He winked at Beth and gave her a leering smile as he reluctantly got in beside his wife, who looked like she could run over him. Beth walked over to Sive.

'What's up? You look like a pressure cooker about to blow, and what's this about being asked to leave?'.

'Nightmare of an evening,' Sive hissed.

'Did you try to convert them all to being a vegan or something, or did Mrs Gallagher arrive and scold them all for having their elbows on the table?' Beth whispered jokingly and Sive pulled her out of earshot.

'If only that was it. Dan came home half plastered, threw up, totally forgot about his bloody dinner party. He went to get a shower and get changed just as they arrived but instead of getting dressed for dinner he arrived down looking like he just came in from a week-long stag party. He seems to be having some sort of crisis and he picked the perfect time for it.' Sive looked like she was about to cry.

'Feck, that's not like Dan, and how did you get everyone to leave?' Beth was shocked.

'He just announced the dinner was off and told them to leave. That was it, no explanation, just basically, piss off!'

'What's going on with him? He always loves a party, of any description.'

'I don't have a clue, but it had better be good after this farce.'

'Where is he?'

'In the kitchen, sobered up but acting totally off kilter. I told him to stay there until the guests had left.'

'Look why don't you go back to him, I will see this lot off and then I will head back, you need to sort out whatever male mid-life crises Dan is having.'

'I feel awful, you have driven all the way down from Dublin.'

'Don't worry about me, I'll go have a coffee and head back to Avara. I'll have a large gin and tonic at home while I catch up on some mails. We can meet up tomorrow for a big gossipy lunch before the art exhibition and you can fill me in on how the midlife man is, now just go on, leave me to handle this.' Sive hugged her.

'Bloody hell, are you sure?'

'Go and stop worrying. To be honest from the couple I met, I'm not that sorry to miss having dinner with them, they look a right pain,' Beth added.

'They are loaded with money but scarce on the charm. So much for Dan getting them to invest. I have no idea why he would want to do business with them anyway,' Sive added. The guests were almost all in their cars. Sive slipped away and left Beth to deal with them.

'What a carry on, I have never been more insulted in my life, being asked to leave after I just got here, disgraceful.' Jennifer Doyle spat as she sat into her gleaming white BMW. Her husband barely acknowledged Beth.

'I am sure there is a perfectly good explanation and Dan and Sive will be in touch again,' Beth said, smiling as if it was perfectly normal to be turfed out of a house when you had only arrived.

'Tell them not to bother,' he replied sourly.

'I am sorry but these things happen, safe journey now and thank you for coming,' Beth said.

They all drove away and Beth was about to get back into her car when Sive came rushing out.

'He's gone, he left in the bloody Jeep,' Sive shouted to Beth.

'Calm down, will you? He probably knew you were going to give him a roasting. Why are you panicking so much? He probably just needed a breather,' Beth reasoned with her.

'There is something going on with him and he's well over the limit.'

'He has the Jeep, he will probably just go over to that neighbour friend he has with the horses and hang out there for a while,' Beth suggested.

'You didn't see him, Beth.'

'Let's go in, have a cuppa and a think. Did you try to ring him?'

'His phone and wallet are up beside the bed,' Sive replied.

'See, he's not gone far then, he will be back before you know it.'

'Maybe, but I think it's more than that, something in my gut is really frightening me. Dan has never acted like this before.'

'Do you think you could be overreacting just a tad?' Beth asked. She rummaged around the familiar kitchen and made a pot of tea, peaking in at the dried out casserole.

'Dinner was going well I see, they don't know what they are missing, although Nigella need have no worries, her place as Goddess of cooking is still safe.' Beth said trying to lighten the atmosphere. Sive was pacing the kitchen floor.

'He's lucky I don't fire that stupid dinner at him. I told him it was a bad idea, but this was a disaster. Something is obviously going on and I have no clue what it is.'

'Just sit, Sive, and drink a cup of tea. Maybe he just needs some time on his own, how was he this morning? Sive sat down opposite Beth and drank the tea.

'That's the thing, I barely saw Dan in the past few days. He is working crap hours and when he is home, his mind is a million miles away. Beth, am I an idiot or something, am I totally missing something here?' Beth sat down beside her friend.

'It's easy to start imagining all sorts of things. Dan is totally devoted to you, if there is something troubling him it's not to do with some leggy blonde or anything. He did look a bit wrecked lately though, maybe he's just having a bit of burn out, you said yourself he is a bit of a workaholic.'

Two hours passed and no sign of him. After more tea and a few discreet phone calls to see if anyone had seen him, even Beth was starting to get worried. Another two hours passed and she was trying hard to keep Sive from climbing the walls. She knew Sive and Dan were very close and he would never put Sive through this without good reason. He knew how much he meant to her. Other than her father he was all the family she had. Beth had no sister and either had Sive so they often joked that they each were the sister that they never had. She had noticed Dan had looked very strained lately. But this was totally out of character.

'My nerves are starting to cave in. I will kill him for putting me through this. I'll call his secretary at her home, I have her number, maybe she can throw some light on it.' Sive said worriedly.

'Good idea,' Beth replied. The doorbell rang, Sive had not bothered to lock the electric gates.

'I'll get it, you chat to his secretary and see can you find out anything,' Beth replied.

'It's probably Dan's mother,' Sive replied..

'Don't worry I'll handle her.' Beth replied. To put it mildly they didn't exactly see eye to eye. But it wasn't Mrs Gallagher. Beth looked out the window and saw a garda car. She opened the door and two gardaí introduced themselves.

'Good evening, are you Mrs Sive Gallagher?'

'No, is something wrong?' Beth asked.

'We need to speak to Dan Gallagher's wife, is she at home?' Sive heard them and followed Beth to the door.

'I'm Sive. My God, are you hear about Dan?' Sive's face went the colour of chalk.

Beth put her hand protectively on Sive's arm. The older of the men spoke, his Cork accent evident.

'I am afraid there has been an accident a few miles from Tinnabearna beach in Wexford.'

'Why, why are you telling me this?' Sive asked with dread in her voice.

'I am sorry Mrs Gallagher but your husband was involved.'

'What! Wexford! Dan! Is he ok?' Beth asked as she moved closer to Sive.

'He was brought by ambulance to Dublin, he was unconscious when they took him off. Our colleagues were at the scene. It was a serious accident. They let the garda station in Wicklow know and we came straight here to let you know. I'm afraid that's all we can tell you now.' Beth grabbed Sive, who looked like she would collapse, her frightened eyes staring at Beth.

'NO! NO! NOT DAN. NO!' Sive screamed. Beth put her arms around her friend and held her as she crumbled to the floor.

Chapter 4

Death and Life.
Gustav Klimt. Leopold Museum, Vienna

Sive ran into the emergency entrance, leaving Beth to look for somewhere to park. She struggled to catch her breath as she saw the amount of people waiting to speak to one receptionist sitting behind a glass perplex. Without thinking she pushed past.

'Please wait your turn, I can only deal with one person at a time,' the receptionist warned Sive.

Sive could feel her breathing get worse, as if there was no air available.

'My husband, he's been in a crash, just tell me where he is?' A man moved back to allow Sive in.

'Please you have to help me?' Sive shouted.

'Give me his name, please,' the receptionist asked without looking at Sive.

'Dan Gallagher. He was brought in by ambulance. I am sick with worry, I tried ringing on the way up but couldn't get through, I am going out of my mind.'

'Give me a moment,' she ordered.

'Please find out if he is okay. Where would he be?'

'His date of birth, please?'

Sive rattled it off, and held her breath. Perhaps she would say it was a big mistake, it wasn't Dan at all, he would be home by now and all was well. He would explain why he went off like that and he would hold her in one of his bear hugs that only Dan could do. He would wipe all the fear away as they marvelled at how the gardaí could get it so wrong. The receptionist looked up from her computer.

'Yes, he's here, he is with the emergency team. I will get someone to speak with you in a moment. Please take a seat.' Sive's legs almost went from under her, and she grabbed the desk to steady himself.

'Is he ok, where have they taken him?' She felt like someone had grabbed at her throat.

'Somebody will be with you as soon as possible. Now please wait over there.' The receptionist pointed towards the seating area.

Her chest hurt, her heart was beating so fast. The sickly grey walls were closing in on her. The voices and the noise were becoming a blur. She was grateful to see Beth arriving in, her red hair like a glint of sunshine in the array of greyness.

'Parking out there is a nightmare, I just dropped the car and ran. Hopefully it won't be towed away. Although I am past caring. Well, what's the story, do you know where he is?' Sive stared at her as if she was looking through her.

'What if, what if it's bad, What if…?' Sive whispered. Beth put her arm around her.

'Look, wait until we see what the doctors say,' Beth said, trying to reassure her.

'Please, please let him be ok,' Sive said, her voice barely audible.

'I know how worried you are, but you have to try and hold it together a little.' Sive looked like she was falling apart, or that she could faint any minute.

Within a few minutes a nurse arrived and brought them through emergency to a cubicle, passing patients lying on trolleys and relatives looking on anxiously. Doctors in scrubs walked up and down the corridor. Nurses writing files. Porters transferring patients onto better trolleys as they became available.

'Is he okay? Can I see him?' Sive asked.

'Your husband is having emergency surgery now. I am afraid that is all I can tell you. One of the team will speak with you shortly.'

'Why is he having surgery?' Sive asked, her voice frightened.

'I am sorry but that is all I know right now. I just need to take a few details.' Eventually a young doctor in scrubs arrived.

'Hi, my name is Greg, I am part of the surgical team looking after your husband.'

'Is he okay? What happened? Can I see him?' The doctor gave her a sympathetic look.

'He will be in theatre for about another hour, and as soon we can we will fill you in a little more.' Sive studied his face.

'Will I be able to see him soon?'

The doctor shook his head.

'Not for a while. I'm afraid that's all I can tell you now, we will know more as soon as he is finished surgery.'

'Why is he having surgery?' Beth asked.

'It was quite a serious accident. We will be able to tell you more shortly. I know how stressful it is not knowing. Actually, it may be helpful if you could give us a little information on your husband?'

Sive looked at him, bewildered.

'Is there anything you think we might need to know? Was he taking any medication, either prescribed or not, or perhaps acting differently in any way?' Sive shook her head. They must mean was he taking drugs or something. Why on earth would they think that? Should she mention that he was half cut when he arrived home and that he had told the dinner guests to shag off? Then she remembered something that gripped her heart. He had wanted to talk when he first arrived in, and she wished now she had listened. Perhaps none of them would be here in this hospital on a crazy Friday night if she had. She could feel the bile rise in her stomach now, thinking back to the last time she had spoken to him.

'Anything at all might be important. Your husband's clothes were soaking wet when the paramedics arrived on the scene. He also had a very nasty gash to his head that we assume happened an hour or two earlier. He had already lost a lot of blood from it,' the doctor explained.

'What? Was he in the sea? How did he bash his head?' Sive asked.

'We don't know. But he was coming from the beach road when he crashed. If there is anything we should know, I urge you tell us. Especially, if he was on any medication?'

'He was not at all himself. He was exhausted and quite stressed out.' She could feel herself begin to crumble. Suddenly a wave of guilt passed over her body.

'No, he was not on medication. He hates taking anything. He would rather sit it out than take a painkiller.'

'Sive, you're shaking, sit down before you fall.' Beth took her friend's hand.

'I'm fine.' Fine, she had never felt less fine in her entire life, she was terrified. She closed her eyes and said a silent prayer.

She could hardly remember the last time she had prayed. As a small girl, she always did. When her mother died, it was a way of being close to her. If she prayed, she liked to think her mother could hear her.

'When I am gone Sive, I will have a bird's eye view from heaven, I will watch over you always. Just look up at the sky and I will be there, right behind the clouds.'

'But what if it's dark, and you can't see me? What if it's the night and I am afraid and I need you?' Sive asked worriedly.

'That's what the stars are for, silly. I will ask a star to shine down on you and then I will see you. Don't worry my little Sive, I will always be there, close your eyes and I will be there, somehow you will know.'

The doctor's beeper went and he promised to let them know any news as soon as he knew. Beth brought Sive down to a quiet part of the corridor to wait. There was an elderly lady lying on a trolley, her eyes like a bird peeping out of her gaunt face, her face full of worry, as if she had suddenly realised that this was it, the end of the line. Sive imagined she was worried about who would look after her cat or perhaps her plants. The things that were her life now. Sive recognised the raw emotion on her face. Fear. It was almost tangible.

An hour passed that seemed like a decade, and still no news.

'I just can't believe this is happening Beth. Where on earth did Dan go? It's all so mad, I feel I am in a dream and I am going to wake up. Why did the doctor ask me was I concerned?' Sive covered her face with her hands.

'That was a strange question to ask.' Beth agreed.

'It's as if there is more to it. What kind of an accident was it? They are telling us so little. You don't think he intended the accident to happen?' Sive asked Beth. She fought down the nausea that was overwhelming her. Dan was the last person on earth she would be concerned about like that. True, he was agitated and had worked ferocious hours lately, but in danger of killing himself? That was ludicrous.

'I'm not sure what he meant Sive, I agree Dan is not someone you would ever worry about.' After what seemed an age the doctor appeared again.

'Your husband is being transferred to recovery shortly. He has had a bleed to the brain but we have managed to stop it. We have had to put him into an induced coma until he is out of danger.

'This is a nightmare!' Sive exclaimed.

'The next twenty-four hours will tell us a lot. The next seventy-two hours will tell us how stable he is. Does Dan have any other family that need to be contacted tonight?' Sive was looking at him in bewilderment. Why did he want his family contacted now, it was the middle of the night? She could feel her breath coming faster. This could not be happening. She tried to speak but the words felt strangled at the back of her throat, asking would make it real, yet she had to know.

'Could Dan die tonight?' Sive could feel her heart beating fast, willing the doctor to say no, dreading what he might answer.

'He has had a serious injury I am afraid he is critical but we will just have to wait.' His voice direct.

'As I said the next twenty-four hours are crucial. After that we will be more confident of how he is.' Beth gave the doctor a knowing look.

'We will contact his immediate family,' Beth said. With that he again promised to let them know as soon as anything changed. Sive prayed it was only a nightmare. She would wake up in a minute and Dan would be sleeping. He would tell her everything was ok, he was fine, they were fine. But it wasn't a nightmare, it was all happening. She could feel herself struggling to breathe. Beth was holding her, the sickly smell of antiseptic overwhelming her.

'Beth, Oh Beth! I need to see him, I need to be near him, please Beth, tell them I need to see him.'

'It's ok Sive, he's in good hands, they will let you see him soon.' Sive could feel Beth cradling her. She buried her face in Beth's shoulder and cried until she felt surely her heart was breaking. Her mind began drifting to a different time, a most happy time.

'I must have done something good in my life to have found you, Sive,' Dan said as he looked up at the twinkling stars in India.

'Love is precious Dan, it's also strong yet fragile, promise me we will take care of it.'

'Always, I promise you. Always,' Dan promised.

The emergency was at last calming down. Beth got tea from a machine and brought it into Sive. She tried to drink it.'

'I better ring his family, how on earth am I going to tell them, Mrs Gallagher will go into meltdown, I should of rang them earlier. I never dreamt it would be this serious.'

'Do you want me to?' Beth offered.

'No, I better ring Tom, Dan's brother. Tom will know what to say to his parents. God only knows how Mrs Gallagher will take the news.'

On hearing Tom's voice Sive burst into tears, it all seemed so surreal. She told him about the accident.

'Oh Tom, I haven't even seen him yet.'

'Have you someone with you Sive?'

'Yes, yes I have. Will you talk to your parents and let them know? It would be probably better coming from you,' Sive replied.

'Of course, and I will be up there as soon as I can. Sive, was there any one else hurt?'

'I don't know, nobody said anything about anyone else.' They talked for a little while more. Sive felt a little better knowing that Tom was on the way. Tom, as they say, was the salt of the earth. The eldest son who had stayed at home to farm. Sive knew he would know how best to tell Dan's parents. Mrs Gallagher would be hysterical. She idolised Dan.

One of the nurses had said it would be another half hour before she could see Dan and then it would only be for a few moments in intensive care. The half hour felt like eternity until eventually the nurse came back.

'You can go in now, but please only for a moment.' Sive stood up, her legs barely holding her up. She wanted to run to him and tell him everything would be okay. They had so much living to do. So much of life left undone. Slowly she took a deep breath and followed the nurse.

Chapter 5

The Denial of St Peter
Rembrandt. Rijks, Amsterdam

A sliver of morning light cut through the trees, dancing into the bedroom. Sive in that half sleep, half-awake slumber reached over for Dan. He must be already up. The old radiators gurgled and struggled to life. At first their sounds had been difficult to get used to, but now they were familiar and comforting. Hopefully he might bring up a cuppa. Still no sound of Dan. Reality like a stab sank in. Dan was not here. She was fully awake now, and with that the memory of Dan's broken and bruised body in intensive care was all too clear.

She pulled herself from the bed, her body feeling like that of someone far older than her years. A text had arrived from Tom to say that Dan was the same. He had been the same now for three days. The bleed had stopped. The doctor had said he would slowly come out of his sleep. She went back to bed, curling herself up. Mrs Gallagher had wanted to know why had he went out driving when the party was on? Sive had said he had got a call, something to do with work. The first of the lies, but Mrs Gallagher was taking it all so badly. Sive was not going to fill her in on the details, especially the fact that Dan was falling apart earlier that evening.

The phone in the hall was ringing, she ran downstairs in case it was the hospital. It was their solicitor, probably ringing to see how Dan was. Well, she had no intention of talking to anybody. It rang again. She went back upstairs and pulled on some warm clothes. She needed to get out. Grabbing her mobile and a coat she headed for the wood behind the house.

It had started to rain again and she ran for the shelter of the trees. It was her place to escape to. She breathed in the woody smell made stronger by the fresh rain. Hot tears ran down her face as she slumped down beside a large oak tree. She often marvelled at its large roots peeping through the brown earth, it had lost its leaves now and would have to wait till spring for a new coat. The buds would always begin early and then the leaves would grow and turn the richest of emerald. She lay against it now, closing her eyes, going over everything that had happened.

Dan had been working ferocious hours since the summer. He had been vague about why he had to work so much. Normally he was full of talk about the newest contract they had got. But in the last few months he had been quieter. If she really thought about it, for the first time since they got married, they had grown a bit distant. Sive had thought they would be grand again when this big contract or deal was sorted. She had no problem spending time alone. It had given her time to paint and to finish the house. She had become quite engrossed in the house. Thinking back Sive knew she had not asked him very much about how things were with work. Guilt now started to seep into her mind. Perhaps she should have showed more interest. Perhaps things were tougher than she thought. When he was better, she promised herself that she would listen more to him. Perhaps it had all got on top of him, a bit of burn out as Beth said. Her phone rang, it was Tom.

'Hi Sive, he looks peaceful, but no sign of him waking up. I wish he would just wake up and tell us he is ok and then he can sleep for as long as he wants. It's torturous waiting like this.'

'I know it's hard, I am sorry for leaving but I was so exhausted. I just had to come home and sleep and freshen up a little.'

'I'm glad you did, we would have had to get a bed in the hospital for you soon, you looked like you would keel over. It's been a very long three days. Mother is taking it all so bad, I am going to drop her and Dad home soon and come back later. I don't want to leave him, but I won't be long. I will just drop them and come back,' he explained.

'Look, there is no need to rush back, I will head up shortly, just in case he does wake.' She didn't want him alone at any stage.

'Okay, maybe I will just check on the farm. I have a lad looking after everything, but I need to check on a few cows that are due to calf. He might miss it.'

'I will ring you if there is any change.' She felt guilty for leaving Dan at all. Reluctantly she left the wood. In the house, she noticed that Barry White, the solicitor, had called again. She would give him a ring over the next few days, right now she wanted to get up to the hospital. Just as she was about to leave, the hospital rang. Dan was starting to wake up, and there was no family there.

She was on the motorway as quick as possible. Eventually she got to the hospital, but road works had delayed her even further. She parked the car in a no parking area and ran towards the ward almost knocking down a man coming down the stairs. She half ran, half walked to the ward. Thank goodness, he was waking up. A nurse stopped her in the corridor as if she was waiting for her. Sive was out of breath from rushing.

'Hi, do you mind holding on for a minute?' the nurse asked.

'I got a call to say Dan, my husband, was waking up and I'm afraid none of the family are here, his brother had just left. I don't want him to think none of us are here.'

'No worries at all, if you could just take a seat for a minute our hospital counsellor needs to see you first.'

'Is Dan okay?' Sive asked in a panic.

'Please just wait a minute,' the nurse urged.

'But I don't want him to wake with no one there,' Sive said. What if he thought she had not been there, or that Tom had never came? He would feel bad enough waking up alone.

'I need to see him now, surely this can wait?'

'I'm afraid not, please do not go in yet,' she said with authority.

'What is going on, is he okay? Please tell me he's not worse?' Sive replied, exasperated.

'No, he is not any worse.'

'But...' There was a bit of hushed talking from the nurse's station and then a small woman came out and walked towards Sive, her court shoes clicking loudly. She smiled at her.

'You must be Dan's wife, pleased to meet you. My name is Bernadette Logan, the hospital counsellor. There is a room in here if you could just come with me and I can explain a few things.'

'What is this about, I just want to see Dan,' Sive said.

'I just need to talk to you about a couple of things. Please take a seat.' She opened a file and started jotting down some notes. Sive reluctantly sat down.

'Has my husband awoken?'

'Dan did wake up for a little while, and he is gone back into a deep, more peaceful natural sleep now. The doctors can let you know more, but by all accounts, he is more stable.

'Oh, thank goodness. I should never have left. Now he must think he was left alone,' she cried.

'He was only awake for a few moments. However, from the few minutes he was awake it became apparent that his mental state is very fragile and he is traumatised. We need to tread very carefully when he awakes again,' Bernadette explained.

'Oh! I wish I had been here. I will stay now until he awakes again. Don't worry, I won't say anything to upset him,' Sive assured her.

'Well this is the difficult part. May I call you Sive?' Bernadette Logan had that annoying habit of smiling most of the time she was talking, as if whatever she was about to say would sound better out of a smiling mouth.

'Of course,' Sive replied.

'When Dan woke up we told him you were on your way, he got himself very upset and told us to stop you. He didn't say why, but he was adamant you were not to see him.' Bernadette kept smiling as she talked. Sive looked at her, her glasses glinting in the light. Could she have misheard what she just said?

Bernadette Logan gave a big, reassuring smile as she looked at Sive.

'I know this is very difficult to deal with right now, and this could be something to do with his head injuries. However, we must look at all angles. Dan has asked us not to let you in to see him, and we must respect his wishes.'

'What are you telling me? I cannot see him? You can't be serious?' The smile started to vanish from the counsellor's face.

'Sive, I am sorry but we can't let you in right now to see your husband, we must respect his wishes.'

'But, I don't understand, why would he not want to see me?' Sive asked, aghast.

'I'm afraid I can't answer that, you will just have to give him some time.' The smile almost turned upside down as a scowl appeared on her face. Bernadette Logan got up to leave.

'I have to see my husband.' Sive could feel herself shaking. The counsellor looked right into her eyes.

'You cannot see your husband today, Sive.' With that she got up and patted Sive on the arm.

'I will keep you informed of his progress, but for now I have to dash.'

Sive sat there staring after her as the counsellor clip clopped down the hall. She stood up but her legs would not work, this was too much, she could feel her breath struggle. She sat back down and tried to compose herself. She had stayed awake for almost three days to make sure she was there when he awoke and now he had banned her. No explanation. It didn't make sense. She wanted to scream, bang at the door. Tell them it was ridiculous, her husband would want her, her husband loved her. She closed her eyes, and the noise of the ward corridor became distant. Their voices became muddled as she tried to calm her mind. She needed to keep it together, there had to be some misunderstanding. Her breath became more even. The panic started to subside. Her eyes remained closed. She began to hear a different voice. At first, she thought it was one of the nurses. But it was only a whisper. She needed to keep her eyes closed to concentrate on it, or she would lose it. She recognised it, pulled from her memory. A memory of a different time. A most precious memory. Her childhood. The whisper almost caressed her like a lullaby.

'Hush Sive, be still. I am here. Hush, remember the sky, look to the sky.'

Sive opened her eyes, startled. But there was no one there, just her alone in a stark hospital waiting room.

Chapter 6

Beechwood.
Gustav Glimt. Private collection.

One of the nurses brought in a cup of tea to Sive. She sat down beside her.

'It's possibly just due to the trauma to his head. I can only imagine how difficult it is for you.' Sive knew the nurse meant well. It was easier to say that, than what they were possibly really thinking, that she was having some hot affair and her husband walked in on them and then he took himself off to the beach to end it all. Or maybe she was a witch to live with and he couldn't take it any more. She winced at the different theories they must be thinking. As if reading her mind, the nurse interrupted her thoughts.

'Try not to over think things, he could be thinking differently by tomorrow.' Sive nodded to her not trusting herself to speak. She would have to let his family know he was awake. How on earth was she going to tell them that she was not allowed to see him? It took some time to absorb the news. She felt like sneaking in when no one was looking to clear all this up with him. But there was no way the nurses were letting her in. The counsellor had been adamant about the fact that she couldn't. It was insulting to be told so. What was she going to do to him, that she was barred? She had never been barred from anything in her life, let alone her husband. But what if she did go in and it was the truth? What if he screamed and shouted for her not to be there? What would they do? Call security and have her removed? Get a barring order against her? This was worse than hearing he had an accident. It was easier to believe it was his injuries. But in the back of her mind the doubt started to creep in. What if he didn't want to see her for some other reason? She had no secrets from him, no hidden affairs. What on earth was she meant to have done to deserve this? There was no doubt that things had been strained lately and he was under pressure with work, but why did he drive off and go to the beach that night? What was going through his mind? It was driving her crazy wondering what was going on with him and not being allowed to go in and ask him what the hell was going on? How would he have handled being told to gently feck off by the holier than thou Bernadette, the counsellor? He would of went mad and refused to adhere to it. But the difference was she could never imagine putting him in that situation.

'Is there any way I can see him even for a few minutes? I know what the counsellor said but perhaps when he sees me he won't be so confused,' Sive pleaded to the nurse.

'I am sorry, but he did make it quite clear, I am sure with some rest he will be better able to handle visitors,' one of the nurses replied.

'I am hardly a visitor, I am his wife, surely I have a right to see him?' Sive cried.

'Of course, but we do have to respect his wishes, please try not to upset yourself, I am sure it will all be sorted soon enough.' Sive grabbed her coat and bag. This was useless, she was getting nowhere. She asked them to contact her and at least let her know if anything changed.

The nurses were passing her on the corridor. No doubt they all thought she was off with her fancy man while her poor husband was barely alive. Well she couldn't control what they thought and it didn't matter now. But she needed to find out what was going on with Dan that had brought them both here. This was no simple accident. She had no doubt he loved her but there was obviously much more to this. A few times during her marriage, she had noticed that Dan's happy go lucky attitude to life would be almost stilled. She never pried too much, she felt that if he wanted to talk he would. But when he did become like that she knew it would pass and sooner rather than later he would be back to his old self. But had she missed something? Was he worried about something and not talking about it? She didn't really understand much about the business, so if he was troubled he was never one to say too much about it, but she would somehow know and that seemed enough for him. Truth was Sive knew she had really showed little interest in the goings on of it. He was doing a major deal with a British company in the last few months. Maybe it had run into a bit of difficulty.

An older nurse stopped her on the way out. She had been on duty for the first two days since the accident and had been very good to Sive and the Gallagher's.

'Sive are you okay? I heard the latest on Dan, I am so sorry I know how upset you must be.' Sive was just keeping it together.

'To be honest I don't know what to think, I feel numb.' She couldn't hold back the tears of pure frustration. The nurse gently hugged her.

'He is on the mend and things have a way of sorting themselves out.' Her face was full of concern. Sive thanked her. She had been so kind and she needed that bit of kindness just then. She needed someone to say that everything would be okay, even if deep down she knew that she had no idea if it would be. Thoughts of her own mother came back to her again. Would she see the same kindness in her eyes? She liked to think she would. From what she could remember, she too was very kind. It was a virtue that was underestimated thought Sive. You didn't need to have left a legacy of something amazing or something unique. Just a legacy of being kind was indeed a very special one. When she was younger she used to wish for her mother, but as she got older she stopped wishing, it was like a form of acceptance that she was gone. But it had been such a loss to an only child. Now she wished with all the might of that lost eight-year-old for her mother. How wonderful it would be to give her a call now to tell her how troubled she was. Her father was fantastic and had done everything he could for his little girl. But right now, all she wanted was her mother to talk to. Somehow, she felt she might understand. She thought back to what had happened earlier. Her mind was obviously playing tricks on her. She had thought she imagined her mother's voice, but that was ridiculous. It must be the lack of sleep.

The shock was subsiding, only to be replaced by something else. A terrible loss had stepped in. The loss of need from her husband. There were so many questions she needed to ask him, how would she cope? It was a relief to step outside into the air. She got into the car and drove the car almost on autopilot. She would have to ring Tom and tell him what had happened. She would just be honest with him. There was no point in telling him anything else, no matter how hard it was.

Back at the house, she noticed the solicitor had rang again. Without even thinking it through properly she returned his call. At least it would stop him ringing. She would just leave a message with the secretary that Dan was out of danger. But when she got through the secretary tried to keep her on the phone a little longer.

'Sive, Barry needs to speak to you rather urgently,' the secretary explained.

'Well surely it can wait for a while, Dan is in hospital. I thought that was why you were calling,' Sive replied.

'Yes, we did hear and we are so sorry Sive. I hope he is out of danger?'

'Yes, he is but it will be a while before he can be in contact with anyone.' She regretted replying to the call.

'Is there any way you could pop in for a few minutes yourself, perhaps in the morning? I am really sorry to disturb you but Barry really needs to go through some stuff with you?' the receptionist urged.

'I don't see why.'

'He can explain it to you.'

'If you insist, but I really know very little about Dan's business. Perhaps he needs some papers signed, I suppose I could do that. I could go in the morning about ten if that suits?' Sive said.

'That would be fine, Sive, and we hope Dan makes a full recovery.' Sive knew the solicitor's secretary, she was a friend of a friend. Everyone in the village knew someone who knew someone else. Everyone would have heard about Dan at this stage. His own secretary had not been in touch yet. Sive was a bit surprised but she was probably busy trying to manage everything without him. She should drop in tomorrow to the office to see if she is coping all right. She made a mental note to ring her and arrange it.

She headed for the bedroom and lay down on the bed, staring out at the trees that were right outside their window. If she was never to leave the room, just looking at them she could tell the seasons. They were bare now, with their branches waving in the wind. She kept watching almost in a trance until she finally fell into a fitful sleep. When she awoke, the bedroom was in darkness. She stared into nothing for a while, too tired to cry although her whole body felt like crying. Slowly she got up and came downstairs to make some tea and ring the hospital. He had woken again. She waited almost without breathing for them to say he was fine now, and wondering where she was. She could leave straight away. But no, he had woken and seemed fully aware of what was after happening. He had made it clear again that he did not want to see his wife. The nurse said she was sorry but there was nothing she could do. Sive politely thanked her and put the phone down. She walked around the room pulling at her hair and then she picked up a photo of both of them in India, her hands touching her husband's face. He was smiling back at her. The words came crashing back

'Always Sive, Always.' Then with all her strength she threw the picture at the fireplace and watched as the glass fell to smithereens.

Chapter 7

Storm Clouds
Karl Fredrik Nordstrom, National Museum, Stockholm, Sweden

The birds were singing when Sive finally fell to sleep. She had taken two sleeping pills, needing the oblivion for a while. She was awakened in a few hours by the ringing of the downstairs phone. The sleeping pills made her even more drowsy, almost like a hangover. The phone was ringing again, she had forgotten to bring the handset up and put it by the bed. Dragging herself from her bed she wrapped herself in Dan's dressing gown to answer it.

'Hi Sive, sorry to disturb you, just checking you can make it in for our meeting this morning?' It was the solicitor's secretary.

'It's Carol, from Barry White's office.' Sive tried to think of an excuse. The last thing she wanted was to go in there.

'I might have to leave it actually, I'm afraid something has come up,' she replied.

'We would really appreciate it if you could come in Sive, even for half an hour, alternatively Barry will pop out to see you. But he really does need to see you today,' she explained.

'Fine, but I have no idea how I am going to help.' She knew she sounded irritated. But why on earth would they drag her in, what was so feckin important?

'If you can just come in Sive, it would help,' the secretary urged.

'Okay, I will see you shortly,' Sive replied, hanging up the phone before the secretary had the chance to say anything else. Her head ached just thinking about it. It would be easier to crawl back into bed and try to blot out the day. She got a shower to try to wake herself up. The hot water eased the tension in her shoulders. She pulled on some dark jeans and a black polo jumper. The house was quite warm but she was still cold. The thoughts of food made her feel ill so a cup of tea had to do. Cradling the cup, she looked around the kitchen. The cupboards had been stripped and painted a duck egg blue to match the old Aga which took pride of place. There was a collection of books, paintings and old china on handmade shelves and a big comfy chair by the cooker that Dan normally plonked himself on when he came home from work. Sive often found him asleep there if she was out in the studio when he came home. Suddenly she felt very much alone. She checked her phone to see if there was any message from the hospital. Nothing. A big fat nothing. How the hell could Dan do this to her? It must be the accident after all, in a million years she would never of thought Dan could treat her like this.

In the bathroom mirror, her naturally pale face was ghostly looking. She tied her damp hair up and put some blush on. The thoughts of talking to anyone seemed impossible. There was a safety in the house. She was in control of who she had to talk with. With a heavy heart, she locked up and grabbed her coat and a warm scarf. The intercom at the gate was bleeping. She peeped out of the window. It was Mrs Gallagher's car. There was no way she was answering it. Her mobile rang and then her land-line. She ignored all of them. She watched as Mrs Gallagher got out and peered through the gates. She had demanded to have a key, but Sive had refused. It was very rare that she would not answer the gate to her but today was certainly one of them. She waited a few minutes until she had left and then left herself. Knowing Mrs Gallagher, she would be back shortly again. She had left a curt message on her mobile to tell her to contact her immediately.

It was unusual to have a solicitor in such a small place but Thornback village was far from ordinary. Everyone seemed to know everyone, except for the large estate out the road that had a lot of commuters living in it. They tended to do all their dealings in the nearest town, not really mixing with the village people or the surrounding neighbours. Sive did not blame them. Thornback was quite a click, and outsiders where looked upon with suspicion.

The village consisted of a local shop, a post office, the solicitors, butchers and two pubs. Other than that, a school, a village hall and a church completed the village. Yet there was a hierarchy bigger than the whole of Wicklow town. Mrs Gallagher was at the height of it. There were many meetings in the village hall that she seemed to be the head of. Indeed, they could hardly be held if she was not there. Sive knew that her mother in law felt she had a certain standing in the village that she held on to for dear life. The Gallagher's had always been regarded as having a certain amount of grandeur. Their farm took over so much of Thornback, and seemed to look over the village like it was in command. Most of the families had lived there for generations. Any outsiders who thought they were going to live in the idyllic friendly village were sorely mistaken. Some of the farmers sold off land for sites in the boom and got an earful from Mrs Gallagher. She had held a special meeting in the village to voice her anger.

'Farmers with no sense selling off any bit of land they can are destroying our village. Bringing in all sorts who have no respect for the way things are done here in Thornback.'

Mrs. Gallagher liked to go to Sunday mass and had been quite upset when Dan and Sive had failed to appear. Nobody could miss Mrs Gallagher at mass, as she would always make an impact in whatever outfit and hat that she would appear in. There had been a terrible row when Sive told her that she didn't want a church ceremony for their marriage, opting for a civil one.

'You can drag me to a hut on the side of Mount Leinster if you agree to marry me, but I am organising the party afterwards,' Dan had laughed. They had a beautiful ceremony and true to his word Dan had organised a party to end all parties. Mrs Gallagher had refused to go at first but after some coaxing from the local parish priest who was a good friend to Dan and Sive, she had attended.

It was the little church in Thornback that Sive found herself driving to this morning on the way to her meeting. She may not be religious or attend mass but she liked to go in when no one was around. She parked near to it hoping she would be alone. Inside there was a small area that was called the area of reflection. It had a statue of Mary. Sive liked to sit there and look at the statue. Unlike some of the other statues of saints that could look quite fierce, there was real compassion on the face of Mary in the statue. Whoever had made it had captured her grace in the cold sculpture. There were candles to light underneath the statue and Sive lit two. In the silence of the ancient walls she could feel the hot tears fall. It felt good to release them.

'Please just give me some strength.' She looked up at the statue and continued saying the words like a mantra. She really liked the little chapel. It was small compared to most of the others scattered in Ireland.

It dated back to the 15th century and she liked to sit in it and try to feel what it was like to exist back then. She could close her eyes and see the monks who had founded it, walking around in their silence, spending their days in total prayer. It must have been a strange life but surely a peaceful one. Perhaps some of their ancient peace remained in the thickness of the walls. She closed her eyes and thought about Dan.

What if he did not want her anymore? Maybe there was someone else and he wanted to leave her. The thoughts of this made her feel nauseated. But she knew in her heart that it was not in Dan's make up to have an affair. If things were not right between them, he would be honest with her and leave.

She parked near to the solicitors. She would just get this over with and go home. It would only take a few minutes but as she was walking she could feel herself grow panicky, it all seemed so unreal. What on earth was she doing here? She wanted to run home and go to her art studio and forget about everything for a while. She could turn on her music, get her paints ready and lose herself for a few hours. She promised herself that she would as soon as she had this meeting.

The office was warm and the secretary looked like she was waiting for her.

'Sive, are you ok? You look so pale.' A look of concern crossed the secretary's face.

'I'm fine, thanks, will I have to wait long?' If she did she decided she would just leave.

'You can go in now Sive.' There was no backing out now so she just went in. Barry White was a large man, who looked like he should be working out on the land rather than in an office. He got up to greet her and shook her hand. Sive had met him out with Dan loads of times but she had never really had a chat with him on her own.

'I'm really sorry to hear about Dan. I am sure you are very worried about him. How is he?' he asked with genuine concern.

'He is more stable now. What is all this about, Barry? Can it not wait until Dan is better and can handle it himself?'

'I am afraid not Sive. Please take a seat.' Reluctantly she sat down.

'Would you like a glass of water Sive?' she asked, giving the solicitor a large file.

'No thanks, I am sure this won't take long.' The secretary left and closed the door behind her. Barry cleared his throat and rustled through the files as if stalling for a few minutes.

'Look, if it's something to sign, perhaps I better wait until Dan is better,' Sive said.

'No, I didn't ask you to come in here to sign anything. I have some rather difficult news I am afraid,' he said hesitantly.

'Difficult? In what way?' Sive asked.

'There is no easy way to tell you this Sive but Dan was in a lot of financial stress.' He looked straight at Sive, who looked confused at what he was talking about.

'What do you mean, was the business not doing well? I know it's a bit slower since the recession but things are building back up again. Dan did say that like every business the recession damaged us but it's improving now. He did seem very stressed recently. Sive looked bewildered, how could it be in financial difficulty? Dan had never said anything about that. She wondered did he know.

Barry put down the pen he was holding and looked at the woman in front of him..

'Sive, did Dan talk to you at all about what is happening with the company, about the trouble that it is in?

'What are you saying Barry, is it serious?' Sive asked worriedly.

'I'm afraid so Sive.' He moved his body around in the chair, loosening his tie as he took a large gulp of water.

'What's going on?' Sive asked, noticing how agitated the solicitor appeared.

'It's not good.'

She could feel her stomach muscles tighten, the nausea she had felt earlier threatened to make her retch.

'What is it for God's sake, what financial trouble is he in, is it revenue or something like that?' The solicitor shook his head.

'Things have really closed in on Dan, he tried everything to stop this happening. I hate to be the one to tell you, but with Dan in hospital, I feel it's crucial you are aware of what is going on.'

'Well, what is it?' What is going on that is so crucial that I know?' Sive said, exasperated.

'Dan's company is with the receiver Sive. It's over. The company is gone.'

Chapter 8

Dance to the music of time
Nicholas Poussin. The Wallace collection, London.

Sive thought she must have been punched in the face. It was as if the air around her had become thick with fog.

'Sive, you had no idea I gather?' The solicitor asked, his voice full of concern. She tried to find her voice, she wanted to scream at him, her body wanting to take off and only stop when she was miles away from the room. But when she spoke it was only a whisper.

'None. I had no clue,' she replied in almost a whisper.

'I see. It must be a terrible shock so.' He rang his secretary to bring in some strong tea.

'How long has it been in trouble?' She tried to keep her voice steady. Was this some mistake? How on earth could Dan's business be gone? He had put years into it. They had put everything on hold to allow him to devote so much time to it. Barry White got up and walked to the window, shaking his head.

'Dan was doing really well right through the recession. His company was expanding. Software development is such a lucrative business to be in and Dan was flying high. Were you aware about the British deal he was involved in?'

'Yes, he said it was huge, he said it would take the company to another level,' Sive replied.

'To be honest it was looking like that, the banks all had put their money behind it. He was liaising with a British company who wanted to act as distributors for his software. It was a super deal that would take it right across Britain in all the hospitals, which was huge. That is why he invested heavily in the company, to help complete the deal. But when all the investment was put in, they had never expected Britain to pull out of Europe. Everything changed overnight in Britain. The deal seemed watertight, but there was a clause. They wanted the deal just as much as Dan did. It was only the finer details that had delayed it going through.

Then when the shock of Brexit happened, they had a knee jerk reaction. Not knowing how it could affect them with Ireland, they decided to go with a British company. Less risk involved. Dan took a risk Sive, investing so heavily, but it seemed worth it, the deal was almost there but it fell at the last hurdle. The company just could not take the hit.'

'But surely after everything with the recession, the bank would not loan money without being fairly sure it was safe?'

'True, but it did seem watertight. Dan's business was secure and he had plenty of assets to use as collateral,' Barry replied gravely.

'I had absolutely no idea, I know he invested some money that my father had given to us.'

Barry White got up and took off his jacket.

'I'm afraid that's gone too, Sive.'

'Oh, my God, what is left if the business is gone and our money? I am sure he has some other investments. What about the land he inherited from his parents, please tell me it's safe?'

'Sive, I wish I could tell you that it was, but the deeds of the land were used as collateral. The land has a lot of good road frontage, so is suitable for housing if anyone can get planning on it, so this did increase the value of the collateral. Any money invested or otherwise was used to keep the business going.'

'So, what are you telling me, all that is left is our home, everything is gone.' The solicitor got up and paced the room, then he walked over to Sive and sat on the chair beside her.

'Sive I am not sure how to tell you this, but you have to know. Dan had your home re mortgaged and used as collateral for the business.' She looked at him, her eyes not blinking.

'You signed it, Sive.'

Sive had no recollection of signing anything of the sort.

'Are you telling me that he forged your signature, you were unaware that your home was used as collateral?

'Is the house under threat?' He shook his head as if trying to find the right words.

'Sive, the house, your home. I absolutely hate to have to tell you this. But your home is also with the receiver.' Sive felt her breath stop. It was as if that moment was frozen. She knew whatever happened in her life from now on, this moment was her turning point. She looked at him as if he was not real, as if the very moment was not real.

'Sive, did you understand what I said?'

'Could you repeat that please?' Her voice was barely audible.

'Sive, the house is gone, everything, even Dan's car. They had given him a final notice the day he had the crash.' She stared at him. She suddenly felt very trapped, like a caged bird, frightened and desperately thinking of an escape route. She expected the building to start crashing around her, matching the turmoil in her head.

'Sive, are you ok?'

She tried to compose herself.

'My home, our home, I don't understand, how can they take it, how could he remortgage our home without my knowledge?'

'I did ring you Sive, and told you what Dan wanted you to sign. You came into the office.' Barry pointed out.

'I remember now, he told me it was only a formality, some stupid clause that he had to adhere to. I thought nothing of it. I never doubted him,' Sive said incredulously.

'But I wrote to you Sive and explained the implications, you had to go into the bank and sign it. Were the details not explained to you? I had said on my letter that if you have any hesitation at all to contact me.' Sive felt sick to the pit of her stomach. She did remember going into the bank. The bank manager had explained it to her. But while the manager had to take a call, Dan had told her not to worry about it, the bank manager was just making a fuss. Dan had said it was to do with insurance and had made light of it. They had both signed it and then went to lunch in the town. They had never talked about it since that day.

'I never read through it properly. Dan told me not to worry about it. I believed him, it was just a formality. Are you telling me I signed our house away that day?' Sive tried to remember. She had trusted Dan completely. That was what she was meant to do, wasn't it? But now she suddenly felt a fool, how could she have signed anything without truly knowing the implications? A tiny voice in the back of her head reminded her that it suited her to let Dan make all the financial decisions. What era was she living in, not to be aware of her financial situation?

'Look Sive, if you signed the documents not knowing what you were signing, we could make a case against it. But I must tell you, Dan could then be up for fraud.

'What! Dan, Fraud! Are you serious?

'Very serious I am afraid, the banks and the revenue are hungry for their money and they will not show any kindness to someone who has tricked them as such into losing their money.'

'How long have you known about this?' Sive could not identify the emotion than was threatening to suffocate her.

'It's being going on for a while now Sive. Dan to be fair hoped things would turn around for him. He tried to fight and look for new investment but it was useless. He was almost denying that it was happening until it finally did. But the revenue had also stepped in and put a stop to any chance he had of keeping his business. It was like a race against time and Dan lost big time.'

'But how on earth was I not aware of any of it?'

'To be honest, I have no idea. But from tomorrow it will become common knowledge Sive, because the receivers will move into the company and begin to wind it up. There must be an announcement to the staff and that is going to be difficult. They will be entitled to statutory redundancy but there is nothing else left. I am afraid they are all out of a job tomorrow.'

'This is a nightmare, is there really nothing to be done?' Sive replied, shocked.

'If there was anything to be done Sive, Dan has tried it.' Fear pulled at every fibre of Sive's being. She knew she had to ask him something and she needed the truth. Something she had tried to push out of her mind since the accident.

'Barry, do you think my husband tried to take his own life?'

He shook his head. 'I have no idea Sive, but I do know he was very tormented and things were unravelling for him beyond his control.'

'He was on the beach earlier that night before the crash. He wanted to talk when he first came home. He was all over the place. Was he going to tell me? We had guests arriving, people he thought would invest in the company.'

'It was too late for that,' Barry replied.

'He was obviously going out of his mind with worry, he forgot to cancel them.'

'But I gather he is able to talk now. Has he mentioned anything about it?'

'Dan refuses to see me. I had no idea why, but after what you have told me, I feel like I was living with a stranger.' There was a knock on the door and the secretary arrived with the tea. Sive knew by the look on her face that she knew what was going on. She handed her the tea but Sive didn't trust her hands to hold it. She had to get out of there.

'I need to get some air, please.' The secretary opened the window and Sive went towards it, breathing in the cold November breeze. Her mind and body were so exhausted, she wondered was it all a dream, or a nightmare more like. She sat back down and took a sip of hot tea and tried to get her body to calm down.

'What happens now?' She realised she sounded stronger than she felt. She was grateful her voice didn't let her down.

'Dan has the documents to state that you were given three weeks to vacate your house and return his car. I could try to talk to them to see if I can delay it, under the circumstances.'

'Is there anything that can be done to save the house?' Sive asked, her voice trembling. He shook his head.

'Dan tried everything, it was so heavily mortgaged there really is no way of saving it. We can certainly try again, as it is your family home, but Sive, I am very doubtful of the outcome, in fact I can be certain that there is no saving it.'

'But surely there are avenues to try?'

'Dan tried everything, the only thing we have is that you signed this without real knowledge.'

'I can't put my husband in jail for fraud, Barry.'

' There is no other way.'

'How long have I got?'

'I will contact the receiver and let you know the details.' Sive could feel herself crumble. It felt so surreal, it was as if she was watching someone else, but this was happening to her and Dan was not there. She steadied herself as she stood up and grabbed her coat.

'What about his staff, they are all so loyal to him?'

'They will get statuary redundancy, but after that there is very little we can do for them. I can fill you in on how it goes.'

'I would like to go too. It's the least I can do,' Sive replied.

'You don't have to Sive, it will be very difficult.'

'I will be there,' she replied, leaving no room for negotiation.

'Would you like me to drive you home Sive, or I can get Carol to go with you?' Barry asked, concerned.

'No, but thank you, and I appreciate your honesty Barry. I only wish Dan had given me the same courtesy.'

'For what it's worth Sive, he thought he was protecting you.' Sive stared at him for a moment, praying she could hold it together until she got out of there. ;She could see the pity in his face. She wondered did he see the anger, the anger at herself for allowing this to happen?

'I'm not a child Barry, I have no idea why he felt he needed to protect me, anyway we can see where that has got us.'

'Dan has lost so much Sive, many businesses went down but were not personally guaranteed by personal assets. I did try to tell Dan, but to be honest it was very low risk, the deal was almost there.'

'I have lost a lot today Barry, but unfortunately I have also lost my trust in my husband.' With that she made her way down the stairs to the street. Her legs were shaking, in a half hour her life had been pulled away from her. She tried to calm her breath, she needed to get home.

'Sive, I almost passed you by, I wasn't sure it was you.' Sive looked at the woman in front of her. Oh no, of all the people to run in to today.

'Hi Imelda, sorry I was miles away.' She watched as Imelda Murphy looked her up and down, taking in everything she was wearing. No doubt to report to her cronies in detail.

'I'm just rushing around, we are off shopping you see.'

'Lovely, sorry I must run myself,' Sive replied.

'I am off to New York with the girls. We go every year. It's a mad shopping weekend but I love it. We love it.' Sive knew who the gang were. A few women who looked down their noses at most of the other people in the village. They competed heavily with who had the biggest house, car and holiday. Sive had nothing in common with any of them. She knew Imelda had had her sights set on either Dan or Tom as a husband, and had been livid when Sive arrived on the scene.

'How is Dan? I was shocked to hear of the accident.' Sive tried to think of how she could get away from her.

'He's out of danger now thank you, sorry, I must rush.'

'We might pop up to see him, myself and Derek, when I get home from our trip.' With that she tossed her freshly blow dried blonde bob, running her spray tanned hand through it.

'Well enjoy your trip.' Sive almost ran away from her before she could ask her any more questions.

'Tell Dan I said hello,' Imelda called after her. Well that will be highly unlikely. It would be difficult to tell Dan anything when he wouldn't speak to her. She rushed to the safety of the car. There was no way she risked meeting anyone so she started it up and drove home. Home, the home that would be gone soon.

When she got to the entrance she pressed the code to open the gates. Sive adored the house and had felt privileged to live in it, She drove in and the gates closed behind her. She was safe now, away from Imelda Murphy or anyone else. She let go of the salty tears and cried as the anguish of the heartbreak of losing her beautiful home hit her properly. Dan must know what she is going through now, and he chose to shut her out of his life. She was alone in every sense of the word.

Chapter 9

A Country Home
Seattle Art Museum, Seattle.

It felt strange walking into the house now knowing what she knew. She had believed that this is where they would grow old together. Have children and rear them. Now everything was a sham. Dan had lied to her and deceived her. It seemed impossible to think Dan would be capable of such a thing. Sive sunk into a chair and stared into space. That night at the beach, what was he really doing there? She begged it not to be the truth. She still had his phone. Her heart pounded, running up the stairs searching for it. She charged it up and went through the calls. There were lots of calls the day of the accident and then there was one text that he had sent to Barry White.

'It's all over so?' the reply from Barry was.
'It's over Dan. You have to tell Sive.'

But he hadn't. He had told her nothing. Had he decided to throw himself in to the sea? But that didn't make sense. Why then did he end up in a car accident? Sive had so many questions. She wanted to drive to the hospital and ask him what the hell was he thinking of? Now she could ask no questions. He had left her to deal with all this. How could he gamble with their life, without even telling her? Their home, their beautiful home. He knew how much she loved it. He had gambled too much.

She looked around at all her paintings in the hall. She had collected art for as long as she could remember. It may seem the hobby of the rich but Sive had deprived herself of so much to save money to buy art. The solicitor had not mentioned the contents of the house, she would have to check with him. But her beloved art would have to be pulled out of her arms. Some of it was worthless to anyone else. But each painting had meant something to Sive when she had bought it or painted it herself. She had spent so long deciding on where to hang them just so the light was right. Now it all seemed such a sham. They didn't even own the wall that they hung on. She had painted the walls in an antique white to allow the paintings to come to life.

The house was cold. Lighting the fire, she took in the smell of turf that was so dry it lit up straight away. Dan had wanted to put in a modern stove but Sive had persuaded him to keep the traditional fire. It carried her back to her childhood home. There was a comfort in it that soothed her. Her father tended to light the small fire in their house before she even got up for school. There was no heating in the house but he lit the fire almost every day so she never remembered being cold there. It was so cosy to get up for her porridge and eat it beside the warm fire crackling away. It was there to welcome her home from school and they had spent many evenings drawing, chatting together and learning to be a family, just father and daughter. She needed to speak to him now, so she wrapped herself up in a blanket and curled up beside the fire and rang her father.

He answered it almost immediately. She had already told him about Dan and had texted him each day. He wanted to come up, but she asked him to wait for a few days. On hearing his voice, she could hardly speak.

'Sive love are you ok, is Dan ok?" She had not planned to tell him everything but suddenly it all came pouring out.

'Oh, Dad, it's awful, you are not going to believe what is after happening.' Quickly she filled him in on all that had gone on. Dan's refusal to speak to her, the house being taken, her not knowing anything. And then she sobbed until finally she stopped and calmed herself.

'The house Dad, our beautiful house. I love everything about it even though we are forever fixing it up. I can't believe I have to walk away from it now,' she sobbed.

'Sive I don't want you on your own, I can be with you about ten. How the hell did he keep all this from you? I was so sure everything was going so well for him.'

'I am his wife and I had no clue, so what on earth does that say about us? I was living with a stranger all these months. He never mentioned a word. The solicitor could hardly believe I knew nothing. What else is he hiding all this time? Dad, there is no sense in you driving all the way here tonight. I will wait until tomorrow and see what the solicitor says about moving out and I would prefer to drive down to you in a few days, when I know a little more.'

'I don't want you to be alone,' her father insisted.

'I know, but you are only a phone call away and to be honest, I think for the minute I would prefer some time to absorb everything. You know me, I sometimes deal with things better with a bit of space.' It was true that Sive could spend long periods on her own, especially if something was bothering her.

'I will call Beth too, Dad, and if I need to I can stay with her so don't worry too much. I am better already knowing you are there.'

'Okay love, but ring me at any stage, even if it's the middle of the night.'

'Thanks Dad, I will ring you tomorrow after I talk with the solicitor.' Putting the phone down she felt better. Just knowing that her Dad would be there helped enormously. She realised not for the first time how wise he was. She had told him everything and he had never judged her or Dan. Beth to be fair was just as non-prejudice. She had told her about Dan not wanting to see her. She was as shocked as Sive and thought it must have to do with the trauma of the accident. The fire had lit up now and the room was warm, her eyes were heavy with exhaustion and she drifted off to sleep.

A couple of hours later she was awoken by the intercom. She had no intention of answering it. Her mobile rang and Beth was almost shouting down the phone

'Are you okay? Will you let me in?' she shrieked.

'What? Is that you at the gates?'

'Yes! Will you let me in?' Sive got up and buzzed the gates opened. She put some more turf on the fire. Beth arrived in armed with bags of food, and almost dropped it on the way in.

'Feck sake, I rang you a few times and there was no answer, are you okay?' She headed straight for the kitchen and put on the kettle. Sive followed her in and sat at the table.

'Yeah I must of went to sleep when I came home from the solicitors.' Beth stopped what she was doing and turned to Sive.

'The solicitors, what were you doing there?' Sive filled her in in on the developments. She trusted Beth as much as her father. She counted her blessings there and then to have her.

'You cannot be serious, Sive, not the house?'

'Yes, the house, our beautiful house.'

'I can't believe it,' Beth replied, dumbfounded.

I still can't quite believe it myself,' Sive said almost to herself.

'Surely they cannot take it just like that?'

'It's being going on for a while, I had no clue. It doesn't say a lot about our marriage, does it? I am so bloody angry Beth. According to the solicitor he's been fighting the banks and the revenue for ages and there was no time left. The solicitor said I could fight it but he was not very optimistic about the outcome. He is a good solicitor, I don't think he would advise me wrong.'

Beth hugged her friend.

'Oh, Sive, this is unreal. I don't know what to say to you. You have turned this old pile of rubble into something so beautiful and now it's being taken away from you on top of having your husband in the state he is in,' Beth exclaimed.

'Not to mention that we are completely broke and the money my father gave us is gone, as well as the land the Gallagher's gave us. Mrs Gallagher will have a stroke when she finds out about the land. You know how she feels about new houses in the village, and her own land may be covered in them now. Everything gone on his bloody big deal. It's not the money, the land, even the house, it's the lies. Lies, lies and more lies. Our whole marriage is a sham.'

'Sive, I know you must be angry, but maybe there is more to it. One thing I know about Dan is that he loves you more than anything. I cannot imagine why he's done this, it seems surreal.'

'I am going to start looking in Dan's office to see if I can make any sense of it all, will you help me?'

'Of course, but should we really be looking at Dan's stuff?'

'He has left me no choice,' Sive said angrily.

'First you can eat something, before you fade away,' Beth replied. Sive was about to say that she wasn't hungry but she knew by the expression on Beth's face that she better not. Beth began looking for plates and cups.

'There is a fab new café and deli after opening near me. You would love it, it's all healthy stuff and has lots of that vegan stuff you eat, I brought some lovely soup and salad for you to try.'

Sive tried a little soup, but her stomach was in knots.

'Thanks Beth, and thank you for being here,' Beth looked at her friend, her face full of concern.

'You'll get through this, I know you will.'

'I probably will, but whether I will still have a marriage at the end of it is another story altogether,' Sive replied sadly.

Chapter 10

Eight Bells
Addison Gallery of American Art, Andover, USA

A large rosewood writing desk with a green leather insert took pride of place in Dan's office. Papers lay strewn, the waste-paper basket full. A photo of Sive and Dan eating ice cream in Venice sat on the table. Ten years ago, now. They had backpacked across Europe for two months, living in hostels, eating slices of pizza and drinking cheap bottles of wine. They had thought about living abroad, falling for a run-down farmhouse in Burgundy. Sive's father had given her a large sum of money that would go a long way towards making it habitable. Dan had tried to suss out how he would start his business over there. Sive could live anywhere, all she needed to do was paint. They both had decent French.

'Can you see it Sive, you and me living here, sitting here on the veranda, growing some vines,' Dan asked.

'Could I live in this beauty, to wake up to the scent of lavender, the rolling fields dotted with vineyards and ancient villages? It would be heaven Dan.'

'Would you miss Ireland too much Sive, you do love our rugged land?'

But in the end, Dan thought it better to start his business in Ireland. They had settled to stay in Wicklow. The money went into Dan's business. Looking at the picture now taken in a little town nestled deep in the Burgundy countryside, Sive could hardly believe how things seemed to have turned out. Then, they were so happy just to be together. It never mattered what they were doing if they were together. So, when had that changed? Or was it the same for lots of couples? Life had got in the way. Ambition and money. But she was happy to go along with it. She knew that there was a need in Dan to prove himself. God knows Mrs Gallagher wasn't very happy when he announced he had no intention of joining them. She had put up lots of arguments, but Dan was having none of it.

Sive had been proud of him standing up to the pressure and doing his own thing. He had made a great success of it. Or so it seemed.

'Right what will I do? I still feel bad looking in Dan's files.' Beth was going through the incoming post that still was unopened.

'You can begin there and open all those and see if there is anything in it about the banks. But first give me a hand, I want to open this filing cabinet,' Sive said to Beth.

'Is it locked? I feel bad enough going through his stuff. But breaking into his files!'

'Well he has hidden enough, if I have to break open an old filing cabinet to find out how I lost my home, I have every right,' Sive replied curtly. It was an old cabinet and with a few tugs and pulls they managed to break it open.

'I wonder what we will find in here?' Beth said dryly.

'It's just, he always seemed so sure of himself, so confident. Almost like he could take on the world,' Beth exclaimed. Sive shook her head in agreement.

'I know. He was always so driven. Once he got his own company there seemed to be no stopping him.' Beth started opening all the post.

'I am sure you're not the first wife to find herself like this,' Sive sat down on Dan's chair and looked out at the woods.

'But that's it Beth, I thought we were different to most couples. I trusted him completely, I have never doubted him in anything. I thought we were strong, devoted to each other.'

'He was obviously trying to protect you Sive,' Beth tried to reassure her.

'The solicitor said the same Do I look as if I need protecting or something? You protect a child from the truth if you think they cannot handle it, not your wife for Christ's sake.' Sive threw some papers to the floor in frustration.

'Did you not notice anything strange with him, Sive? Was he acting weird? Although when I think of it I saw you both a few weeks ago, and he was fine, in the Italian that night, remember?'

'Of course I do, we were the last to leave as usual. Dan got friendly with the owner and they chatted about Italian soccer until the early hours. I was driving and had to drag Dan away at two in the morning. Would you have known then that he was about to lose everything he owned?'

'Here, what's this?' Beth held up a letter that looked like it had been hand delivered. It was from the banks. They read the contents. It was loud and clear. The bank wanted Dan to put the house up for sale. They said they had exhausted all other options and following their last meeting with him they wanted the sale to go ahead immediately. They wanted him to act as the vendor to recoup the money that was due to them. It was dated almost a month ago. Sive reread the letter.

'Jesus, how could he not have said anything? How did he carry on as if nothing was wrong?' Sive stared at the letter in disbelief. Beth took it from her and read it again.

'What the hell had he been thinking, to keep all this from you? It's baffling.'

'Did he think I couldn't handle it, what the hell did he think?'

They sifted through more letters, all telling the same story. Found lots of final demands and solicitors letters. There were tons of letters from the revenue and the banks. There was a letter from the high court. It just went on and on.

'How could he read all these and then come out and say nothing and ask what is for tea? I feel I was living with a stranger. I need a drink.' Beth nodded in agreement, they did need a drink.

'I do too, come on, I spotted a bottle of white wine in the fridge. Bring in the papers to the fire and you can look at them in a bit of comfort.' Beth went into the kitchen and poured two glasses and brought them in. Sive sat on the sofa trying to make sense of all the paperwork. She sipped the wine and after a little while she could feel her muscles relax a little.

'That's it, it's gone, all this is gone and it looks like my marriage is a sham.' She looked around the house. We have only finished it and now it's gone. I can't believe it and I can't even talk to Dan about it.' Her eyes fell on the wallpaper she had searched the internet for. A dark emerald green that seemed to bring the nature outside indoors. It was an original 1930s. Where the hell did everything go so wrong? Why had she not noticed? Was there something strangely wrong with her for all this to happen without her knowledge? Thoughts of utter failure filled her head.

'We have nothing. We don't even have a marriage,' she drained her glass.

'Sive, you don't know that yet.'

'Well it's not looking very good, is it? My husband wants me nowhere near him. Has banned me from visiting him. He seems to have led a secret life that I know nothing of. He didn't trust me with the truth. He chose to lie and keep me in the dark about everything. Not really a Mills and Boon romance, is it?' she said

'Perhaps it is the trauma from the accident Sive, maybe when he comes around properly he will make more sense,' Beth replied.

'According to the nurse, he has come around and he is making perfect sense. He wants me to stay away. Loud and clear. No mistake. Anyway, look at how much he has kept from me. What else could he have kept from me? Maybe he was leaving me anyway. He wanted to talk that night. Now it makes sense, he was telling me he was leaving me. There must be someone else?'

'You don't know that, stop jumping to conclusions,' Beth quickly replied.

'How do you know he hasn't? I feel I don't know what he could have been up to. I am such an idiot,' Sive said loudly.

'All I'm saying is don't give up on him yet, and stop blaming yourself for not knowing. He chose not to tell you. You cannot take the blame for that,' Beth tried to reason.

'Well, I have enough to worry about with this lot. If the bank thinks I am going to sell it for them they have another thing coming. If they want it there is nothing I can do but they can bloody well sell it themselves. When everything is packed, I will leave the keys with the solicitor and they can all do what they like with it. I must start packing. Where on earth do I even start and where the hell will I put everything? Oh, my God it has just dawned on me! We have nowhere to live! I was so wrapped up in the fact that I would have to say goodbye to the house that the realisation that we are suddenly homeless did not enter my head.'

'You are not homeless. You can come stay in my new apartment if you want, and so can Dan.'

'You have only moved in yourself, I am dying to see it. I never thought I might be looking for a bed in it,' Sive said sadly.

'You are more than welcome,' Beth said, hugging her.

'I might just take you up on that offer, even for a short time Beth. I know I can stay with Dad too, but it's such a shock not to have your home, I can hardly get my head around it.'

'Look we will figure it out together, you are not on your own Sive.'

'Thanks Beth, here pour me another glass of wine, it might knock me out.' Sive had barely slept since the accident. Tonight, the wine might lull her into some sort of sleep. She just wanted a bit of oblivion for a while.

'That's the bottle gone,' Beth said, draining the last drop.

'There is lots in the wine rack. There is a really good bottle of red. I feel like getting drunk. Dan was saving it for something special. Now seems as good a time as any. It's not every day you lose everything. I'll grab it and two fresh glasses.' She was just getting up when the intercom at the gates rang.

'Who could that be, at this time, it's past eleven?' Sive exclaimed.

'Hold on, I will get rid of them,' Beth said. Sive brought the wine in to the sitting room and snuggled into the couch, hugging a pillow. She could hear Beth talking to someone but couldn't make it out. The conversation seemed to be getting heated. Beth hung up and pushed the intercom opened. Her face was puce when she came in to the sitting room.

'It's your mother in law. She is a piece of work. I told her you were exhausted and would call her tomorrow. She was having none of it and demanded I open the gates. I told her I would talk to you first and she said that if I didn't open them she would drive through them.'

'Oh, not Mrs Gallagher,' Sive groaned. 'I bet she has found out that Dan has banned me and she is coming to find out why.'

'Sive, you stay here and I will tell her you are in bed,' Beth said.

'She will only march up the stairs and demand to see me.'

'Just let her try,' Beth said defiantly.

'Oh, let her in, I'll have to face her sometime, now is as good as any.' They could hear the car door closing and Mrs Gallagher clip clopping towards the door. She rapped hard on it. Beth went to let her in.

'Mrs Gallagher, how are you?' She made no reply but stared at Beth. 'It's a bit late for visiting, is it something urgent?'

Mrs Gallagher threw her eyes to heaven.

'It is not your place to tell me when is appropriate to call on my daughter in law. This is family business and you have no part in it, let me tell you.' Sive came to see what was happening.

'Beth is the nearest thing I have to a sister Mrs Gallagher, so she is staying.' Mrs Gallagher looked at Beth as if she was contaminated.

'I will not discuss anything in front of her, this is family business. I want to speak to you.' She gave Beth a look that left her in no doubt what she thought of her.

'Kindly leave me to speak to my daughter in law in private.'

'I am going nowhere so whatever you have to say, you better get on with it.' Beth stared right back at her. Sive was afraid Mrs Gallagher would take a swipe at Beth, she looked so angry.

'How dare you speak to me like that? I suppose you have something to do with this cult Sive is in too.' Beth looked at Sive. It was Sive's turn to throw her eyes up to heaven.

'Mrs Gallagher is convinced that Dad is in some cult because he has long hair and eats no meat. She thinks I am in it, too, and has warned Dan not to follow.' Mrs Gallagher turned towards Sive.

'Exactly! But he didn't listen, did he? You did this to my son. You have dragged him into this cult, this terrible cult that has brought Dan to where he is today. I know all about the trouble he is in, oh yes, I know it all now.'

'What the hell are you talking about?' Sive shrieked.

'You know exactly what I am talking about. Oh, yes, the nurses have told us. He wants you nowhere near him. He tried to stay away from your cult but you kept dragging him in. Why else would he not want you near him? You should be ashamed of yourself. Everything he has done for you. Living in luxury and not a care in the world. But it wasn't enough for you. You wanted him to join this cult and he had enough. So, he drove away and crashed the car with worry about you and your cult. No wonder he wants you nowhere near him.' Beth stared at Mrs Gallagher in disbelief.

'Sive is not part of any cult and neither is her father Milo,' Beth exclaimed.

'Call it what you like. It's a cult. Eating all those strange foods and those strange people. I have heard all about it. Oh, we met them at the wedding.' Beth looked at Sive who looked like she might explode with anger.

'The people from the farmer's market,' Sive explained, her voice raised.

'They try to pretend it's all nice and they will look after you in this cult, oh I have read all about it, and then they take your mind and your money. It's a CULT!' Sive stared at Mrs Gallagher.

'What do you know, what do you know about Dan?' she asked, her voice barely under control.

'Only that it is all over the village that the business is gone. My own neighbour Bridie Whelan drove in at high speed in her Mini to commiserate with me about Dan losing his business. I knew straight away what it was. The CULT! I knew it,' Mrs Gallagher cried.

'I tried to warn him. Oh, yes, I did. But he wouldn't listen. Your kind should stick to yourselves. I have nothing against your father or his cult but I don't want it in my family.' Beth looked stunned by Mrs Gallagher's outburst. She was about to say something but Sive put her hand up to stop her. She could feel her heart beating so loud that it felt like it was going to come out on to her jumper. Her body got so hot that she began to get beads of perspiration on her brow. Mrs Gallagher had her mouth open as if she was going on another rant but Sive grabbed her by the arms, staring at her. She didn't know she possessed such anger but it was engulfing her.

'I am not in a cult and neither is my father. Stop it.' Sive screamed. It looked like Sive could hit Mrs Gallagher she was so angry. Beth's mouth dropped. Mrs Gallagher backed away.

'How dare you speak to me like that? Now your true colours are coming out Miss, I knew Dan would rue the day he brought you home.' Sive marched up to her and there were only inches between their faces.

'How dare you accuse me of bringing Dan to this? I have listened to your taunts for long enough. No more. God forgive me but I will not be responsible for my actions if you ever slander me or my father again. Do you hear me?' she shouted. Mrs Gallagher held her head up even higher than usual.

'Well how come he had lost his business? Tell me that then?'

'Dan has lost his business and I knew nothing. I had to find it out from Barry White the solicitor. He gambled on some bloody deal and lost. He gambled it and never told me. Your precious son threw our life away behind my back. He hid everything from me. Stop blaming me or my father or I swear to God I will report you and tell everyone in the town that you are demented, and see how your neighbours like that. As for living in luxury. This was never my choice. I love this house as well you know but I never wanted to live near you. Dan wanted all this. He wanted to prove to you that he could do it alone. Why on earth he felt he had to prove anything to you is beyond my understanding. But for some unknown reason he did. Now he has failed,' Sive said, her eyes burning at Mrs Gallagher.

'Well why does he want you to stay away from the hospital then? Answer me that?' Mrs Gallagher said defiantly. Beth tried to calm Sive down and pointed towards the kitchen.

'Sive has no idea, Mrs Gallagher. Please stop accusing her of causing this or I will ask you to leave myself for your sake as well as Sive's.' Sive had no intention of calming down.

'I have no idea why your son is acting the way he is. Maybe the fact that he hid the truth and that even our home is gone has made him lose all sense. Yes, even our home is gone.' Sive was holding nothing back.

'Mother of God, what are you talking about?' Mrs Gallagher sank into the chair.

'Now you know. It's all gone. The money my father gave us and any money we had, too. Oh, yes and the land too. The land that as you constantly remind us has been in the family for generations. Well it's all gone. Get that in to your head. I knew nothing.' Mrs Gallagher looked like she was going to collapse.

'I don't understand, how did this happen? The land is gone, your house is gone?' She put her hand to her mouth. Sive was not going to keep anything from her now. It was better out in the open, at least then she couldn't be accused of not telling her or hiding something from her.

'Everything, the solicitor got in contact with me as soon as I came home from the hospital. I had no idea why he wanted to see me but he insisted. It was to let me know that everything was gone and Dan knew all about it. Only tonight I have found the bank letters telling him to sell the house, which I might add were sent a month ago, but your precious son chose to keep that little nugget of information to himself and let me plan a dinner party for him.' Mrs Gallagher could barely speak but eventually found her voice. She shook her head in disbelief.

'My God, what must Barry White think of us?' Sive shook her head. Typical of Mrs Gallagher, the first thing she worries about is what will people think.

'Are you sure? Are you sure about this? The house, the land...?'

'I have to pack up and get out. The banks and the revenue and everyone else Dan owes money too want it all.' Mrs Gallagher looked faint.

'How about a cup of tea for the shock Mrs Gallagher, come into the kitchen.' Beth ushered them into the kitchen and made some strong tea. Mrs Gallagher drank it, her hands shaking.

'So, it wasn't the cult.' Mrs Gallagher said, her voice only a whisper now. Sive looked like she would explode. Beth stepped in. She sat down opposite Mrs Gallagher.

'Mrs Gallagher, Sive is not in any cult and neither is her father. You cannot go around making ridiculous accusations.' Mrs Gallagher was about to tell her what she thought of her but Beth gave her no chance.

'No, Mrs Gallagher, I know you are very upset over Dan, but I will not allow you to come over here and blame Sive or accuse her of anything.' Sive was surprised how well Beth seemed to know how to talk to Mrs Gallagher. She was kind but firm with her. She obviously had come across her type before. She sighed inwardly, wondering could there really be anyone else like Mrs Gallagher in the world?

Chapter 11

Woman in the Wilderness
Alphonse Mucha, Mucha Museum, Prague

Sive had a dream that Mrs Gallagher was force feeding her with her prize-winning lamb stew, and awoke with beads of sweat on her forehead.

The familiar sounds of the house that normally gave her a sense of calm and belonging were replaced by a feeling of pure panic. Soon she would no longer hear them. Instilled in her memory, they were to become sounds of her past. They would not be part of her morning for much longer. She loved waking up to the soft gurgling of the pipes or the creaking of the downstairs window that was on Dan's to do list since they had moved in. He would never get to mend it now.

It was bad enough to lose the house, but she had to face it on her own. Say goodbye to it alone. She pulled a robe around her and dragged herself from the bed. She felt like she could sleep forever. Stay in bed and not get up. Pretend the world was existing without her. As awful as it was to lose her home it was the loss of what she thought was real that was worse. She would have said they were unbreakable. How naïve. Couples had gone through worse than this. There were wars and death and couples managed to stay together. Being told to stay away from his bedside was something she had never expected. His denial of her was too much. She knew she could eventually let go of the house in her heart. Someone else would hopefully love it and take care of it. That was what she would wish. She couldn't regret bringing it back to its former beauty. It had looked forgotten and alone and she was proud of what she had done with it.

She could hear Beth in the kitchen. She was glad she had stayed over. Sive was more shocked that anyone at her own reaction to Mrs Gallagher. For years she had allowed her to get away with so much, but she knew she couldn't take it anymore. If Beth had not intervened, it could have been much worse. Sive could feel herself get angry again remembering her mother-in-law's accusations. How dare she make her feel responsible for Dan. But she knew anger was not an emotion she could deal with right now. She had enough on her plate and she vowed that if Mrs Gallagher came back to taunt her again, God help her but she would report her. Sive smiled for a minute to herself as an image of Mrs Gallagher being carted off by the local gardaí crossed her mind. She would probably complain that they were only ordinary gardaí and would demand to be arrested by the chief superintendant. She would ask if the hand cuffs were cleaned properly, and was she going to a first class garda station. No ordinary run of the mill garda station would do.

Sive went down to see what Beth was up to. The smell of cooking met her from the kitchen. Beth was singing softly to herself. She smiled at Sive when she came in.

'I hope you're hungry, I have eggs ready.' Sive sat down at the large kitchen table and helped herself to fresh coffee.

'Thanks, Beth.' She was grateful for the coffee but knew her appetite did not reach to eggs.

'You look like a ghost, did you sleep at all? Although I am not surprised after last night. Imagine thinking you and your dad are in a cult because you don't eat meat. It's funny if she wasn't serious,' Beth said as she munched on a piece of hot buttered toast.

'I know. I get so angry when I think of what she said. I know she never wanted me, but I never realised how much,' Sive replied.

'She has no idea how lucky she is, having a daughter in law like you, Sive.'

'Thanks Beth, although I am not sure if I can still be classed as a daughter in law when my husband is refusing to see me.'

'Dan will come to his senses. Whatever is going on in his head, he is not thinking straight. Maybe somehow he can explain all this mess to you..'

'I am not going to even go there, I have enough to think about without worrying if he is going to decide to grant me a visit. I feel like going in and shaking him. Asking him what the hell is he thinking of, shutting me out? But no I'm not going to think about it.'

'Right, I am ready to plate this up.'

'Just a little for me.' Beth put a plate in from of her and one for herself. Sive barely touched it.

'If you don't eat you are going to get ill,' Beth scolded as Sive pushed her uneaten breakfast away. Beth on the other hand ate every morsel of her own breakfast.

'I know, I just have no appetite at all. I know you went to bother to prepare it.'

'That's not the reason I am saying it to you. Unlike me you have no weight to lose and you have already lost half a stone I would say.' It was true. Her face looked gaunt and her clothes already looked too loose for her.

'My appetite is the first thing to go when I am worried,' Sive explained.

'It's the last thing for me, I tend to eat a lot more when I am stressed. I can put on a half stone in a matter of a couple of days if I don't watch what I eat. I only think about food and it seems to run and grab onto me for dear life. You on the other hand will fade away if you get any thinner.'

'I will try, thanks Beth, just not right now. I am going to start packing today. There is no sense in delaying it. It will only break my heart living here now knowing I must give it up. I really love the house but it's not mine to love any more so I just have to leave and the sooner the better,' she said sadly.

'I still can't believe this is happening to you Sive,' Beth replied.

'I know, but I suppose people have to face worse than this and they get through it.'

'I know how much you love it and you have made it so beautiful, it would break anyone's heart having to leave it.

'I will be back after work to help you.'

'No, I can do this alone Beth. To be honest I want to. But thanks. You go to work and I will ring you later if there are any developments.'

'If you're sure, but ring me if there is anything, especially if Mrs Gallagher comes back with a crucifix and accuses you of being a witch or something.' Sive smiled at the idea of it.

'Last year she accused me of growing hash in the window sill. I had started a little herb garden. She kept warning me that the guards had dogs to smell out drugs. She is always on the lookout for magic mushrooms in my fridge and she examines the tea if I make it. I think she is convinced I want to get her hooked on some weird drug.' They both laughed.

'Right, I'm off to get ready for work,' Beth said. In half an hour, she appeared with her red hair pinned up as if she had just come from a hair salon. She was wearing a black pencil skirt that hugged her curves in all the right places, a cream silk blouse and elegant black stilettos.

'Wow, you look like that actress off *Mad Men*. You really know how to wear clothes to suit you.'

'My job helps, I couldn't afford all the beautiful clothes that I own without some very good discount from my designers. You know me, I adore my silks and chiffons. She hugged Sive, the smell of Chanel Allure filling the air. 'Call me and don't forget to eat.' She picked up her bag and put on an off-white cashmere coat. Sive waved her off as she drove away in her trendy silver car.

Sive got dressed in jeans and a jersey and went to the local shops and hardware. She bought lots of bubble wrap. Tape and labels. When she got home she made a pot of tea. She began with the paintings on the wall. They all meant so much to Sive. She bought her first painting after a summer job working in an ice cream kiosk. Some of the paintings were from Irish artists and others were from her travels or her own. Each painting that came off the wall tugged at her heart. She also had a couple of paintings her father had kept for her that her mother had painted, each one holding a different jewel of a memory.

'Look Sive, that's the fox just at twilight, look at his eyes, misunderstood, fearful but hungry. This is the old bridge, covered in moss where the birds nest under. The Burren at dawn when the dew glistens in the early morning sun. When you look at my paintings, you will remember the smell of paints, the time I washed the paint from your hair with the rain water after eating banana sandwiches and hot chocolate as we waited for the beauty of the Burren to awaken, so we could try to capture it on our canvas.'

He mothers paintings were beyond precious. She wrapped them up securely and when they were all down and carefully packaged and labelled she went about packing all her little trinkets that were dotted around the house.

By evening the house looked very different, with the walls bare and all her treasured things labelled and packed up with bubble wrap. It was like erasing her existence in the house. She felt she was letting it down. Had she cared too much about it? It wasn't like her to get caught up in something material but it was as if the house had a soul and she wanted to bring some love into it. But at what cost? Hopefully not the cost of her marriage. The guilt was starting to nibble away at her. If she hadn't spent so much time obsessing about the house and painting in her studio, maybe she would have realised how much trouble Dan was in.

Was he going to tell her everything the evening of the accident? Was that why he drove off? Because she didn't listen? She was sick of it all going around in her head. It was evening now and she realised she hadn't eaten again. She checked her phone. Still no word from the hospital.

At least her car was staying with her. Dan had wanted to buy her a new one loads of times but she had seen no need for it. Her car was old but she liked it. She was relieved now because if she had anything worth selling the receiver would probably want it. Nobody would take her old car except the scrap yard. She heated up some soup and nibbled at some toast. As she ate her solitary meal she looked out the window, towards her studio. Dan had it built for her thirtieth birthday. It was her perfect place, where she could enter her world and forget about any other existence. The grief of losing it hit her like a knife to her throat. She would leave it until tomorrow to go into.

She was working on a collection for an exhibition. Dan had encouraged her to do it. She hadn't held an exhibit for years. She had taken her time as there had been no rush. It dawned on her that she would have to get a job as soon as she could. She could possibly sell some of the paintings that she was going to use in the exhibit. But that would take time and money to market properly. What on earth she would do for money, she had no idea. Everything had changed now. It frightened her how dependent on Dan she had become without realising it. He looked after all the bills. She wished she had paid more attention to getting some of her paintings sold. It would have been heartening to know she was self-sufficient.

There sitting in her kitchen she vowed never to be dependent on anyone again. Nobody would have the power to literally take the rug from under her and that included Dan. She had no idea where she would live or indeed how. But she had been thought a difficult lesson. No matter what happened she would begin from this day forward being dependant on herself.

Chapter 12

Burren Land
Anne Madden. Crawford Art Gallery, Cork

Boots the cat was curled up in the window taking advantage of the late winter sunshine, stretching out her long fat limbs then curling back up with a large yawn and heading back to sleep. Milo, Sive's father, lived at the edge of the Burren, overlooking the silver Atlantic. He came out from the back with a beaming smile at the sight of his daughter and embraced her.

'At last I get to see you. Come here to me until I give you a hug.'

'Oh Dad, it's good to be home.' There was something about coming home that reminded Sive about the things that were important to her. She always felt closer to her mother too when she inhaled the wild scents of the Burren.

'Can you smell the hawthorn my little Sive, the air is thick with it, hold my hand and we will take a walk through the hazel woods, where the fairies sleep.'

It had been a very difficult few weeks. She had gone to visit the staff of the company on the day the receiver arrived. No doubt the staff thought she was well covered financially.

'Often when companies close, the people directly involved are not hurt financially,' Barry White explained to Sive.

'They are normally a limited company. So, they can carry on without losing anything personally. Literally walk away from the financial disaster. But Dan had put everything he possessed up as collateral. He had given his word and lost,' Barry White explained.

'Everything we both possessed,' Sive pointed out. But the staff had enough to worry about. They had lost their livelihoods. Sive knew they were loyal to Dan and they seemed genuinely shocked at the announcement. They had of course heard the rumours that had spread across Thornback like a forest fire. There was very little Sive could say except how sorry she was. The worst part was there would be nothing left for a redundancy package. They would get statuary redundancy from the government but that was all. They were out of a job. Some of them would pick something up quickly. But they would get no golden handshake for all their years of work with Dan, and some of them had been there from the start. Jack the security guard was getting on and Sive knew he would find it hard to get anything. Dan's secretary came over to Sive. She had talked of retiring to Dan, but he had begged her not to retire for another year or two.

'How is Dan?' Sive knew she was genuinely concerned and she couldn't lie to her.

'Dan refuses to speak to me Betty.'

'Oh, no Sive! He is not seeing clearly.'

'He has banned me from visiting.'

'This is killing him Sive, but Dan will bounce back. I am sure he will, he will see sense soon.'

'You knew what was going on?'

'I did, I begged him to tell you Sive.'

'Why didn't he?'

'I'm not sure, but that is only for him to say.'

'Well there is little chance of that,' Sive replied curtly. Betty was loyal to Dan to the end, if she knew anything more she had no intention of telling Sive.

She hired a storage space for all their furniture. She had left her art studio until last to clear out. She packed up everything. Since the accident, she had not painted. She took one final look at her little haven before locking it for the last time.

On the way down to Clare she had cried for what she had lost, but as she began to embrace the rugged landscape, she could already begin to feel stronger.

'Come on in, you look cold. I have the fire lighting and some lunch ready,' Milo said.

'Great I ate nothing on the trip down so I am a bit hungry. The house looks great Dad.' Sive sat down by the fire and could feel herself relax properly. An old fashioned cream dresser displayed mismatched mugs and some photos. How she had missed her home place, it seemed to calm her mind a little just being there.

'The sea looks wonderful on the drive over, are you up for a walk a little later?' Sive asked.

'Well first we will get you fed, although before you take off your coat I just need to call Oscar in, he will be glad to see you,' Milo replied.

Oscar was a red setter dog that adored Milo and Sive. They both went outside to see where he was. When they called him he came bounding into the yard. He almost knocked Sive down he was so delighted to see her. They walked around the house to calm him down. The trees with their winter coats surrounded the garden and sheltered the house. At the side was an orchard, where Sive had spent most of her childhood, climbing trees, eating apples and painting under their shelter.

'Oscar, stop jumping and come into the garden for a minute and sit.'

Milo had planted a rose garden to the front, he had started sowing it when Sive's Mum had got ill, it was full of sweet smelling roses when in bloom, and in the winter, it lay almost sleeping.

'Oh, it's good to be home Dad.' Nothing ever seemed as bad when she was home with Milo. He had a great way of looking at life. He had an earthiness that seemed to resemble his surroundings. Sive knew that the land and the sea were deep in Milo's blood. There was a certain stability to the Burren and its surrounding countryside. The country could move on or not but certain ancient places and beliefs remained unchanged in the West.

'Come on in, Oscar will lie by the fire. I had him out for a walk so he will quieten down once we get inside.' Milo was right. Once Oscar came inside he flopped down and looked like he was going for a big snooze within minutes.

'Gosh, I miss living so close to the sea Dad. I mean right beside it.'

'Your mother was the same. First thing she would do in the morning was look out to see what colour the sea was. Remember she would insist on keeping you out of school to go and collect sea shells. Then you would both spend hours painting them. The poor headmaster didn't know what to say to her, he would try to explain that she couldn't just take you out whenever she had a fancy for it but she was having none of it,' Milo grinned.

'She would tell him when she brought me in that I had to stay out because it was such a beautiful day, the sky was calling to her and no one in their right mind would stay indoors,' Sive laughed.

' I think he was half in love with your mother to be honest,' Milo added.

'I agree with you, when Mum died, his eyes used to well up when I would meet him,' Sive said.

'Your mother touched so many, she was so wild and free, some people did not understand her, but secretly a lot of people envied her, she adored life, each day was a gift to be treasured.' He smiled remembering.

'When she died, I thought you were broken Dad, but somehow, you got strong again.' As a small child, she watched him walk his beloved Burren and roar at the rugged raw rocks to help him bare the pain of his loss. Amidst the strange beauty of the land Sive knew he found his peace with it.

'How are you Dad? I worry about you too.'

'I loved your mother so much, my heart did break, but I had to try to see the beauty in things again, I had you and you were so lost without your mother, but somehow we muddled through,' Milo said with a hint of sadness at the memory.

'I know it sounds mad, but since the accident, I keep hearing her voice as if she is with me. It's possibly just feeling so tired, my mind playing tricks on me.'

'Your mother was the most unusual woman I have ever met Sive, and she cared for you so much. I like to think she is watching out for you. You do look exhausted. You will sleep now that you are home, there is nothing like a good walk through the Burren to make anyone sleep. There is no need to worry about me Sive. I have some very good friends here. I enjoy my life, it's simple but rich in many ways and the farmer's market keeps me busy. Speaking of markets, does Mrs Gallagher still think I am in a cult?' Milo grinned.

'Don't ask. If I get started on Mrs Gallagher, I might not stop.'

'Oh!'

'She got it into her head that we had brainwashed Dan in to joining our imaginary cult. She thought that he had got involved and lost all his money.'

'That's absurd!' Milo said laughing.

'It was no laughing matter, when she drove up to the house and started accusing me. Luckily Beth was there or you could be bailing me out for murder. I have never found anyone more infuriating in my entire life.

Anyway, we put her straight. But I haven't spoken to her since. I talk to Tom every day and he lets me know how Dan is,' Sive added.

An aroma of fresh herbs and vegetables simmered on the hob in a casserole. Homemade brown bread with nuts and all sorts of seeds was cooling in a clean tea towel. Freshly churned butter he had received from his farmer's market buddies was waiting to be spread on the warm bread. He stoked up the fire and began to serve lunch with a chilled glass of exquisite homemade wine.

'Dad this is gorgeous.' It was a simple meal but so fresh that it was fit for a queen. Afterwards, Milo brought her bags in.

'I painted your old room recently, I hope you like it.' It was a comfort she had taken for granted for many years, but now it meant so much to her to know that she always had a home with her father. Hugging him, she got up to look at the newly decorated bedroom. Milo was also quite an artist. The walls had been painted in a sky blue and Milo had painted different song birds dotted on the walls.

'Dad it's beautiful,' Sive exclaimed. Robins, wrens, corncrakes and thrushes were delicately peeping out. The old wood floor had been sanded and painted white. The bed and dresser had got a makeover of a duck egg blue. A large bunch of wild flowers stood in a colourful old earthenware jug. Sive's eyes fell at the end of the bed. Without saying anything, she walked towards it. There was a beautiful easel with a box of paints and some high quality brushes. She ran her fingers over the brushes. Her hands, going over the easel, like a caress to a new baby.

'A little present for you, I got them yesterday.' Milo smiled.

'Dad.' Out of nowhere, her composure slipped and she could feel herself crumble. Milo put his arms around her.

'There, there, it will be alright, pet, you are made of strong stuff.'

'Everything is such a mess. I don't know what happened. Dan still won't speak to me. I think he must blame me somehow. Although I have no idea why. But why else would he ban me from seeing him? Imagine Dan banning me. It seems ludicrous. I feel I am in a bloody nightmare Dad.'

'We all make mistakes, and can lose our way in life pet. But everyone must take responsibility for their own path. Dan made his own mistake.'

That evening they sat by the stove and talked for hours. Sive talked about Dan and everything that had happened. Milo just listened mostly, unless she asked him something. She had felt better from talking everything out, it seemed more manageable now that it had all been said. They took down the old photo album and spent a happy hour going through their shared past.

'Do you remembere how your mother loved to sew?'

'Of course, I can vividly remember a cream lace dress with delicate flowers that she made for me. She had taken some sequins from her own wedding gown and sowed them on to it. When I wore it she said I was a fairy princess. I wore it so much she was constantly replacing the sequins until my dress had more sequins than the wedding dress,' Sive replied, smiling.

One day after school she came home to find her mother doubled up in pain with her father cradling her. They brought her to hospital and had to leave her there. Sive had cried herself to sleep and prayed her Mother would be home soon.

'But it had been caught too late, there was no more that could be done,' they said.

They brought her home towards her final days. Milo and Sive stayed with her almost all the time. Sive sang her favourite songs to her and brushed her hair. Her mother died in autumn, her favourite season.

'What a beautiful autumn my little Sive. It is such a glorious one. The leaves have never looked so rich, falling in a dream of colours, look at the russet array blanketing the ground.' Sive always knew it was apt for her to leave when nature was at its most wondrous.

It was around then Milo bought Sive her first proper set of paints and easel. Sive started to paint for hours. It was as if she could somehow get the sad emotion of loss and heartbreak out in her childlike paintings.

After more tea that evening and some delicious coffee cake a friend of his had baked for him, she eventually climbed into bed and for the first time since the crash slept soundly. When she awoke the first thing she saw was the easel. She stared at it for a long time. She had not painted since the crash. Then, almost in a trance, she started to prepare the paints and the canvas. At first the strokes felt almost shaky. She was going to stop, then she got lost in the act and all around her was forgotten. Around mid-morning Milo gently knocked on the door. She had been painting for hours. For the first time since the accident, her mind was at peace, if just for a while.

'Are you ok Sive?' She got up from her seat and opened the door. 'I started painting, Dad.' Milo looked at the canvas she had worked on. An array of violets and orchids blending into a splendid sunrise. It was the beginning of a beautiful painting.

'It looks wonderful, Sive.'

'Thanks Dad, I wanted to paint something positive. I feel it's full of light.'

'It is,' Milo said, surveying it.

'I was thinking, now only if you think it might help. I could drive up and see Dan. We could ring the hospital and check if it's ok. At least we might be able to make some sense of why he doesn't want to see you, it's not fair to leave you in limbo like this. If he refuses to see me there is nothing we can do, but I have a feeling he will ,' Milo suggested.

'I'm not sure Dad, I feel so angry with him for all this, that he doesn't bloody deserve to see you or anyone belonging to me,' Sive replied.

'I can understand you feeling like that, but you do need some clarity on this Sive, he can't just avoid seeing you. You are his wife. We need to know why at least?' Milo stated gently.

'Very well, go up and see him and maybe you can make some sense of it all,' Sive replied.

Chapter 13

Pieta
Uffizi, Florence, Italy.

Although it was visiting time when he arrived at the hospital, the nurse said Dan was sleeping and to come back in an hour. Milo thanked her and said he would. He was about to head back to the car park when a loud bellow came down the corridor.

'Milo, is that you?' Milo looked up and took a deep breath. He knew that voice.

Mrs Gallagher came clip clopping down the hall in her kitten heels. She had a lime green dress and jacket on that made her look like she was attending a wedding. Over the years they had met on a few occasions. Milo had noticed that although she disapproved of his lifestyle, they both had one thing in common, Sive and Dan, and this had somehow bound them together a little.

'Oh Milo, what a mess!' He had not been prepared for this.

'I have been up to see Dan but he was asleep. We were only allowed see him for a few minutes and he was sleeping, he seems to be sleeping any time I am here. I have not had a chance to talk with him at all.' Mrs Gallagher explained.

'Join me for a coffee?' Milo invited. He realised that he should have been prepared to meet with Dan's mother. He wished her husband was with her. She had a hat on her head. It was moving with her as she talked. He saw a sign for the hospital café and found a table for her.

'Order some tea for me Milo and make sure the cups are clean and no mugs please. I have no idea why some coffee houses serve tea in mugs. It's a disgrace! It really is. Sometimes I wonder where this country is going, I really do. Or those big thick cups, what on earth are we supposed to do with them? Get a big spoon and drink our tea from the spoon?' she asked crossly. Milo was about to answer her when she cut him off.

'Make sure it's a nice cup. Remember, check it's clean,' she said in a loud voice that made anyone else in the coffee shop look at their own cup to check its cleanliness. He was glad to get to the counter. At least it would buy him a few minutes. There was no escape. He ordered two big cream cakes. He knew she loved her cakes. Luckily the cups looked fine and not a mug in sight. When he arrived back to the table to his dismay she was crying.

'Things have a way of working themselves out, try not to upset yourself.' He gave her some napkins to dry her eyes.

'Oh, Milo what is to become of them? If only they had built a house on Thornback Farm, this would never have happened. I tell you, I would not have allowed it. If only I had known, we could have talked with the bank. The Gallaghers of Thornback have a very solid name with the banks, let me tell you. Not a penny is owed to them. Tell me Milo, what are we going to do?' she demanded. He hesitated before answering. The last thing he wanted was to get into some big discussion about his daughter and Dan with her.

'How is Dan?' he asked lightly, trying to steer the conversation away from Sive.

'Well, he is out of danger, but between broken bones and ruptured spleens, he's a mess. But Milo, all is gone! Their house, money and the land.' Mrs Gallagher began to cry again. Big loud sobs. He shifted uncomfortably in his seat.

'Where is Sive?' she asked crossly as she took a large bite of her cream cake. Milo cleared his throat.

'Sive is giving Dan some space.'

'SPACE!' Mrs Gallagher almost choked. 'He is in bits in a hospital bed, what can he do with space?' she demanded as she looked up at Milo as if he had all the answers. Milo had no answer for her.

'I am afraid it is at Dan's request.'

'Why on earth would he ask his wife to give him space in his hour of need, can you tell me that?' she said curtly. Mrs Gallagher moved closer to Milo. He took off his jacket, the heat of the coffee shop getting to him.

'We can only respect their wishes, and hope that things will get better,' Milo said, trying to calm her down.

'They can hardly get any worse, my son is in a right state, and your daughter is nowhere to be seen.' Milo could feel his patience melting.

'You can be assured that if Dan wanted Sive by his side, she would be there in a heartbeat, right now he does not and you or I cannot do anything about it. Secondly, I would not think it advisable to accuse Sive of neglecting him or of anything else for that matter.' Mrs Gallagher shook her head in dismay.

'The young of today, they have no understanding of marriage or what it should be. We never looked for SPACE! We just got on with it.' She scraped up the last of her cream cake and dabbed her mouth with a napkin.

'Life is complicated for them now. All we can do is be there for them and hope they work it out,' Milo said as he drained his coffee cup. Mrs Gallagher was signalling over to one of the girls behind the counter.

'I think it's self-service.' Milo quickly added.

'Nonsense, she is just standing there, chatting to her colleague,' Mrs Gallagher replied.

'MISS, MISS! SERVICE!' she hollered, much to Milo's embarrassment. The other customers looked up to see what would happen. The girl was clearly annoyed but she came down.

'We are finished here, you may clear away,' Mrs Gallagher stated grandly. Milo looked at the girl and gave her his most apologetic smile. She picked up the cups noisily and without saying anything scowled at Mrs Gallagher and walked away.

'The service here is a disgrace, I will be calling the management. I certainly will. That's what you get employing foreign people. No manners whatsoever!' Mrs Gallagher said, pursing her lip. To Milo's relief, Desmond her husband arrived to collect her. Milo marvelled at his patience with his wife. Milo liked Desmond. He was a good man. From their few meetings, he reckoned he should be up for sainthood to manage Mrs Gallagher so well. They chatted for a little while and then Desmond decided it was time to go home. They promised to keep in touch about the whole situation. Milo made his way back down to see Dan.

'You can go in and see him for a little while, I told him it was his father in law and he seemed happy to see you.' Dan thanked the nurse and gently knocked on his son in law's door.

Dan's face was grey, with yellow bruises. Milo tried to hide the shock he felt on seeing his son in law. He looked so different from the man he knew. They had always had a good relationship. Milo admired Dan's zest for life that was infectious if you were in his company. He knew he was a good man and was glad Sive had met him. He never expected to find Dan like this. But life had a way of throwing enormous challenges in your way. Milo knew all about this. When you were least expecting it, your life could take a turn. It was then up to you and only you how you navigated yourself around it. Some people managed better than others. Unfortunately, some people could never overcome the obstacles. Looking at Dan in his hospital bed he hoped Dan would find his way. Yes, he was bruised and battered from the accident. But he was more worried about the despair that was almost tangible, that seemed to seep out of him. His heart seemed to be broken. He had thought he would be angry and frustrated, not this terrible sadness. Dan looked away and Milo could see he was crushed.

'Well, I fucked up badly,' he said angrily.

'Things got out of control for you Dan, it happens,' Milo replied.

'But I've lost everything, it's all a disaster.'

'You still have your life and people who care about you. Everything is not lost.'

'The house, our home, after everything Sive did with it, I gambled it away,' Dan replied.

'Look, you took a risk. It didn't work out. In fairness Dan, you never expected Brexit to happen. I believe that was the deciding factor on the deal?'

'Maybe I was heading for this anyway, too many lies,' Dan whispered. Milo didn't comment, he wasn't quite sure what he meant.

'How is Sive?' Dan asked, his voice barely a whisper.

'She is stronger than we give her credit for. It's very diffcult for her to understand why you refuse to see her. To be honest I would like to know why myself?' Milo said.

'I have let her down so much. I can't face her. I'm shocked she would want to see me,' Dan replied.

'Is that the only reason you are keeping her away?' Milo needed to know if there was more to it.

'It's a big reason Milo, how on earth can I look her in the eye after everything I have done?' Dan asked.

'But shunning her is not the answer Dan, she needs to see you, be with you. Sive is terribly sad about losing everything, but she is your wife.

She loves you. You must see that. She has handled worse than losing anything material.'

'But the lies, how can I explain the lies?'

'You can't! But shunning her is no answer. I know you thought you were doing the best for her. Protecting her from the truth. That was your mistake. But I do believe you hoped this was the best way not to hurt her. What's done is done Dan, you have to talk to Sive.'

'I feel she is better without me.'Dan replied bluntly.

'That is for her to decide surely,' Dan made no reply but turned his head. Milo decided to say no more. At least he knew now why Dan had refused to see his daughter. It was shame that was driving it. Shame was eating him up and not allowing him to move on in any way. They could fix him medically, but unfortunately his wounds ran deeper. Eventually Dan fell asleep. Milo got up and before he left he pulled the blanket up more snugly on his broken son in law.

He left the hospital and hit the road home, his heart weary suddenly. He had expected Dan to be angry or annoyed with Sive. But from what Milo could see Dan was melting into a deep depression. He wondered about the crash, had it been deliberate? Was money to blame for all this, or was there more? They seemed to be so happy, he wondered would they ever find their way back? The frightening part was there seemed to be no hope in Dan. He had always been such a fighter. Milo had admired his drive and ambition, it was a huge part of who he was, that now had vanished. But sometimes when someone is at their lowest they can find some clarity and begin to move forward. He hoped for both their sakes that Dan would find the strength and courage to want to live again.

Chapter 14

The Night Café
Vincent van Gogh. Yale University Art Gallery, U.S.

The next evening Sive joined Milo to meet with some friends in a pub in the village for a bite to eat. After much coaxing, she agreed to go with him. Milo changed into a tweed jacket, with his customary scarf and Sive was struck by how handsome he still looked.

'You look very dapper Dad,' Sive smiled. They walked into the village huddling close together against the sea breeze that bit at their faces. The heat from the pub was enticing as they walked in.

'Ah, Milo, here I kept a seat for you both.' An old man with a beard that resembled Fagin out of *Oliver Twist* called them over. The heat was just what they needed. They were an eclectic group of people who were not all native to the village. There was a French couple who ran a local restaurant. A couple of friends from the farmer's market. A retired doctor who had spent years away in the poorest parts of the world who was chatting to the local goldsmith. One lady who was called Ruby was about the same age, if a little younger than Milo. She had a trace of an American accent. She had a soft cashmere shawl over her shoulders fastened with a cameo brooch. Her blond grey hair was feathery and very flattering and showed her high cheek bones. Sive had thought she had seen a secret smile pass between Milo and her and wondered was she some special friend of Milo's.

'The wild mushroom risotto is only delicious; would you like to see the menus?' Ruby asked giving Milo a big smile.

'I'll go with the risotto and a pint of Guinness,' Milo replied.

'Me too and a glass of chardonnay,' Sive added

'Are you on holiday?' Sive asked Ruby.

'Goodness no, I have adopted Clare as my home. I have lived here for over two years. When my husband died a few years ago, I decided to travel. My first stop was Ireland. I am still here,' she laughed. I love to bake so I have a stand at the market. It's right next to your Dad's,' she added. Sive looked at Milo. He had never mentioned Ruby up to now. He was chatting to one of the other men. He had never started another relationship since her mother. It struck her that it would be wonderful if he did have someone.

The risotto was piping hot with delicious fresh herbs. Afterwards, over an Irish coffee, some of the group began to play some music. One man took out a flute which looked a bit worse for the wear. The flute may have looked shabby but in the hands of its master, the music was beautiful and stirring and had a lonesome air to it. Sive felt she could have been in the National Concert Hall, he was so talented. Afterwards she could not get Dan out of her head. He would so love this setting. Even though he loved his flash cars and fancy suits he adored something rustic like this.

'You look a bit far away there, are you okay?' Ruby asked.

'Yes, my husband is not well and I can't help but wish he was here, he would love it,' Sive replied.

'You can bring him when he is better, and I look forward to meeting him,' Ruby said reassuringly.

'Yes, I will. He loves Clare. The first time I met him I was in Doolin. Shortly afterwards I brought him to see the Burren. He loved how ancient and mystical it is. There is something about the West, it can capture you,' Sive said.

'I agree, it certainly can,' Ruby added. Sive sat back and listened to the various artists get up to do their piece. A man who reminded her of another era began to play the tin whistle. 'The lonesome Boatman.' It was hauntingly beautiful. It was good to meet with her fathers' friends.

She had learned a lot about friends in the past few weeks. She knew true friendship was hard to come by and needed to be treated with care. There were lots of people ringing about Dan, but Sive felt they were just looking for the details. The worse the news the better the gossip. When it broke about the business being with the receiver, it was all that was talked about around the village for a week. But there were some genuine callers who knew Dan since he was a child who were genuinely sorry for him.

They stayed for another while in the pub and then said their goodbyes. Sive noticed that Milo took a little longer to say goodbye to Ruby than anyone else.

'Ruby is lovely,' Sive remarked casually.

'I have known her a few years, she made the coffee cake that we had earlier.'

'Oh! That was nice of her.' Sive waited for Milo to elaborate, but he said no more. If there was something going on, Milo made no reference to it and they happily chatted about the evening. When they got home, Sive's phone rang, it was the hospital.

'Hello, Mrs Gallagher.'

'Yes, it's Sive, please call me Sive.'

'Sive, we have some good news for you. Your husband is asking to see you.'

'Oh!'

'Yes, he is much the same but he has asked to see you tomorrow if you can?'

'I will be up first thing in the morning,' she replied.

'Great, if we say about 11.30 I will get the doctor to see you first and have a chat with you.'

'Ok, and thank you.' As she put down the phone, she burst into tears, it was hard to know how to feel, so many emotions were building up and it was all too much, she cried with relief at being able to see him, and sadness that he had ever stopped her. Her father hugged her.

'Imagine being so happy that my husband is allowing me to see him.'

'These are very unusual circumstances Sive, perhaps he has seen the light a bit.'

'I don't know Dad. I think he blames me in some way for what happened. If I had taken more interest in his work, I would have known. Instead I was happy to allow him to be the bread winner while I dilly dallied renovating the house and did a bit of painting.'

'Hardly dilly dallied, you project managed a huge restoration on your home and did a lot of the work yourself.'

'Don't remind me. All the hours I spent stripping walls and skirting, not to mention the floors,' Sive said remembering.

'Exactly, not to mention the hours you spent on the internet looking for replicas of its past.'

'All for what?' Sive asked.

'I know it's hard to see the time you spent on it as anything but a waste. But you brought back a beautiful old house that was falling. It was a work of art itself by the time you were finished with it. You should be proud of what you achieved. Nobody can take that away, not even the bank.'

'Thanks, Dad. I will try to remember that when I hand back the key,' she said with a touch of sarcasm.

'That's not going to be easy.'

'I know. I am dreading it, but in another way, it might help me move on to the next step in life, whatever that is.'

'You know you are welcome to stay here if you want, and Dan too. It's your home and always will be.' Sive gave him a hug.

'Thanks Dad, but I will find our own way somehow. I think I will take Beth up on her offer and stay with her for a little while. Now that Dan is not barring me I will try to be closer to the hospital.'

'Don't expect too much from him pet, not yet anyway.' Milo remembered the despair that Dan had seemed to slip into. At least now he was allowing Sive to visit him, and hopefully it would help him. But Milo had seen that he had a long way to go.

'Right, I'm off to bed.'

'I think I might paint for a little while, night Dad.'

She knew she wouldn't be able to sleep if she went to bed, so she continued with her painting. It gave some calm to her head as she concentrated on the paint strokes. She kept going over everything in her head. How your life could turn upside down so quickly. After a couple of hours, exhausted, she fell into bed.

When she got up the next morning she could not decide what to wear. It seemed ridiculous to her that she did not know what to wear to see Dan. Eventually she decided on a warm winter wool dress in a charcoal grey that Dan had bought for her when they were abroad. She washed her hair and put on a tiny bit of makeup and a spray of his favourite perfume.

She brought her stuff with her to stay with Beth. It would be only half an hour from her house on the motorway to the hospital and it would give Sive a few days to figure out what she was going to do about where to live.

'Bye Dad, I will keep you posted on any update. I am just hoping Mrs Gallagher won't be up there.'

'Her bark is worse than her bite love,' Milo added.

'Well her bark can be pretty bad let me tell you,' Sive grinned back.

'Here is a flask of tea for you, just in case you need it for the journey.'

She hugged her father good bye and arranged to see him soon. It was a long trip back up to the city but eventually she was there. Arriving into the hospital, she suddenly felt very vulnerable. They all knew that Dan had requested her not to see him. She went to the nurse's station and let them know she was there.

'Take a seat and someone will be with you shortly.' Sive hoped it was not Bernadette.

She waited about ten minutes and then, a young doctor who introduced herself as part of the psyche team that was looking after Dan, appeared. Sive felt comfortable with her straight away.

'I think, it's a positive step from Dan that he wants to see you. I have chatted with him and he has refused to talk about your relationship at all. I would ask that you give him plenty of time and let him talk when he is ready. Just by being here as I say is positive, that he is ready to face reality again.'

'How is he?'

'Well physically he is much improved, afterwards you can talk to someone on his medical team, but his mental state is very vulnerable. We will monitor him over the next few days. As his physical health is stronger, it could be a case that we move him to the psychiatric ward until the heavy depression he seems to be in has lifted.'

'Oh, I didn't know it was serious enough for him to have to go there.' Alarm bells were ringing in her head.

'Well, we are not sure yet, we will see how he is over the next week, but the present state of his mental health is very weak. But it will be Dan's decision if he does. Any information that you could give us may help. I understand that things have been very difficult for him financially, and is it true that you have lost your home?'

'Yes, I am afraid it is, I haven't sorted out anywhere for us to live just yet. I have been with my father. It's been such an enormous thing to happen to us.'

'Of course, I can only imagine, and of course this is not helping Dan in any way. I think though that hiding the facts from him is not going to help, if he asks you anything, you will have no option but to be honest with him.'

'The house and the money is nothing, if only Dan could get well.'

'We are doing everything we can. Hopefully, we will see a little improvement soon. We will keep him monitored. Now if you would like to, go in to see him, but just for a short while.'

'Thank you.' Sive made the small journey to Dan's room and knocked on the door.

Chapter 15

Myth of the Western man
Art Gallery of New South Wales, Sydney, Australia.

The icy rain hit Sive's face as she stepped out of the hospital entrance. After scanning the different areas, she spotted the car. It was dark now and she had parked there mid-morning, but for her it felt a life time ago. Her hands were shaking with the cold as she opened the car door and let herself into the sanctuary of it. On the passenger seat was the flask her dad had gave to her before she left. It was still hot and she gratefully poured the tea and tried to gather herself. There were Christmas lights glinting in the rain on the distant street, they might as well have been from a different planet, she felt so far removed from them.

The image of Dan's stricken face in the bleak hospital bed was something she knew she would carry for a long time, and the raw guilt was like bile in her stomach reminding her that she may have had a hand in putting him there. Nobody would say that but it was becoming apparent to her that she had not been there for him and the reality of it frightened her. The phone beeped interrupting her thoughts. It was Beth.

'Where are you? I have tried to call you? Have you seen Dan?' Hearing Beth's voice full of concern was suddenly too much, Sive couldn't speak. She started to sob and heave right into the phone.

'Oh, God are you all right Sive? Is it Dan? Is he worse? Where are you?'

'I'm in the car park at the hospital.'

'Are you in the car?' Beth asked.

'Yes,' Sive replied, trying to compose herself.

'Stay where you are and I will come get you,' Beth instructed.

'No Beth there is no need to do that, I will be fine in a minute.' Sive tried to regain her composure.

'I have just come out of the hospital, I just need a few minutes to get myself together, it was such a shock seeing him. I hardly recognised him.'

'Is he that bad?' Beth asked.

'His injuries were bad enough but it's more than that. The damage is much deeper, Beth.' Sive knew he was broken. In every way a man can be.

'I'm not sure what I expected but to see Dan so far removed from the man I knew was shocking.'

'Oh, God it sounds like he is in a bad way, Sive.'

Sive replied but it was as if she was talking to herself.

'If only I had known, but I just didn't want to, I was so wrapped up in my own little world, how did I miss that my husband was heading for this? What kind of a wife was I? He had tried to tell me how things were, but I didn't want to know. I had no clue he was this bad. What if he never gets better, I will never forgive myself.' Sive could feel herself crumble again.

'Will you stop berating yourself for feck sake? It wasn't your fault Dan ended up in such a state, and Sive, I don't think you should be driving. You sound in a right state,' Beth exclaimed.

'Beth, it was so strange to see him this way. I'm better now honestly, I will get on the road in a few minutes.'

'I can pop up for you Sive, and drop you back for the car tomorrow.'

'No, honest I'm fine now, it was just the initial shock.'

'Drive carefully!' Beth warned her friend.

It took Sive ages to get out of the city and onto the motorway. Thankfully she took the correct exit off but then almost jammed into a car at her side that she failed to see. The driver blew the horn and shouted at her.

'Get off the road you fucking idiot!' It took all her strength to keep her hands on the wheel and stay calm. She felt like an idiot she didn't need anybody yelling at her. She eventually took the exit to Avara, then turning off to a quieter road. Avara came into sight. Christmas lights lit up the little village making it look magical. A large Christmas tree stood in the centre with boxed lights giving it a Victorian feel. She could feel a calmness envelope her body. She found the entrance to the apartments and buzzed herself in at the gate. Beth answered almost immediately. Her voice was loud and clear on the intercom. Sive thought she had never been so happy to hear her friend's voice.

'Did you take a diversion through Donegal or what? I was beginning to think you were never going to arrive!'

'I know, it took me longer than I thought it would,' Sive replied.

'Drive on in and I will meet you outside, I can't wait to see you.'

The apartment block was overlooking the coast and was very plush. Sive parked her car between a Jag and a Mercedes. Relieved to have finally got there she suddenly saw Beth coming towards her, her red curls wild in the wind. She was wrapped in a dark shawl and Sive thought she looked like a Goddess from long ago.

'Wow! Beth, it's so good to see you. What a fancy place you have here.' Beth wrapped her up in a huge hug.

'I am so glad you are here. Let's bring your stuff in.'

'I hope you don't mind, I brought my art stuff with me, just in case I am here for a few more days?' Sive asked.

'I have told you to stay as long as you need and you know I mean that, it's just so good to see you. Come on and we will get you sorted,' Beth replied and Sive had no doubt about how genuine she was.

The large, very tastefully decorated open plan sitting room and dining area was overlooking the pier. A small kitchenette with glasses of all descriptions shone from illuminated presses. Sive took off her shoes and her feet sank into the deep pile cream carpet. Yellow roses were dotted in unusual jars around the apartment, and modern art decorated the walls.

'Wow, can I have a quick look out the balcony?' Sive asked. The balcony was just off the living area and was outside a large sliding door.

'Of course, but it's cold out there,' warned Beth. They opened the large balcony door and closed it quickly behind them, keeping in the warmth of the apartment. They both stood as the wind swept their hair over their faces, there was a lighthouse in the distance, and some twinkling lights far out at sea of a ship passing by. It was picture postcard stuff. They came back in quickly, glad of the heat.

'God, that would certainly blow the cobwebs away, but it is beautiful, it reminds me of home, being so close to the sea. What a stunning view. It's so calming to get the smell of the salt water, I feel I am at Dads,' Sive remarked. Beth smiled in agreement.

'I do love it, and the village is great too, quite a quaint little place and it's so close to the city now with the motorway, I wouldn't want to live anywhere else. I am thrilled to have found Avara. There is something pretty special about it to be honest.' She busied herself in the kitchenette getting out glasses and plates. 'I have some dinner ready for you but would you like to take a shower first and settle in I know you have had a rough day? I have your bed made up in the guest room.' Beth explained. Sive decided to take a shower, she felt so drained.

The bathroom was state of the art with lots of very expensive looking potions and lotions.

'Use whatever you want, there are fresh towels on the radiator,' Beth called after her. The power shower was so strong that it almost knocked Sive over. She felt so much better afterwards as she wrapped herself in the softest white towels she thought she had ever used. The guest bedroom was completely white. From the walls to the bed and the furniture. A beautiful African motif full of colour hung on the largest wall. She sat down on the brushed cotton quilt on the bed and tried to gather her thoughts. Today had been a shock, but at least she felt she understood a little more.

Dan had told her that he had felt so overwhelmed by what had happened that he couldn't face her. This had broken her heart. It was easier to be angry with him but now she hardly knew how to feel. She pulled on a tracksuit bottom and loose top and headed back to the living area, admiring Beth's bedroom on the way as the door was open wide. It was decorated in French chic and looked like a boudoir for a film star. There was a tantalising smell from the kitchen. Beth was busy plating up some delicious looking lasagne.

'Before you ask, calm yourself, it's vegetarian,' Beth explained.

'This looks delicious, you've been busy,' Sive said.

'I can't take the credit I'm afraid, it's from that healthy café that I was telling you about,' Beth replied.

'Wow, sounds right up Dad's street all right,' Sive noted.

'Some of the villagers are not impressed though. They think it's strange she serves no meat. She has a job trying to convert them.'

'God, I must visit it,' Sive replied, delighted.

'I'll take you over for a coffee in the next few days. When are you seeing Dan again?'

'Not sure, perhaps the day after tomorrow. Tomorrow I am going to go back to the house for one last check. I need to pick up the post and make sure nothing is left behind.' Sive was dreading it but she knew it had to be done. When she had spoken to Dan she had not mentioned it, his mind was far too fragile to deal with anything like that now.

'I can take some time off and come with you if you want some company. It might be better not to be alone, I can only imagine how you feel having to face that.' Beth offered.

'Thanks Beth but I think I better go alone. I thought losing the house was the worst that could happen, but now it pales in comparison to worrying about the state Dan is in. I need to see the solicitor again too, but thanks for offering to come' Sive knew she wanted to go alone, she needed to get used to trying to deal with things alone. She now knew she had depended far too much on Dan and it had done her no favours when the tables were turned.
'How is all that going with the solicitor?' Beth asked.

'Well, he is handling most of the financial part with the receiver.' She still could hardly believe the financial mess they were in. Sometimes it completely overwhelmed her.

'I am still trying to deal with the fact that I was oblivious to the whole thing,' Sive said as if to herself.

'There is only so much you can do Sive. The most important thing is to get Dan well and let the solicitor sort the rest out for now,' Beth replied.

Sive agreed but her mind was worn out worrying about everything. Just the basic worry of where she was going to live.' Beth and her father had both said that she could stay with them and Dan too when he came out, but Sive knew that living with her father or Beth was only very temporary. It was up to her now to sort out where she could live and financially how she could live.

The next morning the smell of freshly roasted coffee awakened Sive. She could hear Beth in the kitchen, she threw on her dressing gown and went in to see her. Beth was dressed for work in a very expensive cream crocheted long sleeved top and skirt.

'Gosh that is exquisite,' Sive commented

'The perks of working for designers. This was made by a very talented lady who has crocheted for years and only started selling her work in the last few years. I met her by accident on a trip to the Aran Islands,' Beth explained. Sive sipped her coffee, looking out over the bay. It was one of those beautiful Irish mornings that although a crystal frost glistened, the sun was emerging, making everything look golden.

'What a beautiful view.'

'I know I feel blessed to have found this apartment. I really do love it here since I moved from the city. I was afraid I would miss being so close to work, the theatres, restaurants not to mention the shops. But when I finish work I long to get home. It really feels like I have come home, maybe for the first time in my life.' Sive caught the melancholy in Beth's voice. She rarely talked about her own home, but Sive knew the relationship was very strained and she only visited her home-place in Limerick once or twice a year. She had a brother whom she didn't really get on with and her mother was a bit of a strange person. Sive had met her once but found her quite cold. Her father was dead a few years but again there seemed to be no closeness there between them before he died. Beth never really talked about them or where she came from. Sive was glad she had found Avara and seemed to be so happy here.

After breakfast Sive set off. Her first stop would be the house, before she handed over the keys. She felt a lump in her stomach. It felt surreal to be having one last look at her home.

When she opened the door, a load of post greeted her. She sat down to go through it. It was mostly addressed to Dan but she opened it. All the details of the financial crisis they were having was there in black and white. A flashback hit her of the dinner party she had held. What on earth was going through Dan's head when she was talking about what she would cook?

All the personal stuff was packed up and she had one last walk through the house to double check. The bank wound not care that she had trolled the internet to get the original Victorian rose wallpaper for the guest bedroom. Or the gold edged bathroom accessories that she had imported especially from Italy. She looked at the cornices and moulding that had been specially commissioned and then she couldn't take any more. She had closed her art studio on the last day she was here. She was glad she didn't have to go in again. It was too painful. But the garden, she needed to see it one more time.

The garden was almost asleep now but she knew it would bloom beautifully come the summer and the front avenue in early spring would be awash with daffodils. She closed her eyes to try to picture how it would look, but somehow, she failed to picture it and then it didn't matter anymore. She hoped that perhaps a family with some children would end up in it. She had imagined it would have been her and Dan and their children. She had pictured them running around the garden and then escaping into the wood to be wild and free. The wood, how she would miss it. Especially in spring when it had a wonderful blue haze from the carpet of bluebells. Her time was over in it now. She took one last look around and locked the door, fighting the tears. She was shocked she could still cry. She was so tired of crying, it seemed to drain all her energy away. She didn't look back as she drove away. That door was closed. She drove straight to the solicitor to give him the keys.

He was waiting for her. He filled her in on the legalities of everything. The receiver would sell stuff off and what was remaining would be divided up amongst the creditors. There was nothing left for her or Dan.

'I am so sorry it's come to this Sive. Are you coping?'

'Just about, I am lucky I have a good friend and my father of course.'

'Good, and if there is anything else I can help you with, please contact me.' She got up and shook his hand before leaving.

She pulled her coat closer to her as she felt the air colder suddenly. All the anxiety in her body was hard to keep under control. She kept walking down the street hoping to God nobody would recognise her, she couldn't face anyone. There was a pub on the corner that she seldom went into but found herself walking into now.

'May I use your bathroom?' Sive asked the girl behind the bar.

'Just on your left, are you okay?' she asked kindly.

'Fine, thank you.' She was relieved the girl didn't seem to know who she was and there was no one else in the bar except one man reading his paper who didn't even look up he was so engrossed in it. In the bathroom, she was taken aback by her own pallor. Dark circles under her eyes were more noticeable by the paleness of her skin. Her eyes looked tired and strained. Weary suddenly, she washed her face and hands. When she came into the bar she ordered a pot of tea and sat in a quiet corner. The girl arrived with the tea and a scone with cream and jam.

'Compliments of the bar, I have just made a batch in the kitchen.' Sive thanked her and smiled to herself. Again, it struck her how much a bit of kindness could mean. She was touched the girl had brought down the scone to her. Human kindness meant so much. It reminded her that even if it was such a difficult day, she was lucky she had her father and Beth. At least Dan was talking to her now. He had such a long way to go, she knew she had to be strong for both of them. She tried to think about things. It was a strange feeling to have lost your home. There was the material side of it. Everything Dan had worked for, all the money they had spent on renovating. Everything gone now. And then there was just a feeling of loss. As if she had let the house down by not being able to keep it and look after it. The garden was the hardest part to leave. Her mind found it hard to leave it behind. The roses that she had spent so much time maturing needed so much care. Would anyone care for them now or would they be just left to die? There was an area that she had cornered off for wild flowers and in the height of summer it was a buzz with honey bees and birds. It was where nature was at its finest. Would the new owner even appreciate this, or perhaps they would just think it wild and overgrown and plough it up? She knew she would have to let it all go but it was hard. Feeling a bit better after her tea and scone she thanked the girl and ventured back out onto the street.

There was music coming from the village hall. The local choir was rehearsing. Mrs Gallagher had always been part of the choir but recently had had a falling out with the organ player

'I told her that a choir should sing proper religious songs. I have no time for this modern stuff. If you don't like it, then you should not be in a choir, I am sure all the ladies here agree with me.' But Sive had heard from a neighbour that they had sided with the organ player and Mrs Gallagher had left in a huff.

'I am not going back until they stop this ridiculous music, I have written to the bishop to tell him. If I don't hear from him soon, I will pay him a visit.'

'But if that's what they want,' Sive had tried to intervene.

'They have no idea what they want. But the choir will sing religious songs by the time I am done with it and that is that,' Mrs Gallagher had replied bluntly. Sive would never go in if she thought she was there, but now she couldn't help but quietly walk in and listen in the hall where no one could see her. The choir began to sing a beautiful version of *Ave Maria*. It was her mother's favourite hymn. Suddenly, her mind was full of images of her. Lately she was on her mind so much and as she listened to the music and closed her eyes she could almost see her mother laughing and running on the beach. She could see herself, wild and free running after her.

'Feel the wind little Sive, feel the salt air on your lips, this is the beauty of the universe, this is life's gift to us.' The song came to an end and she quietly stepped out of the building.

Chapter 16

The Dream
Frida Kahlo, Private Collection.

Dan could hear the rustle of the breakfast trays making their way down the corridor. The trays were getting closer, and he silently prayed it would not be Lily who was on today. The others came in and silently placed the tray on his table, only stopping to ask if the order was right. He didn't care so he tended to just nod his head. Lily liked to chat unmercifully even though he made no reply to her. She insisted on pulling the curtains and ignoring his pleas to leave them closed. The door opened, it was her, she had her victim.

'Rise and shine! Rise and shine! That's what I say! Let in God's good sunshine, that's what I say!' Her squeaky voice like icicles in the silence of the room.

'Come on, we will puff up those pillows. Yes, we will. There's a good lad. We will give those pillows a good puff up.' Dan leaned forward, there was no escaping her.

'My grandchildren love their pillows puffed. It's good for their brain. That's what I say and my God do they have good brains? The best that there is! Going to be something big they are. Oh, they sure are, that's what I say.' Dan tried to turn his back to her, but quick as lightening she was at the other side.

'Did I tell you our Darren got twenty out of twenty for his spelling test? Imagine! Not one wrong. Not a tiny single one.' She settled the tray in front of him, looking right up into his face, making sure he could not avoid a word.

'A genius! That's what he is. Going to be something big. Sure is with that big brain. That's what I say.' He closed his eyes, locking out the brightness. If only her voice could be locked out.

'I'll leave you now love. I'd love to stay and keep you company but I must go. Eat your breakfast now, you will be much better then. That's what I say. Ta da then, lovely chatting to you.'

Like a bad dream, it was over and she was gone, he could hear her in the corridor stopping to fill in one of the porters on the spelling test. If only he had the strength to get out of bed and close the curtains, the brightness was like a razor to his brain. He could ring the bell for someone to close them but then he risked having to converse with them. He would wait a while. Then with as much strength as he could muster up he pushed the tray away and threw down a pillow and pulled the sheet over his face. He willed himself back to sleep. There at least he didn't have to think or be.

Because thinking hurt too much, too much guilt, too much pain. But it was impossible to stop the thoughts, tearing at him, tormenting him, if only he could breathe but not think.

The corridor was busy now, doctors and nurses getting ready for rounds. He said a silent prayer that they would not come near him. That they would leave him alone. Just come in and close the curtains but leave him alone. He needed his mind to go to a different time. A time when his mind was free.

He is running through the fields, his boots making great squelching noises in the wet grass. A ten-year-old and his beloved dogs by his side, searching for rabbits and hares. Down in the ditches rooting out something for them to chase. They never catch anything, but oh, how they do love the chase. A hare with her hind legs skipping in the air takes flight. A three-legged terrier with the heart of a lion and a sheepdog that wags his tale all his waking hours take after her.

'Go on lads, we will catch him,' Dan shouts in glee at his two companions. He is in the chase too, dirt splattering his face. He can barely catch his breath he is running so fast, they see her now, they are getting closer. Her back legs are the last thing they see as she disappears near the river. The dogs dive in, the hare has lost them. They run into the water splashing, barking and panting. The two dogs come back out, shaking themselves off with their fun, jumping on Dan, the three amigos.

He can almost smell the grass. He heard the knock on the door and tried to ignore it and go back to his dream, where he was free.

'Dan, I have someone to talk to you this morning.' The ward sister had a woman with her. An attractive lady in her mid-fifties.

'Good morning, Dan. My name is Doctor Purcell and I am the consultant psychiatrist. Is it ok to have a chat with you?' Dan looked at her as she started getting out a file. He wondered what her reaction would be if he told her to piss off. He wanted to go back to his dream, away from anyone with files and questions. Away from nurses with high pitched voices who nagged him worse that his own mother. Away from everyone including himself. So yes, he did mind if she sat down, he did mind if she started talking. Could they not understand, he just wanted to be left alone, alone with his broken thoughts and broken life?

'I would like to talk to you Dan, about how you are feeling,' she said.

'I want to be left alone, is that too much to ask?' Dan replied curtly.

'Can you tell me why, why you want to be left alone?' she asked.

'No. Can we do this another time?'

'It would be better if we could talk a little now,' she said.

'Is it really too much to ask just to be alone?'

It obviously was, as the session with the doctor lasted over an hour. Afterwards she told Dan she would be back to see him soon. It was over. He could close his eyes again. It was his only peace. There were no words to express how he felt. No conversations were going to make him feel less alone. The curtains were opened again. Sleep would not come and give him the nothingness to kill the feelings.

He looked out his window at the grey sky. There was so little colour on the trees with the bleakness of winter. He looked at his hands. They were pale and softer than he remembered. He loved the outdoors and this had kept them rougher. He had a firm hand shake. He believed it said a lot. How many people had he met over his life time? How many people had he shaken hands with? Yet now he wanted none of them.

Thoughts of Sive came to him but he tried to push them aside. He did not want to think. He felt dead to himself. Sive his life. It was as if he couldn't reach her, he wondered if he ever could again. Could it ever be like it was? They were so happy, he loved her more than anything. But you cannot hide the past it has a way of creeping up on you when you least expect. When you are at your most vulnerable. Exhausted from thinking he closed his eyes and mercifully sleep came, where he was back chasing the breeze with his dogs.

Chapter 17

Lady at the Tea Table
Metropolitan Museum of Art, New York.

Sive had a meeting with the psychiatrist to talk about Dan. She felt almost guilty discussing him but it was becoming apparent that Dan was sinking into a very dark place. Sive desperately wanted to pull him out, but she knew she needed help. She could not do this alone. She grabbed her bag from the car and headed in for her appointment. She knew Dan was very low and instead of improving he seemed to be sinking even lower. It would be good to see what the specialist said. She found the office and waited outside until she was called. Doctor Purcell greeted her and invited her in to her office.

She was quite matter of fact when Sive met her but Sive could see a warmth of compassion in the other woman's eyes.

'Please take a seat.'

'Thank you.'

'I'm afraid your husband is deeply troubled, but his physical injuries need to heal a little more before we know where we are,' she explained.

'Is this a result mostly of the crash?' Somehow if it was, Sive felt she could deal with it a little better. It would be more difficult to hear that she had simply not seen it beforehand.

'It's hard to say now, but there is no doubt his mental health is very low. I will assess him again shortly. The surgical team has prescribed something to relax him so for the moment with all the medication he is on I am not going to prescribe anything else.

'Dan is normally so upbeat so much has happened, but it's just so unlike Dan to be like this.'

'I know about the business collapsing and the loss of your house. Is there anything else I should know about?' the doctor asked.

'How do you mean?' Sive asked.

'Is there something about his past that I need to know? I asked for any old records to be transferred up to me. Has Dan ever suffered any previous mental health issues?' Sive was taken aback with the question.

'No, not at all. I would never have worried about him in that manner. As far as I am aware he had a good childhood and teenage life. I know he was sick for almost a year with glandular fever and was off school. But that was when he was sixteen. Other than that, he has been fine.

'Really, glandular fever?'

'Yes, he was quite bad, but he was at home as far as I know for most of it. He did go to some special hospital for treatment in England I think.'

'For glandular fever?'

'Yes.'

'That's interesting!' The doctor scribbled down some notes as she listened to Sive.

'As I said he is really positive,' Sive added.

'Okay, so he was just his normal self beforehand?'

'Well not quiet. He had a lot on his plate obviously and had hidden it all from me. There is one thing about Dan that contrasts with the Dan that everyone knows.'

'Go on,' The doctor urged.

'Since I have known Dan I have noticed at rare times he can retreat a little into himself. But really, I suppose most people do at some stage in their lives. Not many people if any notice it about him. He is great at always keeping up a good front. But there have been times when I suppose he feels down, like any of us can. But when he is I am just aware of it and I know in time he will be back to his usual self. It's difficult to explain. But I have never worried about it or even said it to him. It has been like an unbroken truth between us. Something I understand yet it has never been said. But he has never had to seek medical help. It's as if he goes to somewhere that is hard to reach him. But he knows I am there and that I understand he needs that time to just think about things. As I said it's hard to explain to be honest. But now that you ask me I thought I should mention it.'

'OK, well as I said I will have a look at all his old records just to be sure and I will assess him again very shortly. We will keep a close eye on him. If you could chat with his immediate family about our concerns. It is better that they are made aware of it. We need to tread very carefully with Dan until he regains some mental strength,' she explained.

'Of course, I will meet with his parents and his brother today if I can,' Sive replied.

'Good and I will keep you informed of how he is, we will take it day by day.' She got up and showed Sive out.

Sive headed to the coffee dock for a cup of tea. Dan was still very distant with her and talked very little. She knew she would have to talk to the Gallaghers about what the psychiatrist had said. She had not spoken to Mrs Gallagher since the big row at the house. But that was the strange thing about her mother in law. She would act as if nothing had happened. For Dan's sake, she had to contact her. There was no time like the present.

She took a deep breath and dialled her number. She picked up immediately and gave Sive very little time to tell her anything.

'Sive we need to talk about Dan and about where you are going to live. I have decided you can come here until we sort things out, at least I can look after Dan and see that he is getting something nourishing. Nothing like some solid cooking to help him along. He loves my roasts. I will make sure he gets plenty of nourishing food. Once he has a bit of strength in him he will be as right as rain.' Sive tried to remain calm.

'When the time is right for Dan to leave hospital, I will discuss where we will live with him. No decision on our future will be made by anyone but Dan and myself. Do I make myself very clear Mrs Gallagher?' There was a stony silence on the other end of the phone.

'Well where do you propose to bring my son, might I ask? Some caravan down on that Burren, where he will most definitely get pneumonia and be back in hospital before you know it?' Sive knew better than to get into an argument with Mrs Gallagher on the phone.

'As soon as any arrangement has been made you will be informed. For now, the subject is closed. I am ringing to discuss his recovery and I refuse to discuss anything else on the phone.' She arranged to call up to see her so that they could talk properly.

'Afternoon tea at four,' Mrs Gallagher instructed.

'Very well, we can talk then,' Sive hung up and immediately could feel the anxiety building in her about her meeting. At least Desmond and Tom would be there if any fist fights broke out.

On entering the avenue, Sive realised she had never visited her in laws on her own, Dan was always with her. The avenue was about a half a mile long with ash trees bordering. It was a large sprawling farmhouse with ivy growing all over it. There were lots of rose bushes planted, that of course were prize winning. The farmyard dogs signalled her arrival. Sive had other friends who lived on farms but none of them were quite like Mrs Gallagher.

Mrs Gallagher was at the door wearing a bright green twin set and a flowery skirt. Her hair was freshly set and her pink lipstick was perfect. Sive gathered she spent very little time on the farm herself, preferring to give her instructions from her parlour amidst her china collection and her Waterford crystal. Sive grabbed the flowers she had brought as a gift and greeted her mother in law, who looked with distaste at her jeans, jumper and boots.

'We will have tea shortly, but I think we will have a chat first so that we are all agreed on what's happening,' Mrs Gallagher instructed. Sive could feel a row brewing, somehow this was not going to go down as she planned.

'Please sit down dear in the living room, I am just going to call Desmond and Tom. Sive stepped into the living room which was more relaxed than the parlour. The walls were filled with photos of the family. Pictures of Dan and Tom in their communion and confirmation outfits were pride of place on the mantel piece. More photos of almost every occasion adorned the walls. Mrs Gallagher went to the back door and bellowed her best.

'Des..mond.., Tom..., come inside.' Sive was amused at her mother in law shouting like a banshee. Within a few minutes Desmond arrived, unusually dressed in a crisp white shirt and pullover under his farm jacket. Sive knew he must have been forced into it for her arrival. Tom arrived shortly afterwards, and despite his work clothes, looked as handsome as ever. He winked at Sive and whispered.

'She is fairly fired up now, try to take no heed,' Mrs Gallagher came in and checked that they had both left their work boots outside and then took control of the conversation.

'Now, let's get straight to the point. We are here to discuss Dan and what's best for him, I think....' Before she could continue, her husband broke in gently.

'Sorry love to interrupt you, but Sive has come to see us, let her tell us what the specialist has to say.' He smiled encouragingly at Sive. Mrs Gallagher looked daggers at her husband and then questioningly at Sive. Sive nodded gratefully at her father in law.

'Yes, I was in this morning. To be honest he still has a long way to go but at least the injuries are starting to heal and his leg should be fine with physio. He is still very weak though but the injury to the head is healing. They are very concerned about Dan's mental health now. They have had the consultant from the psychiatric department visit him. They are taking it day by day, but it's important we are aware that he is under psychiatric care and we must be very careful what we say to him for a little while.' When Sive finished speaking she could feel Mrs Gallagher's eyes bore into her and her mouth was pursed tightly, you could hear the animals outside, breaking the tangible silence. Her father in law moved uncomfortably in his seat. Tom broke the silence.

'You can be assured we will say nothing to upset him in any way Sive, but it's serious then, they must be very worried to have him under psychiatric care.' Mrs Gallagher had found her voice and it bellowed out of her.

'What is this talk about psychiatrists, as if it was as common as a sore throat to have one visit you?' She rose to her full five feet five inches and with her kitten heels an extra two inches. Her face had become very red and her eyes seemed larger than possible.

'I have never heard such a load of nonsense in my living room.'

Tom looked at her and then at Sive.

'For Christ's sake mother, don't be daft, Dan is not well,' he implored.

'I do not want any more talk on this subject, thank you very much, we will go up to the hospital tomorrow and sort out any misunderstanding. Psychiatrists indeed. Nobody in our family ever needed to see one of those,' she replied curtly.

'Mother, are you mad? Of course we have to get Dan help if he needs it,' Tom added.

'Pearl, it's a shock surely, but we have to listen to the doctor, they know what they are talking about.' Dan's father tried to get her to see reason. At that the phone rang.

'Do not answer that Desmond, it's probably Bernie down the road after spotting the car coming into the drive and wondering who it is, I don't want her getting hold of any of this, I might as well put it on the radio. The most important thing is that this does not get outside this room. I am not having anyone talk about one of my family in this way. Some of his cousins and aunts want to go see him, we will just say he has the vomiting bug and can't see any visitors, and we will keep saying that until this is sorted. As I say the most important thing is to keep this quiet.' Sive knew her mother in law would be upset, but this was ridiculous.

'Dan's mental health is very low, he needs all the support he can get. Pretending it is not happening is not going to help. His mental health is what is important, Mrs Gallagher.'

'I want no more talk of anyone mental in this house,' Mrs Gallagher roared at Sive. Tom looked directly at his mother.

'Sit down mother. Woman have you lost your reason? Dad will you talk to her and make her see sense. She is acting like a crazy woman.'

'Pearl, Tom is right, you have to see reason here, you cannot sweep this under the carpet.' He scratched his head with anguish. Sive stood up and looked Mrs Gallagher straight in the eye.

'Dan is sick. He needs the best treatment we can possible get for him. I thought that you wanted to talk about Dan, not talk about how you are going to hide the fact he is unwell from everyone. I don't particularly want to let people know this, but I am not ashamed of it as you seem to be,' she pointed out. Mrs Gallagher was quick to retort back.

'I see nothing of the sort. Yes, his business is gone, and if he had stayed in the farming sector nothing like this would ever have happened. But our Dan always had different ideas, well we can see where that has got him. We never wanted him going off starting that business. The land is in his blood. He should have stayed here. But no! He had to go off and got notions of something different. Look where that has got him. He has not the shirt on his back, or do you Sive, so don't tell me what my son needs.' Sive felt like she had been struck.

'That's it, I'm leaving.' Sive had heard enough and got up to go.

'You are a piece of work, Mrs Gallagher. How dare you speak to me like that,' she said as she was grabbing her bag. Desmond stood in front of her.

'Sive, don't go. Please just sit down. For Dan's sake,' he added. Then he looked at his wife.

'Pearl will you get a grip on yourself for God's sake, you have gone too far.' His voice was calm but firm. But Mrs Gallagher could not be stopped.

'I am only speaking the truth Desmond, it needs to be said, and I am the only one willing to say it.' Mrs Gallagher eye balled her husband, putting her hands on her hips. Desmond raised his voice.

'We have all made mistakes, Pearl, throughout our lives even you and me. Who are we to judge how Sive and Dan live theirs? It is their life and we have no business judging it in any way. Now I know you are upset but the last thing we want is to fall out. At least for Dan's sake can we all please try to calm down if only to somehow help him?' Mrs Gallagher was clearly taken aback by her husband's stance and for once was quiet. Her husband looked kindly at Sive who was barely sitting on her chair, as if ready to go at any time.

'What we want to say to you Sive is we are here to help in any way we can. We wanted to let both of you know we want to help. We were thinking of expanding the farm. The beef herd is Tom's domain, but we may look at getting into some tillage. Dan was always good with tractors. He could even go out for hire, with the machinery. It's there if Dan wants it.' Mrs Gallagher had to get her tuppence in.

'There is a nice site up in the front field, we can get started on a house. I was thinking a nice bungalow, with a sun room, a good solid oak kitchen, none of that Ikea business. Something sensible and easy access to the farm, that way we can keep an eye on Dan too.' Sive looked at Dan's parents. She knew in their own way they meant well, but living so close to her mother in law was truly not going to happen. But that conversation was for another day.

'Look, I appreciate you are trying to help but all I am worried about now is getting Dan better, and from what the psychiatrist said support from his family is crucial in his recovery, and trying to cover it up will not be helpful.

'Dan will be fine when we get him home, Sive. I've known Dan longer than you. He will be fine.' Sive was about to interject but Mrs Gallagher was back to her earlier stance.

'Dan has had a car accident and with the vomiting bug he is not up to visitors. That is what we will say if anyone asks. Now that's settled we will have some tea.' She bustled off to the kitchen to organise the tea. She was humming out of tune to herself as she busied herself. Sive stared after her as if questioning was this really happening. She looked at Tom for some sort of explanation. He shut the living room door as Desmond got up, shaking his head with frustration at his wife.

'Please excuse Pearl, Sive, I am afraid she is in denial about Dan. I will talk to her when she cools down. She just has no idea how to handle it. Of course, we won't tell people he has the vomiting bug, but perhaps he could do without any visitors for the moment anyway. I realise he is very ill, and his mother must too, but she needs some time to adapt to the situation. Whatever her methods, when it comes to Dan her heart is in the right place. Sure, she is cracked about him, he was always the apple of her eye. Give her a bit of time, Sive, to get used to it, just for Dan's sake. Despite their differences, they are close.' Sive had to agree with her father in law. Dan found his mother infuriating but he deeply cared about her, and her him, and for Dan's sake she would try to give Mrs Gallagher some time to adjust.

'I didn't realise Dan was that affected from the accident.' Tom's face was very strained and pale. He had said very little throughout the argument.

'Well, I am afraid it was before the accident, he had a lot of pressure that I was unaware of. He carried on as normal. I wish I had picked up on it sooner, he may not be in this position now,' Sive replied.

'Well, we could all say that Sive. Sure, I thought everything was going great from him,' Desmond added. Sive nodded in agreement.

'Tea's ready,' bellowed Mrs Gallagher.

'Dan will be ok in the end Sive. He has a strong mind and it will pull him true, and he has you to fight his corner, he is a lucky man.' Desmond put his arm around Sive and they all went into the kitchen for tea. Mrs Gallagher dominated the conversation with talk of her prize plum puddings and Christmas cakes that she had made in abundance to give to certain neighbours who would appreciate the art that went into them. Sive was always amazed at how Mrs Gallagher could have a full-on row with someone and then act as normal as if it was just part of the day. There was no more talk of Dan or his breakdown. They were just discussing her apple tart when a car pulled into the yard and the dogs went mad barking.

'Co..ee.. its only me oh no, have you visitors? Sure, if I had known I would have left it till later, but as I am here...' A small woman Sive recognised as Bernie arrived in.

'Come on in, you will have some tea and tart,' Mrs Gallagher replied as she put her eyes up to heaven.

'Sure, who could refuse your tart Mrs Gallagher,' replied Bernie who was already seated and pouring herself a cup of tea. She turned her attention to Sive.

'Sive, how is poor Dan? I heard he had a right accident, myself and Jim are thinking of going up to see him after mass on Sunday, bring him up a few tractor magazines I have, you know to pass the time.' Mrs Gallagher almost dropped the tart.

'Dan is doing really well, thank you very much Bernie. Sive just dropped down to tell us about the vomiting bug in the ward where Dan is, she has just come from there. Sive seems to have escaped it we hope, but you never know.' Bernie stared at Sive who had just given her a large bowl of cream for her tart. She stared at the cream as if it was contaminated.

'The vomiting bug, merciful hour, that's the last thing me or my Jim needs, I'll leave the tea,' she said as she pushed her chair back, almost knocking over Mrs Gallagher, who was hovering over her.

'Tell Dan I'll leave it till he is out and I will see him then, give him my best.' With that she was on her feet and her little Mini was giving off steam getting out of the yard.

'I might as well of put it in the *Evening Herald*, Bernie will make sure everyone in the village knows about the vomiting bug and steer clear of Dan,' Mrs Gallagher said triumphantly as she sat at the top of the table. Sive, Desmond and Tom couldn't help but laugh.

Chapter 18

The Stages Of Life
Casper David Friedrich, Leipzig, Germany

'I just can't believe how Mrs Gallagher reacted Beth, it was unreal. Imagine pretending to everyone he has a vomiting bug. She really believes that her homemade cooking is going to make everything go away.'

'It sounds hilarious about her neighbour.'

'It was, we were in hysterics, despite ourselves. She is unbelievable. She will do anything to make things look good in front of her relatives and the neighbours of course.'

'You had a very open-minded dad but not everyone had. Look at my parents, they had a way of thinking that seemed in the dark ages but it's not that long ago. What the neighbours thought was the guide that some of them lived by and still do,' Beth explained.

'But surely today, with all the talk of mental health, how can anyone not know that it is just not right to treat it like that?' Sive asked, bewildered. Beth shook her head in resignation.

'I suppose they are so long living a certain way it's difficult for them to change. Ireland, live! My family would probably handle it no different. Actually, thinking about it they would be much worse.' There was a shift in Beth's tone, like a darkness crossing over her.

'Are you ok Beth?'

'Yes, I'm fine, to be honest I was just remembering something,' she replied.

'Oh, what was it?' Sive asked gently.

'Nothing,' Beth said, as if to herself.

'It might help to talk about it,' Sive added.

'No, sometimes the past is better left there. In the past.' With that Beth pottered in the kitchen and Sive knew to leave well alone. But she wondered what she meant. She decided to change the subject. Whatever it was, Beth had no intention of talking about it right now.

'What are you up to for the evening?'

'I have a meeting with some of the designers we have for our new spring/summer fashion show next week.'

'It must be hard to think of summer clothes in the middle of winter.'

'I know, you get used to it though. How about you, you are probably exhausted after the day?'

'I think I'll paint actually, it will be good for my mind, it's all over the place,' Sive replied.

'Okay. I'll see you later, and try not to worry too much.' Sive made a strong cup of tea and set about her painting. Before she knew it, she was lost in another world, and her mind was eased as she immersed herself in her art. A few hours passed without her hardly stopping. She had begun a painting of the Burren while on her visit home to her father's. Inspired by the rugged landscape, Sive was trying to capture it as dawn breaks, when she believed it's ancient beauty was at its most glorious. It captivated the wild orchids that grew in abundance, almost dancing as they welcomed the dawn. In the morning mist the echo of the Aran Islands could be seen in the distance. Sive never tired of painting the Burren and knew like her father it was deep in her blood. It had been like a tonic walking through the heathery landscape, which somehow had brought some peace to her mind with the loss of her home. She continued painting for hours, totally losing track of time.

Beth came back after her meeting. The conversation earlier was not mentioned and Beth was full of news about her fashion show.

'The colours and the fabrics are amazing, I am so excited about it. The designers are just so creative it's as if there is no limit to their imagination, and the most important part for me is that a lot of it will sell.'

'Do you have a favourite designer?'

'I just love when I find a new one that I want to sign, one that is not anywhere else in Ireland. It leaves me with huge possibility as it's not just for Irish designers, even though seventy percent is. Still, I have thirty percent to peruse anywhere in the world and that gives it a great edge. I have one designer from Rome that I am chasing and she is amazing. I think our buyers would love her designs. They are so elegant. By the way I got a beautiful coat as a gift from a designer but it's about three sizes too small. I have no idea what she was thinking. Here, would you like it?'

It was a fabulous tweed coat in a dark russet colour. The lining was in n emerald green silk.

'Wow it's gorgeous,' Sive said as she put it on.

'Great, it's yours, your mobile is ringing.'

'It's Mrs Gallagher.' Sive sighed. 'I better answer it or she might hunt me down.' She grinned.

'Sive, myself and Desmond are going to the hospital in the morning to see what is going on with Dan I need to clear all this up, so they can concentrate on fixing his broken bones. We can meet for tea if you wish, I can fill you in on what I will discuss with them.' Sive was going to tell her that she had no right to interfere, but that was for the hospital staff to take care of. Whatever the visit was about there was sure to be some drama so she thought she better go, if only to be there for Dan. She agreed to meet them for a coffee afterwards.

The hospital car park was busy as usual and it was with a heavy heart she walked into the coffee shop. Mrs Gallagher had a very colourful purple and green two-piece suit on with cream shoes. Sive noted at least there was no hat today.

'We are over HERE,' Mrs Gallagher shouted for everyone in the coffee shop to hear. Their eyes followed Sive over to her mother in law who was holding court at the table.

'He was having a session with some therapist, so we have yet to see him. No idea why on earth they are having that with him. I am sure when I have a good chat with him all this nonsense will be cleared up,' Mrs Gallagher explained. Sive tried to figure her mother in law out. Could she really think that a chat with her was going to bring her son back from the darkness that he was in?

'Therapists and sessions, I have never heard the like. In our day, you just got on with it. If trouble came to your door, you did the best you could, there was no one there to have sessions with no, you just got on with it. Now never let it be said that I would say anything, I would not interfere. It's the last thing I would do, but therapists, now really. All our Dan needs is a little rest, some good home food and he will be as right as rain.' Desmond looked at Sive and shook his head. Sive gathered that he and Tom had not managed to get through to Mrs Gallagher about the seriousness of the illness. Well at least Tom was good about it and Desmond was really trying to come to terms with it. But Mrs Gallagher, that was another story. Desmond made a last attempt to help his wife see the light.

'But Pearl we must see what the doctor says.'

'I tell you now Desmond, I am not listening to any nonsense, I am going to give him a piece of my mind if he starts on about anything mental about my son.' Mrs Gallagher was adamant.

'Pearl it's his mental health.' Desmond corrected her.

'Call it what you like, but my Dan is not one of them.' Sive and Desmond resigned themselves to saying nothing. God knows how this was all going to go. Sive had images of Mrs Gallagher dragging poor Dan off his bed and shoving him into the car to come home to eat her apple pie. That was not going to sort it, even if it was prize winning.

They went down to the ward, and met a nurse. Sive stayed in the waiting area and allowed Dan's parents to see Dan on their own. The nurse sat down for a minute with her.

'Are you OK, you look very worried.' Sive told her how Mrs Gallagher was taking the news.

'Don't worry, I am not going to leave her in there for long, the last thing we need is Dan to be upset by her. I am afraid there is no improvement, he is still very low.' The nurse knocked on Dan's door and after a few minutes the Gallagher's appeared. Desmond looked ashen and was barely able to speak. Sive was unsure what to do, she had never seen this side to Desmond, he always seemed the same, always agreeing with Mrs Gallagher and always in the same mood. Mrs Gallagher looked like she had shrunken a little since she had gone in. She clutched her matching cream handbag and put her free hand over her mouth.

Sive found a quiet corner for them all to sit. Mrs Gallagher just kept shaking her head, all the fire had gone out of her.

'I don't understand, he is not himself at all, he hardly spoke. He looks terrible. What is going on? Up to now he was asleep or very groggy when we saw him. He is awake now and it is nearly worse. I demand to speak with his doctor.' Thankfully the nurse came over to them.

'Dan needs a second opinion, there is obviously something wrong with whatever treatment you are giving him. You see it's not in our family at all, this, this... mental health thing.' Mrs Gallagher explained to the nurse.

'I see, but I am afraid it can hit any family at any stage, the most important thing is that Dan feels supported now. I am sure the doctor will tell you more, he may not get a chance to talk to you now, but I can get him to call you if you like.' Mrs Gallagher seemed to sit up a bit straighter at the mention of the doctor.

'Yes, get him to call me please. I will discuss this with him, I am sure there must be some mix up with medication. Tell him to ring me as soon as possible dear. Thank you that's what I will do, sort this out with the doctor, there must be some explanation. Make sure it's the consultant that rings me, no young trainee, I need to speak to the top, do you understand?' The nurse gave Sive a knowing look and went off. Desmond put his arms around his wife. Suddenly she started to cry big, heaving sounds.

'Hush pet, there, there.' For the first time Sive could see the strength of their relationship. Mrs Gallagher was all fire and brimstone but Desmond was the one who gave her strength. He cradled her like a child and Sive could see how deeply they cared for each other.

'I am going to bring Pearl home,' he said eventually when Mrs Gallagher had finally stopped crying. Sive smiled reassuringly at him She watched them walk down the corridor, Mrs Gallagher leaning on her husband, her heartbreak evident after seeing her son.

She waited a little while and then decided to go in for a few minutes to see Dan. They had got him out of bed to sit on a chair. He was sitting with his eyes closed. Sive wasn't sure if he was awake so she only whispered.

'Dan it's me.'

Without looking up or opening his eyes he whispered back, 'Don't let my mother in to see me again, Sive.'

'Oh.'

'Just don't let her in, I can't deal with her. Will you pull the blinds please?'

'Okay Dan, but it's not going to be easy, you know your mother.'

'I know her more than anyone. I can only imagine what she is saying.'

'She finds it difficult to understand, Dan.' Sive was surprised that she was standing up for her, but in her heart, she knew Mrs Gallagher adored her son.

'Well, let her find it difficult, I don't care anymore, just keep her away from me.' Sive wanted to tell him how hurtful it was to be shunned and shut out. But she bit her tongue.

'Very well Dan, I will have a word with your mother.'

Chapter 19

Portrait of a Woman
Unknown, Louvre, Paris, France.

Beth had arranged to meet a new Irish designer that she was about to sign. Normally she would be upbeat at the thoughts of signing such a new artist, but today her mind was elsewhere. She couldn't shake the feelings that had been stirred up by the conversation with Sive. Although she thought about the past, it was safe in her memory. When she allowed herself to think about it she was always on her own, as if she needed that safety net of her privacy. There was no way Sive knew anything but still it had upset her and she wished she could shake the feeling away.

On impulse, she drove near St. Stephen's Green and just by luck got some parking. She had a while before her meeting, she had planned to go into the shop and do some prep work but for once her heart wasn't in it. She paid for her parking ticket and walked towards the park. She hadn't been there in a long time. She walked for a little while before finding a bench to sit on near the lake to watch the ducks. Out of nowhere hot tears fell down her face. Years ago, it happened a lot, she had no control over it. She had kept herself to herself then. Building a barrier so she could cope. Only for Rose her landlady she would have been totally alone. There was no network of friends that she could turn too. Coming up to Christmas, the fairy lights always brought it back.

She was alone now but it was her own choice. She was happy with her life, she loved her job and her apartment. She had friends to socialise with if she wanted and anything more she did not want. Happy families had never played a part in her life, she would never risk having one of her own, it was safer being alone, at least she knew where she stood. The rug could not be pulled away from you when you were on your own, she looked up to heaven and allowed herself to grieve for what might have been.

She could see how frustrated Sive was with Mrs Gallagher's behaviour. But Beth had been a victim of keeping up a good front for her family.

She had played by the rules set out to her. Time does heal she thought, but it doesn't forget, the memories of the past are embedded in your heart. She had decided long ago not to allow bitterness to rule her life, but keeping a distance from her family was part of keeping the bitterness away.

Reluctantly she got up and headed to the new French restaurant to meet her designer. She checked her make up in the bathroom first. It was busy but she had a table booked. The designer arrived. She was young not long out of college.

'What an amazing collection you have so early in your career.' Beth looked at her recruit. She was blonde and glamorous with a maturity more suited to someone older.

'My parents always encouraged me from a young age, so I feel I have been designing for years to be honest.' She smiled confidently as she ordered in perfect French.

'My goodness, you are so fluent.' Beth was taken aback by her confidence.

'Oh, I love French, so I did an exchange for a year to Paris when I was in college. My mother came over and visited me so I wasn't too lonely and of course I loved Paris. It was an amazing year.' Beth couldn't help but compare her own adolescent and early twenties to this young, self-assured girl sitting in front of her. It may have been a different era she had grown up in, but comparing it, it felt like a different planet. Normally she would be so focused on a lunch like today but today her mind fought the memories that were rushing in to cloud her mind. As she listened to the designer talk about her collection and her inspiration she had to fight the image of herself as a young girl. The ghost of her past as a frightened youth, oppressed and lacking self-belief or confidence, was haunting her. If she had come from a different family how would she have turned out? Was it just pot luck to whom you were born to? How lucky this young girl was with all the opportunity and encouragement that she had gained. She tried to brush the past aside and concentrate on signing this new dynamic designer.

She went into the bathroom of the restaurant and looked at her reflection. Her flame red hair was set off by a silk blouse in a deep turquoise colour tucked into some black tailored trousers with Italian leather high court shoes. Her skin glowed with the hint of makeup. She looked the part. Successful, together and professional. Nobody but her could see the ghost in the mirror, she washed her hands and shook the past away. If only it could be rewritten, would it take the pain away? She touched up her make up with a delicate blush and some rich lip gloss and went back to her newly signed client who was waiting outside, with her Prada bag on her shoulder, for Beth to show her more of the boutique.

Chapter 20

White House at Night
Vincent van Gogh. Hermitage Museum, Amsterdam.

The rain pelted down on Sive's bedroom window and then, true to the Irish weather, the sun came dazzling out, impatiently waiting to shine. After throwing on some clothes she set out for a walk. Her head hurt thinking about everything, the house, the solicitors, the banks, but mostly Dan's broken body and mind. It was like he had given up.

Deep down, she knew she loved Dan and she had to believe her marriage was worth fighting for, even though he was indifferent to her and that hurt like hell. She knew that he might need her now more than he ever did. She thought about the shock of all she had lost. Now when she awoke the bile didn't greet her. The sheer loss of handing over her home had been physical. But now that it had passed, she knew she had survived.

Avara village was just waking up. A lake in the centre was home to some swans, who guarded it like a castle. She sat beside the lake and watched the hustle of the early morning.

The smell of freshly baked bread and coffee wafted through the air. People came in and out of what looked like an old-school house but was actually a café. Wind chimes hanging over a craft shop mingled with the slow move of traffic. The boutique hotel in the centre of the village was painted an old-fashioned green with dusky pink shutters giving it a French château look with loads of winter flowers hanging in baskets. A spiral of smoke came from its old chimneys. Some very expensive cars were parked outside. A mature, elegant lady who could have walked off a Parisian side walk came out of what looked like a dress shop, checking her window display. A tractor and trailer slowed the village down to a quieter place. The farmer was an old man with a cap and a pipe in his mouth. He drove with such ease that he looked like he was more on a day out than working. Some tourists came out of the hotel as a large swanky bus arrived to take them off for the day. Sive could hear the American accents and watched with amusement as they stuck big name badges on their chests. They were decked out in enough rain gear for a flood. She decided to walk around and discover the village a little more.

A short way down the pretty road there was a row of stone cottages, each one as individual as the next. On one of the gates was a for rent sign. She walked over to have another look. It looked run down and the garden to the front was over grown with weeds. Like a lot of the buildings in the village it was from another era. Opening the gate, it creaked as she closed it behind her and walked up to have a closer look. It certainly did not look lived in. Peering in through the windows it looked deceptively larger than the outside. Suddenly, she tripped over something, almost falling. It was an old wooden sign, more a battered piece of wood. It read: 'Hawthorn Cottage.' She couldn't resist having a peek out the back, there was something about it that almost drew her to it. Smiling she took in the garden with its stone walls surrounding it, wild and forgotten with rambling honeysuckle and fuchsia. Although neglected it was a beautiful space. Touching the walls of the house she could feel the sense of the past contained in it. It could be a couple of hundred years old. What secrets were contained within the walls? Something told her she wanted to find out more.

A small orchard was at the back which reminded her of her childhood. She was just coming back to the front when she heard a male voice.

'Good morning, lovely house isn't it?' An elderly man spoke. Sive was a little startled but he looked very friendly.

'Yes, it really is. I was just having a little look out the back.'

'Shame the garden is in such disrepair, the owners used to keep it beautiful, they would be broken hearted to see it. Bill Maher, lovely to meet you.' He held his hand out to introduce himself.

'Pleased to meet you, my name is Sive Gallagher. I didn't mean to intrude into the garden,' she replied as they shook hands.

'Oh, don't worry, the owner would welcome you. He was that sort. He hasn't lived here now in a few years.' Truth was Bill Maher missed his neighbours dearly, he worried about who would rent the house.

'It's very reasonable rent, to the right tenant,' he pointed out, smiling.

'Really, it is a lovely house.'

'It needs some work, but it's very solid if you like old houses. Most young people like the new modern thing with lots of space.'

'I adore old houses, they have a story to tell and I like to think they hold the memory of who went before.'

'How interesting, I never thought about it like that, well this house has some very good memories, so. Many an evening I spent here as did many others, enjoying wonderful hospitality. It would be great to see it occupied again. It's a friendly road if you are interested. A lot of us are old stock now, so we need some new blood to come in and bring some life into it.'

'It does seem lovely, I am not sure if I am looking though,' Sive said.

'Well if you are looking for an interesting little house, Hawthorn Cottage is a little gem. It needs a bit of tidying up, but it's very solid. Just a little patience and time, like lots of things in life really. Patience and time and a bit of understanding.'

'Wise words. It was lovely to meet you,' Sive shook his hand.

'You too, better get back to the wife, she has the breakfast ready and she does not approve of me being late,' he grinned.

Arriving back to the apartment she saw a familiar Land Rover and knew it was Tom, Dan's brother. Beth had given him the address at the hospital. Suddenly, a panic hit her, hopefully Dan was not worse.

'It's okay, I just came down to have a chat.' He smiled reassuringly, standing up to give Sive a hug. It reminded her of Dan's big hugs. He sat back down to his tea and a large slice of carrot cake.

'Beth was very kind and gave me some of this cake, even the mother would approve of it,' he grinned, then his voice became more serious.

'Speaking of Mam, I came to apologise to you. You have enough to worry about without Mam giving you a hard time.'

'You have nothing to apologise for, Tom. Your mother's attitude to Dan is pretty unreal, but at least she doesn't blame me and the cult anymore,' Sive grinned. Tom threw his eyes to heaven.

'Beth, you must not know what to think,' he replied, beaming at Beth. Sive could see Beth fussing a little too much, which was unlike her.

'Your mother is so long thinking that way, it's difficult to change. She was possibly brought up with that attitude and knew no different.' Beth smiled reassuringly at Tom. Sive thought she sensed a tinge of something between Beth and Tom and smiled to herself at the thought. It suddenly dawned on her how well they would suit each other. They were both very ethical and strong minded. They may have totally different lives but there was something right about seeing them together that she could not explain. Beth got up and grabbed her coat.

'I have a couple of things to post. It was lovely to see you again Tom.' Tom got up to say goodbye. Sive smiled at his chivalrous charm. Since she met Beth though, there never had been anyone serious. Yes, there were a few frivolous relationships, but Beth never got very involved. She got herself a cup of tea and sat down beside Tom as she watched his eyes follow Beth out the door.

'Well it's good of you to drive down Tom,' she said smiling to herself. Tom was smitten. He turned his focus back to Sive.

'I just wanted to see how you were after yesterday. I am sorry you had to put up with all that fuss with the mother the other day and I want to tell you we want to help in any way we can.' Sive hugged him, he looked very like Dan but older and maybe a little wiser.

They chatted easily for a while longer and eventually he hugged her and made his way off.

'Tell Beth thanks for the cake.'

'No problem, why don't you call soon again Tom, it's great to see you.' Tom gave her a wink.

'I might just do that.' Sive had a feeling that he would be delighted with any excuse to come visit Beth again. She busied herself in the house and decided to bake. She rooted around Beth's kitchen and found some wholemeal flour and pumpkin seeds and spices. A couple of hours passed till she sat down and surveyed her work. She had made some gorgeous brown bread with cinnamon and pumpkin seeds. Some bran and yoghurt muffins that smelt heavenly. She had also made a quiche with roasted veg and herbs. Just as she was putting the kettle on, Beth arrived in.

'My goodness what a beautiful array of food, I had no idea you had such talent, is Tom long gone?' she asked casually.

He didn't stay much longer after you left, but I get the feeling he will be calling here again soon though.'

'Oh.'

' Tom is a great guy Beth, but he had more on his mind than coming to see how I was.'

'What do you mean?' Beth asked.

'I mean, I think he came to hopefully see you,' Sive said.

'Don't be silly, I don't think I am his type.' Beth replied a little too casually.

'I think you are exactly his type. But promise me if anything does happen between you, I get to tell Mrs Gallagher. She will need to be resuscitated if Tom follows Dan and falls for someone that she has not picked out for him and, insult to injury, my best friend,' Sive grinned as she dished her out some piping hot quiche.

Mrs Gallagher need not worry, I have no intention of getting involved with anyone,' Beth said. Sive wanted to ask her why. Why decide that fate for yourself? But something stopped her. If Beth had something to tell her, she would in her own time.

'Sive, I called into that café that I was telling you about, you asked me to keep a look out for any type of job. I know it's not much but Kaitlin the owner is lovely and is looking for someone part-time.'

'I would love it, have you got her number?'

After a quick chat with Kaitlin, Sive arranged an interview.

'I am meeting with her tomorrow. Right, I am exhausted and I am going for a bit of a lie down, my sleeping pattern is still a bit shook up.'

In the warmth of the bedroom, she was soon in a deep sleep. Before she awoke she was in a slumber where she was neither asleep or awake, and her mind drifted, dream - like. She could see a house, familiar yet unfamiliar, with the unforgettable smell of roses. They were beautiful in shades of yellow and palest pink. In the window, she could see cut roses in glass bowls on the table. The house was so inviting yet she was hesitant to go over the threshold. She was looking for Dan but she couldn't see him. She looked back at the house she must know it? Suddenly she awoke, she did know it, it was Hawthorn Cottage.

The next day she went into the village, the rain had come in torrents the night before and everywhere looked even greener than usual. Sive thought how beautiful Ireland was with its forty shades of green. She retraced her footsteps from yesterday and found herself back at the cottage. The For Let sign was still there. She took out her phone and called it. She was surprised to hear the estate agent was in the village and could show her the house in twenty minutes.

Michael Sharry was dressed in the tightest suit Sive reckoned she ever saw anyone in. He was extremely business like and matter of fact.

'This is the siting room, to the left is what they refer to as the parlour. Then in here we have the kitchen and small conservatory. Very basic,' he added with distaste.

' I think it's very quaint, and look at the light coming into the kitchen and conservatory, it's beautiful,' Sive replied.

'Huh! Whatever you are into,' he added.

An old-fashioned washroom and toilet completed the downstairs. Upstairs had two cosy bedrooms and another bathroom with a big standalone old fashioned bath. The windows showed the thickness of the walls. The wallpaper was peeling off the walls, but other than that there was no damp or disrepair. It just looked like it needed a bit of care. Sive felt protective of it as she walked around; somehow she felt this house needed her as much as she might need it.

The conservatory led on to the garden, which was south facing. Sive could see how precious it could look. The stone wall surrounding it had rose bushes climbing it. She could only imagine how magical it would be when in bloom. She wondered what colour they would be, would they be yellow and palest pink? She certainly didn't ask the estate agent, who looked with distaste at the garden.

'I suppose the landlord could be persuaded to remove everything growing in the garden and put in a large patio. It would be very minimalistic with little or no maintenance.'

'I think that would be a dreadful thing to do, it needs some care and some work, but to me it is a huge feature of the property.'

'Whatever! This house may have to be sold in a few years, but if you become the tenant, I can make sure you have first refusal.' They discussed the cost of the rent and the condition. She looked around the house again, she knew it was a special little place.

'I would like to take it.' She looked calm on the outside, but inside her heart was racing. Yet somehow, she knew she was meant to take it. After discussing the rental, she left the estate agent and decided to go into the hotel for a coffee to celebrate. It was early but the hotel was full of bustle. An open fire in the reception area gave a welcome retreat from the iciness of the morning. A middle-aged lady in formal waitress gear welcomed her and showed her to a lounge.

'Coffee please,' Sive ordered. It was decorated like an old estate house with hunting pictures and deep brown leather couches. The coffee arrived in a beautiful silver coffee pot. Sive began to figure out how she would pay the rent for the cottage. If she even got a few hours in the coffee shop, with the little she had, she would manage it. There would be money needed to make it liveable. But a lot of it she could do herself. Excitement was bubbling inside of her. She had found a new home, and hopefully Dan would love it as much as she felt she was going to.

Chapter 21

The Kiss
Gustave Klimt. Osterreichische Galerie, Vienna.

Later in the day Michael Sharry called to say that he had spoken to the landlord, who would be quite happy to give a longer lease and a clause to say he would not sell it for three years at least.

'Great, when can I have the keys and start getting it ready?'

'Well, you can have the keys, I know there is a good bit to do to make it liveable, but the rent is low. The cottage is at the lower scale of what we deal with here.'

'Well I am quite happy with the cottage, I will be in with the deposit tomorrow.' Sive replied, ignoring his attitude.

It was really happening, she would soon have a place to live again. All she needed now was a job. Beth was fantastic about having her stay, but somehow, she knew she was meant to rent this house.

She headed off to meet with Kaitlin. The coffee shop was bright and trendy. An array of beautiful food of every colour was displayed behind the counter. One of the waitresses asked if she would like a table.

'No, I am actually here to see Kaitlin.' The waitress told her she would be back in a moment. Kaitlin came out from the back. She looked slightly younger than Sive and there was a glow of health that emanated from her, with her blonde hair tied neatly up behind a cotton cap.

'Please sit Sive. Would you like a coffee? I think I will have one.'

'Thank you, I will have a tea.' They discussed the job which would include waitressing and preparing some of the food. The hours were very flexible and the money was above what Sive expected.

'Sounds great, I would love the job,' Sive said enthusiastically.

'Well I need someone straight away. I am a single Mum and I am a bit stretched now to be honest. How about you start tomorrow and I can show you the ropes? See how you feel tomorrow, I am going to have to throw you in at the deep end, but tomorrow evening I will have a couple of hours when the café is closed and I could run over some stuff with you.' Sive was thrilled. Any extra bit of money would help now that she was going to rent somewhere. It would not be a lot of money but her first taste of independence felt good.

'Thank you, Kaitlin, I am looking forward to it.' Sive smiled at her new boss.

'If you could wear that with black jeans, that would be super.' Kaitlin gave her a black tee shirt with The Healthy Cabin written on it. She headed off with a bottle of wine to tell Beth her good news.

When she arrived back to the apartment there was crying coming from Beth's bedroom. Sive gently knocked to see what was wrong.

'Are you ok Beth, has something happened?' Beth opened the door. Her face was blotchy from crying. She looked like she had seen a ghost, her face had such a haunted look to it.

'It's nothing really,' Beth whispered hoarsely.

'Beth, look at yourself, please tell me what's wrong?' Beth tidied her hair and tried to compose herself. Clearly, she was not expecting Sive back so soon.

'Look I know you must be worried but I'm fine I promise, just one of those days.' Sive didn't reply but kept staring at her. Beth got up and went to the bathroom, and when she came back, she seemed to have regained her composure.

'Look I'm fine now, I was just having a bit of a bad day. I am going to make a cuppa and something to eat. Will you have some?' Sive knew not to pry any more, Beth was not for telling whatever was going on.

'Yes, I'm ravenous, let me help.' They pottered quietly in the kitchen for a few minutes, both lost in their thoughts.

'Tell me, how did your morning go?' Sive had completely forgotten about the house after seeing Beth. She just wanted to know what had happened but she knew better than to push her. She felt so bad suddenly, the last few weeks had been all about her troubles, she never thought that Beth had some of her own. She told Beth a little about the cottage.

'I have a bottle of wine, we can have a toast later,' Sive said.

'Love too, I'm going to grab a nap now though. I am wrecked to be honest.' Beth said.

The afternoon was quiet, with Sive painting and Beth staying in her room. When she emerged, she looked back to her old self and the earlier incident wasn't mentioned. Sive was tidying up her paints. Beth looked at the painting.

'Your painting is finished, it's beautiful.'

'I am happy with it. It reminds me of my childhood, spending time in the hazel woods with my mother. There was an abundance of wild orchids growing there. I am going to call it 'The Dance of the Dawn'. I love painting the Burren, I know it so well, but each time I paint it I discover something new and magical about the place.'

'Well it's beautiful, there is something mystical about it. Right, I must go to work. Sive there is no rush moving out, is there? To be honest I will miss you when you do move.'

'I am not going very far, I will be only a stone's throw from here. Avara has me well and truly hooked. I am here to stay.'

Sive was soon starving again and decided to have some of her home-made scones. She heated the scone and put a big dollop of cream and raspberry jam on it. At least her appetite was back again. She was just about to put the kettle on again when a neighbour of Beth's called in. He was quite a large man of about sixty and dressed in a very elegant Italian suit with a rather colourful tie and handkerchief. He had a gentle Devon accent.

'Good evening, awfully sorry to disturb you, but is Beth in by any chance?' he asked.

'I am afraid not, can I give her a message?' Sive replied.

'I was actually wanting to ask her to a little dinner party my wife and I are hosting on Friday evening. We were hoping Beth could join us,' he explained.

'I'm Sive, a friend of Beth's. I am staying with her for a while. Would you like a coffee?' She wasn't accustomed to asking strangers in for coffee, but Beth had mentioned the Watsons, and she knew she was very fond of them.

'I would love a coffee, how kind.' He gave her a broad smile and came in and closed the door. Sive set about making the coffee.

'My goodness, I love that painting, my wife would adore it.' It's breath-taking, so full of hope and joy. Who is the artist? I have tried to think of something for her birthday, and something like this would be perfect, is the artist in Ireland?'

'I did the painting, it's just completed, to be honest,' Sive replied.

'My goodness, is it for sale?' Sive only had to think for a millisecond,

'Yes, it is, but I haven't priced it yet,' she replied quickly.

'Okay, well let me know. I am sure we can come to a price we are both happy with,' he replied, delighted.

'You can have a think about it if you like, come back and see it later, when it's fully dry,' Sive replied.

'It's a beautiful painting dear, I am sure wahtever you charge for it, it will be worth every penny. She is looking for something for her new piano room, this would be perfect.'

'I will ring you later with a price,' Sive said, secretly thrilled.

'Excellent, please come to our little dinner on Sunday and you can bring it with you. My wife loves to meet the artists of her paintings and this will be hand delivered, splendid, now will we seal the deal with a coffee and one of these delicious scones?' Sive laughed and nodded.

'Your talents know no bounds,' he said as he munched into one, and they sat like they knew each other for a long time and chatted about art and his home in Devon.

Sive settled on a price and he was more than willing to pay it. She hadn't sold a painting in so long, in fairness she hadn't tried either. She was so looking forward to telling Dan all about the sale and the cottage. He had said very little about where they would live afterwards. If she could only get him to the cottage, she felt he would love it just as much as she did.

'Don't expect too much from him today, I am afraid he is very low, just give it time,' the nurse whispered.

'I will,' Sive replied.

When she came into the room, he was turned the opposite way. He didn't turn around but kept his back to her. She went around to the other side. He was staring into space, his face white and gaunt. For the first time Sive realised how much weight he had lost. She sat down beside him and reached for his hand. He didn't pull it away. He looked at her and she smiled back at him. Then he looked away again.

'Hi love.'

Dan made no reply.

'It's really cold out there, I will just take off my coat. I brought you some homemade cookies and some muffins. Would you like me to get you a cup of tea?' He shook his head.

He closed his eyes. She was shocked to see tears streaming down his face. She knelt and kissed them away.

'I love you Dan, please come back to me,' she whispered as she fought her own tears. He closed his eyes again and she gave him a gentle last kiss on the lips. How she missed him. Missed his strong arms wrapped around her. She missed the smell that was natural to him. His touch that was so gentle.

When she came out of the hospital she couldn't help herself, and she allowed herself to cry and cry. She sat outside on a seat even though it was freezing. As she looked up some snowflakes were starting to come down. She wanted to rush back up to tell Dan to come down and watch the snow with her, help him see the beauty in life. But for now there was nothing she could do. She hadn't even told him about the cottage. He wasn't ready.

Chapter 22

Lady Writing a Letter with her Maid
Johannes Vermeer, National Gallery of Ireland.

'You are a natural Sive, the customers love you. Beth told me that you are a wonderful artist, a woman of many talents,' Kaitlin said.

'Thanks Kaitlin, it's actually really fun working here, it's a credit to you that the atmosphere between everyone is so good,' she added. In truth, it gave her head a break from worrying about Dan. The food was certainly different than the usual - all vegetarian and super healthy.

'I want a full breakfast please, with toast and tea.' A large woman ordered who looked like she would devour Sive if she gave her any argument. Sive noticed that she had not even opened the menu.

'We can do eggs, tomatoes, mushroom and beans. Or an omelette. Unfortunately, we do not serve meat.' Sive explained. The woman looked at her as if Sive had just declared that they served no food at all.

'Well that is not what I ordered. Unbelievable. No meat at all?'

'No meat, it is a vegetarian café. Would you like a look at the menu. There are some lovely alternatives.' Sive was opening the menu for her.

'Just give me the omelette and make sure it's a large one, with some white toast and a very large pot of tea,' she ordered crossly.

'I have some lovely sourdough bread or wholemeal bread. I could toast that for you.' Sive gently explained.

'Brown!' the woman replied, her voice raised.

'I have green tea, Earl Grey, peppermint or….'

'Barry's tea. Good and strong,' she said demandingly.

*

When she was finished her shift, she got the keys for the house and went to see it for the first time on her own, armed with lots of cleaning stuff. She was going to meet with Kaitlin later to learn a little more, especially about dealing with non-vegetarians.

It was as if time had stood still in the house. Although musty from being locked up, there was a rich scent of the past. Dust sheets revealed ornate handmade furniture in a rich dark velvet mahogany. Antique leather-bound books in browns and dark blues were on wall to wall book cases. Opening the windows to let the dust out, the afternoon sun dappled the room. There was almost a tangible peace in the house. The furniture, Sive realised, was perhaps antique. Sive could imagine how wonderful it would all look. How gorgeous to sit in the little conservatory and look out at the walled garden.

An old rosewood bureau caught her eye. With a bit of care, it would come up beautifully. She tried to open the drawer of it but it was stuck. Eventually with a tug it opened. Inside was a box, bigger than a shoe box, with flowers carved into it. It was heavy as she took it out. Debating what to do, she opened it. The contents were wrapped carefully in a lace pillowcase. She unwrapped the delicately embroidered pillowcase, feeling like an intruder. Her eyes locked on a photograph, a black and white portrait photo of a very pretty lady with wavy dark hair dressed in uniform with a broad smile on her face. There was a medal pinned to her jacket. Underneath the medal lay a bunch of handwritten letters, opened but in their envelopes, and tied together with a lavender silk ribbon. The handwriting was gentle and artistic. There was a small box which held a medal that looked like the one in the photograph. A piece of delicate white lace contained a lady's rose gold watch. Sive carefully picked it up and engraved on the back it read *'Gretta' love J.* There was another photograph of the lady in the picture and a handsome man standing beside her. Sive recognised the background, it was on O'Connell Street in Dublin. The couple in the photo looked so happy, as if life held everything for them. The photo was from another era but the happiness on their faces brought the picture alive. Sive wondered had she ever felt that happy. She thought back to the earlier days with Dan and knew she had. Instinctively she knew she was meant to find this precious box. She carefully put everything back in and closed it again. Suddenly, the house took on a new meaning. Did these people live here? Were they happy? Where are they now? The wind was starting to howl outside, but there was a stillness in the house. She would make sure whoever owned these precious items had them returned.

She called Michael Sharry. She felt that whoever they were they would like to have them. The agent answered eventually in a bored voice. Sive explained her find.

'Oh, just throw them into the shed, anything that is of no use to you just throw it out,' he replied.

'I would like to return them to who owns them,' Sive insisted, wondering what kind of an idiot he was.

'The man who owns the house is up in the Brambles Nursing Home near Avoca, throw them into the office sometime and if I am passing I will throw them into him,' he replied irritated. Sive felt like throwing him somewhere, he was such an ass.

'If you give me his name, I can drop them into him?' she asked trying to keep her cool.

'Sure, it's Jim Bishop, but seriously, I wouldn't bother yourself. He is very old, just throw them up in the attic or somewhere, and any other rubbish with them that you come across,' he replied oblivious to Sive's irritation.

'I have no intention of throwing them anywhere, and I am sure that even if he is old he would like to have his photographs,' Sive replied crossly.

'Suit yourself, but throw out anything else if you like.' Sive hung up before she told him to go throw himself somewhere. Thinking of the smiling couple in the photos, she wondered was it Jim in the picture. Perhaps it was him in the nursing home, but where was Gretta? Well, she would bring the stuff up herself to him tomorrow and try to find out.

She spent the rest of the day happily hoovering, dusting and cleaning. The windows shone. The bathroom now gleamed and any sign of dust had vanished. She took the curtains down, they had seen better days. A full day of cleaning had made a huge difference to the place. The fire place was brick and looked like there could be anything living up in it. She would have to get it cleaned out before lighting it. She could imagine it, though, with the fire lighting. It was such a cosy little house, she couldn't wait to get properly started on it. She decided to wait for her dad to come up to give her a hand putting a face on the garden. Her phone rang - it was Kaitlin from the coffee shop.

'Are you busy cleaning?'

'Exhausted to be honest, just going to finish up.'

'I am in the café, its closed but I am fixing something for myself and my son Daniel, why don't you join us? It would be a chance for me to go over a few things for work. Being a vegetarian only café can throw up a few issues and I want you to be aware of them.'

'Great, I'll just lock up and I'll be with you.'

Daniel was playing on the floor with some Lego and smiled as Sive walked in the door.

'Well you must be Daniel, my name is Sive.' A boy with the most amazing blue eyes looked up at her.

'Sive just in time, food is ready,' Kaitlin called out. Kaitlin had an aubergine tart, couscous salad and fresh rosemary bread; it looked delicious and to Save's surprise, Daniel tucked into a plate of it too.

'Wow, look at him eat, most kids that I know just do not eat that kind of food,' Sive commented.

'I know, I had a standoff with a customer today, because my children's menu didn't include chicken nuggets and chips. I shudder to think what some kid's digestive systems looks like,' Kaitlin said.

'I know, but it seems to be the norm today,' Sive replied.

'I told her I could do a veggie burger in a pita and a baked potato and she asked me was I mad? Then she asked for a toasted special with extra ham. When she found out we didn't serve meat she got up and told me I shouldn't call this a café, and that it was obviously run by a nutter. I told her it was and tried to look a little bonkers, which to be honest the day I was having it wasn't that difficult, and she ran out of the place.' Sive laughed at the image of it and she tucked in.

'She is probably off reporting you as a new cult in town. My mother in law is convinced that my father and I are in a cult because we are vegetarian. She thinks it's a disgrace that we don't eat meat. I have had some very difficult Sunday lunches with her,' Sive said with amusement. Afterwards they had a slice of fig and pine cake with pistachios.

'I do admire you Kaitlin, here you are with this amazing business that you have such a passion for. Thriving after a recession, and raising a child so well all by yourself.'

'I wouldn't quite say I have done it all by myself, I have had a lot of help along the journey. My parents have been a tremendous support and still are, to be honest I have no idea how things would have turned out if it wasn't for them. When I came home and said I was pregnant, they could not have done enough for me. I could not cope with being pregnant, I had my whole life ahead of me and my college education not even finished. I was doing a degree in food science. I stayed in bed for weeks. My poor mother kept bringing me in soup and tea and toast, it was all I would eat. They said they would rear the baby for me and let me finish my education. When he was born, I fell in love with him and everything changed.'

'Did you go back to college?' Sive asked.

'No, my hormones were all over the place. I couldn't quite get my head around the fact that I was responsible for him. Eventually I got on my feet and knew I had to build a life for us, even if it is on our own. I have always loved food so opening this was a dream. At first everyone thought the idea was good, but could not work. It took a lot of convincing. My dad loaned me some money as the bank wouldn't look at me and then I started looking for premises.'

'Why here, why Avara?' Sive asked.

'I have always loved this village, and my parents don't live too far away, so Daniel has family and they are great to still help out with him. Thank God, I have made a profit this year, which is beyond my expectation. Anyway, enough about me, how about you? You got the keys to your cottage. I really hope you like it here. It is a special little place.' Sive agreed but worried that she may have a lot of convincing to do with Dan.

Chapter 23

Presence of the Past
Gunther Gerszo, Private Collection.

The picture-perfect family Christmas was certainly not Beth's. She would be the dutiful daughter and bring her presents down today. She had telephoned her mother. They had agreed to go to the local hotel for lunch and call to her brother's after that. She could leave the next day. She bought the usual voucher as a present. Her mother insisted on only buying in one shop in the local town. It was family run and was a small department store. She had shopped there all her married life and insisted she was not going to stop now. Beth had bought the voucher over the phone and they had posted it up to her. She also put a substantial amount of money in with it. The money and the voucher was easy, it was the card that was difficult. She had picked a holy card as her mother was extremely religious and disliked all the commercialism around Christmas. It was a picture of the Holy Family. What to write on it she always stressed a little about. She didn't want to write the word love anywhere. It was not a word mentioned by her parents ever throughout her life. In the end, she wished her a peaceful and holy Christmas. There was no kiss or sign of affection at the end of her signature, her mother would be most uncomfortable with anything like that. No, what she had written was exactly what was expected of her. She did put a lot of thought into what to buy her three nieces. They were beautiful little girls, all under ten. She didn't want to go over board as to make Santa look bad, so she bought three beautiful dolls with exquisite hand knitted clothes. The dolls had long, curling glossy curls and bonnets made of satin to tie on top. She also bought them a complete set of Enid Blyton books. When she was their age, she had loved Enid Blyton and it had been a huge source of escapism for her. She had a bottle of Chanel Allure for her sister in law and some chocolates. She hadn't bought anything for her brother, he didn't really approve of Christmas presents and would only have something to say about it, so she decided not to.

Last year she had brought him some aftershave and he told her to keep it as the smell was too strong. His wife had been mortified and apologised to Beth. Beth had told her not to worry at all, as he was her brother and she was well used to his ways. With everything wrapped she placed the gifts in the boot of the car, got changed into a navy wool dress and boots. She looked smart but not overdone. She put a small bit of make up on and put her hair up with a few pins. Going out the door she could feel the tension build in her stomach. The journey to her home town took about two hours.

When she arrived into the town she noticed a few changes since her last visit. The corner shop that she had loved to go into if she had a few pence when she was young had weathered the storm of the recession. It looked like *Morrison's Pub* had closed. The street had a big Christmas tree in the middle of the town. She parked easily and got out. She saw some girls dressed in her old school uniform. She wondered was her art teacher still there.

Miss Durand had adored the pupils who showed a passion for art, encouraging them in every way that she could. She told them about Monet and Klimt. She told them about the beauty of their paintings and how their paintings told a story that no words could ever say. Beth loved to listen to her.

'Girls, you must go to France and see the sunflowers and watch their gaze follow the sun all day. The lavender fields will make you dizzy with their scent. The smell of garlic and thyme and the rich berried juice that we make into our wine. Follow your talent, girls. It will help you make sense of the world. You are so full of talent and hope, keep it with you as you experience the beauty of life, it will sustain you when you need it most.'

It was fabrics that held such fascination for Beth, and with the help of her art teacher, she secured a place in college studying textiles.

Her father opened an account for her and gave her the bank book. He would put money in it every year she was in college to aid her.

'After that you are on your own girl,' her mother had warned her. Beth had thanked them both and had set about making plans to move to college. She had got digs close to the college. It included a meal in the evening and it was safe. The woman who owned it opened the door when Beth had arrived. She had the tightest dress Beth had ever seen on

anyone. Her hair was the same blonde as the doll she had since she was a child. Her crimson lips were in a big smile. She hugged Beth like a long-lost daughter and her big hoop earrings jangled as she spoke in her rich Dublin accent.

'Oh, look at you, aren't you beautiful with that rich hair and the bluest of eyes. And look at that porcelain skin. What an Irish beauty you are, you are so welcome.' Beth had never been told she was beautiful by anyone and she almost died of shyness as the landlady complimented her. Her new landlady was called Rose. The house was painted every colour you could imagine. The kitchen was pale blue with a pink dresser and pink wall units. A big, baby blue table with chairs of every colour were seated around it. The sitting room where the students could study was bright yellow with pictures of colourful flowers in heathers and purples on the walls. A window seat with cushions of the palest primrose. A large mosaic on the wall of a girl as if waving her hand, had tiny bits of glitter of every shade. The fireplace was cream with little flowers of yellow painted on it. The hall was papered in big flowery wall paper and the communal bathroom was a dusky pink. Beth would have her own room which was so tiny she could barely turn around in it. It was painted a pretty lime green. A locker painted in cream with primroses delicately painted on was beside the bed. A quilt with all the colours of the rainbow was on the bed, and a thick pink rug was on the ground. Beth had never seen a house decorated in such a way. Her mother would detest it.

'I love it.' Beth replied. Rose had given her a big hug and brought her down for tea with fresh scones, raspberry jam and cream. Beth couldn't wait to start her new life.

There had been no great ceremony at home about her starting college. Her mother bought her some sensible underwear, flannelette pyjamas and new sheets and pillow cases. She had some jeans and jumpers. She had managed to get some beautiful green silk and had made a gorgeous top which seemed to set her red hair on fire. She had also made a skirt to go with it. Her father had driven her up to the digs with all her clothes and stuff that she needed.

He didn't wait to get her settled. Once he took everything out of the car, he wished Beth good luck in college, and warned her not to go anywhere in the evening. He said that they would call her to see that she settled in.

With that he left. Beth would have liked to have given her father a hug but knew that he would have felt too uncomfortable. She thanked him and assured him she would return home each evening to study.

Her first night in her new digs, Beth had felt her first piece of freedom. There was no mother to tell her to turn off her lights. She ate biscuits in bed and read a book for ages. She managed to rearrange the bed a tiny bit so that she could use a small table to set up her sewing machine. She couldn't be happier. Rose had sent her off with a fry up that first morning. She said it was a treat for the first day. Beth had been shy meeting the other students but they had all been friendly and she enjoyed listening to them chatter. Rose had smiled at her and told her that she hoped she would be very happy there.

Rose had remained a loyal friend right throughout the years, and Beth was going to visit her on Christmas day like she had done from that first Christmas.

She walked past Doyle's shop. How she had adored looking at the sequins and buttons. She could imagine the gowns she would love to sew them on. It was opened and she knew she had to go in. Her childhood past was calling her.

Chapter 24

Mona Lisa
The Louvre, Paris.

Beth opened the shop door. Perhaps it would have changed too much inside. The counter was where it was all those years ago, right beside the bargain basket full of bits and bobs and the odd treasure. Her feet almost knew the steps to take. Buttons glittered like tiny diamonds. Threads in rainbow tints dazzled before her. Rolls of silks and lace lay on a large table, brocade, chiffon and satins trailing in luscious hues. Baskets of decorative crystals in violets and reds shimmered in the light. Time was forgotten as she touched the silken rolls. How she had craved the feel and touch of such precious fabrics. But they were far out of her reach.

Sarah Doyle, her mother, thought them wasteful and more suited to fallen women and not her impressionable daughter.

'Tweed and cotton are sensible materials and best in dark colours except for a clean white starched blouse for Sunday mass.' Beth still hated the smell of starch.

She left the shop with her purchase of some exquisite russet organza and some cream Chantilly lace, her next stop was a new bakery with a tantalising aroma of melted chocolate. She purchased a rich fruit cake laced with brandy and spices. Her mother just might approve of it.

'Baking is for brown bread and soda bread,' she liked to say. Anything more than that was unnecessary. Unless something served a useful purpose, it would not be tolerated in the Doyle home.

Beth's bedroom had been her sanctuary where she could escape to with her sewing basket and the odd scrap of material or few buttons that she could save up for. All her dreams had been made in that room. She had bought wallpaper for it which her mother had thought frivolous and a waste of money. It was a delicate rose wallpaper that Beth adored.

In the long winter evenings when all the work was done she would steal away to Mrs Earls. By a hot fire, sweet tea and biscuits, her kindly neighbour had taught Beth how to sew. That winter she had made a patchwork quilt with scraps of material blending into a kaleidoscope of colour and crocheted the ends with a delicate lilac wool. It had been her magic quilt. Underneath the quilt, away from the watchful eye of her mother, was where she could dream of what she would be and who she would be without any judgement.

Getting back into the car she met a neighbour whom she hadn't seen in years. He was an elderly man and had aged a lot since she had seen him.

'Well if it's not the lovely Beth Doyle, looking as radiant as Maureen O'Hara from *The Quiet Man'*.

'Great to see you John Jo,' Beth replied smiling as he held her hand.

'We don't see you very often in this parts Beth,' he replied kindly.

'No, no, I don't get home much I suppose.' Beth was going to give the usual line that suited most people on why she rarely came home, but she knew John Jo was a wiser man than to believe it.

'It's good for you to return to where you were brought up Beth, whatever the circumstances, if only to remember. Your home place is a funny thing, we can all run away, but it has a habit of turning up all the time.' He bid her goodbye and Beth watched his frail figure walk up the street. Perhaps he was right, trying to bury the past does not work, but embracing it could be a difficult task. She took a last look at the town before taking the road for her childhood home.

It was a few miles outside of the town on a byroad. There were a lot more houses on the road since the Celtic tiger. She wondered how some of these monstrosities had got planning permission. They certainly did nothing to add to the natural environment. They looked more urban than country, it was as if the bigger the better, forget about taste or quaintness. She wondered how they even heated the houses, and one or two looked like they had been abandoned before being finished. She had loved the road she had lived on, it was where she had picked blackberries and turned them into jam. In spring, it was abundant with primroses and honeysuckle brambles and an abundance of other wild flowers. In winter now the leaves were gone but she drove slowly, remembering every turn and tree on it. The bridge where she had sat on, waiting for the world to go by. Traffic had been very scarce when she was a child and it was unusual not to know almost every car or tractor that passed. It was customary to wave or say hello to anyone who passed who might then stop and roll down the window to enquire about the family or comment on the weather. There was also neighbours that she liked to visit. Mrs Pierce who lived on her own depended on her for all her shopping. Beth would get it for her every Friday. It never changed. She could still almost remember it. Flour, buttermilk, butter, some meat from the butcher, mostly salty bacon and sugar. She bought her vegetables and potatoes from the neighbours and she had her own hens. She would always tell Beth to buy herself a Turkish Delight and Beth would savour the bar as she sat on Mrs Pierce's green forum chair.

'My lovely Irish Colleen with the heart of gold, lucky the man that gets you.' Everything in Mrs Pierce's little house got a new coat of green paint in the spring. There was a flag stone and a big open fire. Her own chair was a nice comfortable fireside chair painted green with a flowery pattern on the arm rests. The chairs and dresser which proudly held the willow pattern teacups and saucers were the same shade. Come hail or shine there was a turf fire in the grate. As Beth passed where Mrs Pierce had lived, she tried to visualise the house which had been knocked down and another big monstrosity put in its place.

She came to her home place, she could see her mother's car at the front of the house. It was a bungalow built in the late sixties. As she went in the front door, the smell of disinfectant hit her. Her mother liked to disinfect the house almost every day. She suddenly appeared at the door. She was a tiny woman and her pale face was smaller than Beth remembered from her last visit. Her hair was cut short and naturally grey. Her clothes sensible and unremarkable. Beth parked and got out to greet her. There was no warm embrace but a slight awkwardness between mother and daughter. Beth followed her mother into the sitting room. Heavy netted curtains allowed very little light in and the room was dark except for the sacred heart light under the holy picture. She brought in the presents for her mother and put them on a coffee table.

'I'll put the kettle on for a cup of tea, the lunch in town is not booked till one, I had to ask Mrs Earle to come along, is that OK with you?'

'Of course, how is she?' Her mother gave her a rundown of Mrs Earle's health for the next few minutes. Secretly Beth was relieved her neighbour was coming. Her mother and her neighbour were most unusual friends. Mrs Earle was as warm as her mother was cold. Her neighbour had a habit of saying the wrong thing at the wrong time, too, and was known for her great sense of humour. It would make the lunch less awkward altogether, and now Beth was looking forward to it. They had a cup of tea and some of the fruit cake and her mother filled her in a little on the news of the district. Beth gave her the card and vouchers and brought in some chocolates.

'I have your old room with fresh clothes on the bed, I told your brother we would visit later as you were staying the night and not rushing back. I bought you a jumper in Ryan's, it's up on the bed in your old room. Maybe you won't care for it. Leave the tag on and you can pick something your own style if you like.' Beth was surprised. Her mother usually gave her something practical like a good pottery bowl or a coffee pot. It was a very long time since her mother had given her clothes. And even then, it would always be practical. In the last few years, when Beth had come home it was always for only the day, and most of it would be spent visiting her brother or her aunts with her mother. She couldn't recall spending enough time in the house to visit her old bedroom. On opening it she was shocked to see that other than being dusted and hoovered, very little had changed. She tentatively opened her old dresser. Little doll's clothes she had made lay in an old box. She took them out and caressed them as she remembered every detail of making them on her mother's sewing machine. Her home-made patchwork quilt still covered the bed. Her room seemed haunted by her younger self. She saw the bag on the bed and opened it. She took out an exquisite red jumper in the finest cashmere. Her hands gently caressed it, taking in its softness. How she would have longed for something like this when she was growing up. The tears pricked her eyes. It was so obviously beautiful and expensive. Her mother never bought bright colours. Anything that would wear well and would wash. What had possessed her mother to do this? She delicately folded up the jumper and put it back in the bag. Her mother was in the kitchen when she came down.

'It's beautiful, but it's too much.'

'Well, I just saw it in the shop and I hadn't got you anything, you can change it if you want, it doesn't bother me,' her mother replied.

'I wouldn't dream of changing it. I love it.'

'Very well, we had better get moving soon and collect herself, I want to get a good table, not squashed in with someone else having them listening in to our conversation. We will get a nice table if we go early.' There was no more discussion of the jumper, and Beth helped her mother lock up the house. Shortly, they were at Mrs Earle's who insisted they come in for a few minutes and have a drop of Bailey's or port wine.

'How often do I get to see Beth, and look at her as radiant as ever. Come here and give me a hug, it is so good to see you.' Beth hugged her neighbour, who she knew had genuine affection for her. She sipped at the Bailey's and sat down at the fireplace. A new stove had replaced her big range. The photos on the wall of all her grown up kids and grandkids were interspersed with holy pictures and medals from her constant pilgrimages to Lourdes and Fatima. A cuckoo clock tick tocked loudly on the wall.

'You still have the cuckoo clock?' Beth smiled at Mrs Earle.

'Yes, and how you loved to sit and wait for her to come out and sing for you, your little face would light up at the sight of her,' she smiled.

'Oh, I remember so well, and I remember your raspberry buns, you always seemed to have some freshly made.' Sive almost licked her lips remembering how she would eat them just as they were cooked.

'I used to make them on the fire on the old griddle pan. I had loads of jam that I made having the raspberry bushes outside. If we had nothing else, we had raspberry buns. Sure, they were half reared on them,' she replied laughing.

'Do you still make the jam?' Sive enquired.

'Indeed, I don't, I spin into Tesco every Friday now and get what I need. It wouldn't pay me. Oh, I made enough jam in my day. And bread for that matter, I have far better things to do. I go to the bingo a couple of times a week, and I like a couple of little sherries down in McCarthy's with my friends on a Friday evening. I help in the new charity shop too, sure we have a great bit of craic down there, you should see some of the stuff people leave in. And then others, you wouldn't put the dog to sleep on it. Sure, you get all sorts. Enough, tell me about you, how are you and how is life treating you?' she asked.

'I think we better get moving, I want to get a good seat,' Beth's mother interrupted.

'Ah, Sarah, you are always fussing, sure what does it matter where we sit?' Beth knew her mother wanted to get moving. She would have loved to stay a little longer in her neighbour's house, she had always been happy there and she recalled she had spent a lot of time there. Possibly when she shouldn't have been there. But Mrs Earle had never made her feel unwelcome. Quite the contrary, she had loved having her and they had spent many afternoons chatting and sewing over the raspberry buns.

'We better go, I want to get a good seat, not cramped in with anyone else.' Beth's mother's voice was sharp.

'Fair enough, before your mother here gets her knickers in a twist about where she sits, you better let them know the queen is coming!' Beth tried to hide a giggle, only Mrs Earle could get away with saying something like that to her mother.

'Really! Mrs Earle,' her mother replied, very put out.

'A musha I'm coming, I'll just drink down this sherry. Waste not want not.' She drank her sherry in one swoop and they were out the door in the next ten minutes.

The hotel was old world without trying to be. It had just never moved on since Beth was a child. But walking in the familiar doors, there was a certain comfort in it. The menu even looked much the same, with the addition of turkey and ham because it was close to Christmas.

'Do they think we don't get a bit of turkey over the Christmas, shoving it down our necks the minute they mention that Easter is over?' Beth's mother commented.

'What are you having to drink, my treat now?' Mrs Earle rooted out her purse.

'Not for me Mrs Earle,' replied Beth's mother.

'Oh, go on Sarah, we are not going to have a knees up or anything. Have a glass of red wine. What about you Beth?' Mrs Earle asked.

'Beth here is driving she can't have anything.' Beth's mother was quick to point out.

'Beth is well able to speak for herself, Sarah.' Mrs Earle retorted. Beth and the waiter watched them both in amusement.

'I'll just have a sparkling water, thank you,' Beth replied.

I'll have the beef if it's not too tough, what will you have Sarah, you have good teeth, you could have the beef too?' Beth's mother scowled at the mention of her teeth and ordered the salmon. They finished ordering and soon the place started to fill up. They had got a table close to the fire, that was in a good position to see all that was going on.

Lots of different neighbours and friends came up to talk to them. They all said hello to Beth and her mother, but it was Mrs Earle's laugh that could be heard throughout the meal. After coffee and apple pie they sat for a while chatting. Beth's mother had mellowed a little with another glass of wine at Mrs Earle's insistence.

'We must go Beth, you need to call in to see your brother.' Reluctantly Beth dropped off Mrs Earle after the meal and went to visit her only brother.

Chapter 25

Woman
Willem de Kooning, Brooklyn Museum of Art, New York.

Her brother's house was a modern monstrosity of a house that had been built in the boom. The site was quite close to the road and did not lend itself well to such a big house, but that had not stopped her brother. The girls threw themselves on Beth as they opened the door and she was struck by how much they had grown. They all looked so similar, with big brown eyes and blonde hair like their mother. Mary, her sister in law, came to the door. She looked washed out but gave Beth a big smile of welcome.

'Michael will be in shortly, he just had to run out for a few minutes.' Beth brought in the presents and there was much excitement as to what they could open now and what would be left till Christmas day. She gave Mary her gifts.

'God, they are all so lovely, you are so good to us Beth.'

'I feel bad to be honest, I hardly ever see the girls.' Beth watched them as they tore open the presents, hugging Beth with excitement. A car then arrived into the yard.

'It's Michael!' Mary said looking out through the window.

'Quick girls, tidy up the mess, your father is here.' She started frantically cleaning up the mess the girls had created. The girls gathered up the discarded Christmas paper and tidied their gifts as quickly as possible. Beth watched as Mary's demeanour seemed to change as her husband strode in. He was a small man who had once been handsome, but his features had now seemed to end up in a permanent scowl. There was no big smile of welcome from him and certainly no embrace for his sister.

'Well you are here.' He almost spat out.

'Hi Michael, Happy Christmas,' Beth said, ignoring his big scowling face. He looked around and saw the array of presents.

'I hope you didn't bring too much rubbish for them,' he barked back.

'Michael, she brought some lovely stuff, and look what Beth brought me.' Mary was about to show him the perfume set Beth had given her.

'Not sure you will be going to too many fancy places that you will need that stuff. The fire is nearly out, could you not keep a bit of fire on, or do I have to do everything myself?'

'I'll get some, I forgot with all the excitement of Beth arriving,' Mary said apologetically.

'Leave it, I'll get it myself, have you the kettle on?' he said gruffly

'Jesus give me a chance Mick, you are only in the door,' Mary replied.

'I see you are still your charming self, Michael,' Beth said. He made no reply. Beth followed Mary into the kitchen.

'You OK, Mary? How do you stick him?' Mary's face told the real story.

'To be honest sometimes I don't know why I bother, but you didn't come here to hear about us, let's have some tea.' They prepared the tea quietly and then they heard another roar.

'Jesus, are you gone to Newport for the tea or what's happening to it?' Beth could feel herself snap. She stormed out to where her brother was sitting.

'Come in and make it yourself if you want it any quicker or keep quiet.' She felt like killing him. He had really gone off the boil. He had turned into a big pain since she saw him last.

'Mary how do you listen to him?' she asked, exasperated.

'I am used to it I suppose,' Mary replied. Beth noted the tone of resignation in her voice.

'Still, he shouldn't treat you like that.' Beth could see that her sister in law was at the end of her tether and was barely holding it together.

'Any sign of the tea, or have you forgotten us out here?' her brother shouted in.

'Michael, just shut it will you,' Beth shouted out, her voice irritated. Typical, she was in her brother's house as a guest, but she was waiting on him. He really was from the dark ages; women's lib had had no effect on him. They all had the tea and talked about the weather and the state of the economy, her brother's anger at the country very apparent. Beth knew financially things were not very good with them.

'They would all want to be bloody shot, the government and the banks. Good people like ourselves having to bail them out.' He didn't mention anything about the piece of land he had bought and built a fleet of houses on. The houses had not been finished when the bank crisis came and only half the houses had been sold. Beth felt sorry for the poor families who had purchased any of these houses who were left with vacant houses as their neighbours, and a housing estate that looked a lot less like the finished product that they were shown in the glossy brochures when they had bought them. The green had not even been finished and there was a legal battle going on between her brother and the residents. She could see her mother getting agitated, this talk of banks had made her look very uptight again. She wondered what her mother thought of her son's financial predicament. They had been brought up to believe that you should never borrow anything. This knowledge had obviously been totally lost on her son. Funnily enough it dawned on Beth that she had followed this advice without realising it. Her apartment was hers and she had money in the bank for a rainy day. She had worked hard always and had been lucky with her work, which had enabled her to be very financially independent.

'Well, I think we will head on back home now, I would like to light the fire and catch the news,' her mother spoke up. Beth realised that to wear out their welcome with her brother would not be a good idea.

'Where are those young ones, tell them to tidy up that sitting room. The state they left it in, there is no rearing on them, Mary is far too soft on them,' he complained.

'I was thinking of bringing the girls out for their tea this evening if that suits Mary?' Beth said.

'That would be lovely Beth, they will be delighted, I would love to come too, I could do with getting out,' Mary piped up. Her brother looked at her as if she had said she was off to Spain for a mad weekend of drink and drugs. Beth caught the look and spoke before Mary had time to back out.

'We can bring you something back Michael, I am sure you can fend for yourself for a few hours.' He looked at Beth with distaste. Mary winked at her sister in law.

'Great, I will drop Mam home and be back in about an hour. See you Michael.' She felt sorry for him, too. It can't be easy being that miserable.

'See you,' he replied without even looking at her. She looked at him and wondered how she was related to him. If it wasn't for blood she knew she would have nothing to do with him. He was as cold as a man could be. She was looking forward to spending some time with her nieces away from the watchful eye of their father. Her mother was not at all put out by her going out. In truth, she was probably relieved.

Chapter 26

The Card Players
Paul Cezanne. Musee d'Orsay, Paris.

The Brambles nursing home was a beautiful house set in large manicured gardens with gleaming sash windows. It could have been a stately home, it looked so grand. The cold air caught Sive unaware as she got out of her car. She had the precious box with her and some chocolates. It felt strange visiting someone she didn't know, and perhaps he would refuse to see her. But she felt a funny sense of duty to make sure this box got to him.

The woman at the reception introduced herself as the owner of the home, Marjorie Murphy. She looked like she must be wearing her entire jewellery collection, topped off with a heavy layer of make-up, and her hair contained at least a half can of hair spray. She gave Sive a quick and automatic smile. Sive explained why she was here.

'Only approved visitors can see our patients, but I will see what I can do,' she said with an air of authority.

'Thank you, I really appreciate it,' Sive replied as the woman rang a bell and a young woman of about twenty, in a blue uniform, arrived. After hearing what Sive was doing here, she smiled, delighted.

'Hi, I'm Stacey, one of the carers. Jim's awake, he's in his room. I will just tell him you are here, I am sure he would love to see you, he doesn't have many visitors. Take a seat for a few minutes.' The signs of a nursing home became apparent to Sive, a strong smell of disinfectant mixed with the perfume of the owner. A very fragile little woman came into reception, shuffling in slippers, her long white hair falling down her back. She smiled at Sive and in an almost angelic voice spoke to the owner.

'Is it time for the music?' she asked, almost in a whisper.

'No, Elizabeth, it's time for your nap,' Marjorie replied crossly.

'Oh, that's disappointing,' she replied with the same gentleness.

'Elizabeth, back to the day room, good girl.' Marjorie instructed.

'I do love a bit of music,' Elizabeth replied. Despite her years, Sive could see that once upon a time she was a great beauty, and there was a twinkle in her eye that sparkled. She turned to Sive, looking hopeful.

'Are you here for the dancing? I do love the dancing. Have you got dancing shoes on?'

'I am afraid I forgot them,' Sive smiled.

'Never mind, no one will notice once the music starts, all we will think of is the dancing.' Her eyes closed and she waved her body to and fro, lost in a dream.

'Back to your room now Elizabeth, and I promise the dancing will start soon,' the owner said firmly. Elizabeth's eyes sparkled. Sive noticed they were a beautiful blue and bright as a shilling.

'See you at the dancing.' She smiled at Sive before shuffling out, her delicate frame walking down the corridor. Marjorie began filling in some documents, her diamond rings shining in the light. Stacey returned.

'Hi, I have told Jim and he is thrilled to have a visitor, he is in his room after having a little nap. I'll introduce you to him, he is a lovely man, one of the nicest here.'

'Please just stay a short time, we have to make sure our patients get sufficient rest,' Marjorie added.

'Of course,' Sive replied and followed the carer. As they left the reception Stacey whispered to Sive.

'Ignore Marjorie, she is terrified of the health inspector calling unannounced. She is only suspicious you might be a reporter or something, working undercover,' Stacey said, smiling to Sive.

The nursing home was painted in oranges and yellows. Bars were along every wall for the patients to hold on to. They passed the common room, where the slipper-clad aged were passing the morning. Some were dressed and looked like they could be off somewhere, others looked like they would never leave. Although every effort was made to make the place feel homely, light and airy, Sive could feel a tangible sadness hit her as she watched them get through their day. Elizabeth spotted her and came up to her.

'Is it time for the dancing, I do love a bit of dancing?' She waltzed around the room.

'I'll put some music on for you in just a tick Elizabeth, how about some Glenn Miller? You do love that, I'll be back in a jiffy.' Stacey smiled at the little woman. Like a light being switched on Elizabeth's face became alive again.

'I'll just pop on my dancing shoes.' She pottered off down to her room.

An elderly woman dressed fully with a coat and umbrella on her arm came walking up the hall. She had a handbag on her shoulder. She smiled at Sive.

'Just popping to the shops, is there anything you need?' she asked her. Sive shook her head in response and thanked her for asking, looking at Stacey for an explanation.

'That's Mary, she walks around all day going to the shops. Come on in, Jim is in here.'

'Has Jim been with you for long?' Sive asked.

'Just over two years, a little after his wife dying, here we are.' They came to Jim's room and Stacey went in first to tell him she was here. The room was painted in a pale blue, with a blue and white striped chair beside his bed. A photo of a dark-haired woman in a beautiful lace bridal gown sat in a silver frame on his bedside locker. It was the same lady as in the other photos, Sive knew it must be Gretta. A man in perhaps his late eighties sat in the striped chair. He looked frail but when he spoke his voice was clear and articulate, with a hint of an English accent.

'How kind of you, to find me. I believe you are moving into our house, please sit and welcome.' He pointed to another chair for Sive to sit down.

'Thank you, yes I am moving in, I'm Sive, thank you for meeting me,' Sive replied.

'It's a pleasure, delighted you got past Marjorie. That was quite an achievement,' he smiled.

'Well she did tell me not to stay long,' Sive pointed out.

'Oh, she just likes to show a bit of power, her bark is worse than her bite.' Sive liked him immediately, there was something very welcoming yet intriguing about him. He had a gold bound book with hand writing in it that he seemed to be reading. He noticed Sive looking at it.

'It's just my poetry, I like to do a little most days,' he explained.

'Really, I would love to hear some sometime,' Sive replied.

'You are very kind. I do have a little book that Gretta my wife got published for me, I will show it to you, but tell me what brings you to visit me, as delighted as I am to have a lovely woman come to see me today, so unexpected.'

'I found something that belongs to you.' Sive carefully took the box from the bag and placed it on his lap. He was dressed in a very gentlemanly dressing gown, which together with his voice gave him an almost aristocratic air.

At first it was as if he didn't recognise it, and then he slowly opened it. He unwrapped the frame and his eyes locked on the photo. He let a small gasp and he stared until his grey eyes became cloudy.

'Gretta, my beautiful girl.' His hand gently stroked the face in the picture, and in that one tender stroke, Sive could see how much he had loved his wife. He then picked up the smaller pictures and he smiled as his mind travelled back to a different time.

'I remember it as if it was yesterday. How the years have gone, it doesn't seem that long since we had all the years in front of us.' He held one of the small photos to show Sive.

'This was taken in Dublin, look there is Nelson's pillar,' he pointed out. His hand shook as he tried to hold the photo up to Sive.

'We were just walking together outside the GPO when this man with a box camera took our photo. Of course, we were delighted and bought the photo from him. He was always there with his camera taking pictures of the people. We were so in love with life and each other it was as if it could never end.'

'You do look very happy,' Sive smiled.

'That was the day we left Ireland, we eloped,' he replied.

'Eloped?'

'We were childhood sweethearts, but it was not a smooth road I am afraid. I was protestant and Gretta was from a very catholic family. It was not a marriage that either of our families wanted.'

'We ran away, it was all that we could do. We went to London and got married over there. Two complete strangers were our witnesses. We didn't come home for many years.'

'It must have been hard leaving your family.'

'Times were different then dear, I was an only son and my father was the local vicar. My mother was English and my father Irish but both staunch protestants. Mary's family was as catholic as mine was protestant. Both families were totally against us getting married. My parents disowned me and Mary's were no better. I had no brothers or sisters and Mary had one brother. Thankfully over the years, they had contact again and we had many good times with him and his family. He had one daughter who lives in Arizona so we have no close relatives. We didn't have children, do you have any?' he caught Sive unaware.

'No, no, I don't. I am married but we don't have any yet.' It was strange sitting down talking to this kind man, yet in another way it seemed the most natural of conversations, as if he was waiting for her to come visit, and neither of them realising it until she did. There was something about Jim that intrigued her, and she knew she needed to know more about him.

'And the house, the house helped us, you know,' he looked straight at Sive. She got this strange feeling that somehow, he knew she needed some help, too.

'How do you mean?' she asked.

'Well, life threw challenges at us like it does, but somehow being in the cottage seemed like a refuge when we were at our weakest. It seemed to give us some strength, just to be there. We travelled a lot but always it was the cottage that brought us home.

'The cottage is very old, was it always in your family?'

'Well when the war was over an aunt of mine had left it to me in her will. She was my mother's sister and had never forgiven my mother for disowning me. I had no idea what to do with it at the time. We decided to move there for a short while, to work on it and see what our next move was, and we never really left.' He sat back now in his chair, lost in his memories. She got up to leave and he put his hand out.

'Thank you Sive, you have brought great comfort to me, bringing these photos. Nothing could erase my lovely Gretta from my mind but it is lovely to see the photos, they are gentle reminders of a great life. Please come again to visit me and let me know how you are getting on in the house. It is a special little house you know, and I am so glad you found it.' His eyes had regained some sparkle, and Sive promised that indeed she would love to return soon, she got up and touched his hand and left as his eyes went back to his memories. Walking past the patients, she thought about Jim's words. There was something about the house, she couldn't explain it, perhaps it was the peace she felt there when she was in it. Now all she had to do was get Dan to agree to come home to it. Somehow, she knew if they were to have a chance of a future, the house would help them to move on.

Chapter 27

Woman Holding a Balance
Jan Vermeer. National College of Art, Washington.

'So, where would you like to go?' Beth asked the girls.

'McDonald's,' they chorused.

'McDonald's, it is,' Beth laughed. They enjoyed the next hour or so, as they ate their way through Happy Meals.

'Can we go over to the play area?' they chorused as soon as the last chicken nugget was eaten.

'Off you go,' said Beth.

'It's so good to get out. We very rarely do now, to be honest,' Mary said when they were out of earshot.

'Oh, Mary, I had no idea things were so difficult. I would really like to help you and the girls.'

'Ah thanks Beth, but having no money is not the worst thing. My family would help me out if I asked them too, but money is not our only problem. It's the only problem if you ask your brother, but for me it's much more than that,' she said with sadness.

'Are things that bad?' Beth enquired.

'I am trying to make it work, but at times it seems impossible. Only for the girls I would be gone long ago. To be honest I said that I would wait until after Christmas but I am beginning to think that to leave is our only option,' she said with resignation.

'I had no idea it was that serious.' Beth knew her brother was difficult to say the least, but for Mary to be talking about leaving.

'Well now you know, sorry Beth, we came for a nice tea and here I am telling you all our woes.'

'I am just glad you did. Is there anything I can do, does my brother know how you feel?' If he knew Mary was thinking of leaving, surely, he would cop on a bit.

'He is too pig-headed to even listen to me. Anytime I try talk about stuff, he tells me that I am dramatizing everything and that it's nonsense.'

Beth could just imagine him saying that. Her own father would have said the same if he was in the situation.

'Can we have some ice creams, is it ok to ask?' Molly, the littlest of the girls, asked. Beth could see that Mary was trying to compose herself, as talking about things was very emotional.

'Here of course you can pet, you take the money and give it to your big sister and get yourselves an ice cream sundae.' Molly grinned broadly and ran with the money Beth had given her, then she turned and came back and gave Beth a big hug.

'You are the best Auntie.' Beth hugged her tightly back before she ran off.

'They are a credit to you Mary, they are so well mannered, and really nice kids,' Beth exclaimed.

'God, they are and that's what worries me so much. Is it better to stay because at least they have a father, even if he puts them down constantly, or is it better to go and leave them with a broken family?' Beth thought about her dilemma and tried to answer as honestly as she could.

'I don't think there is any right answer to that Mary, but it is very difficult to stay together just for the sake of the kids and not love each other. But probably a lot of couples do,' she added.

'I just don't know if I am brave enough to go it alone either. I went straight from my own family to one of my own. I have never lived on my own without either my father or my husband to look out for me. How pathetic is that?'

'It's not pathetic at all, you have made a great job of raising your family through a difficult marriage, and not every woman could do that.'

'I suppose I could have taken to the drink or something. Funny, all I want is a bit of peace in my life.' They sat in silence for a little while, watching the kids. Beth was trying to take in everything Mary had told her, and Mary was enjoying the peace of mind she craved while she sat in a busy McDonald's at Christmas time.

'It's the loneliness that is the worst, Beth,' Mary was talking as if half to herself. Beth looked at her, not fully understanding.

'I know that may sound strange considering I am the mother of three girls and married. But being in a relationship that is so lost and soul destroying is much worse than being alone. It's the worst type of loneliness. I feel so trapped in it both physically and mentally.' Beth tried to understand, she did remember being part of a family and living with them and feeling very alone. She now lived alone by choice but thankfully was not lonely. She was very content with herself and enjoyed her own company immensely.

'Somehow I can't see Michael changing. He was in better form of course when the economy was up, but greed got in the way and destroyed that for him. I begged him not to get involved with the housing estate. The plans were so out of character with the town. But all he could see was the money he was going to make. The town was up in arms, trying to stop him, even starting a petition. The girls were getting bullied in school because of it, but nothing could stop him going ahead, and now it's not finished and a total disaster and we still have to live here.' Beth knew from her mother that people were unhappy about the estate but she had no idea to what level. Typical she wasn't told about this, it might put her brother in a bad light. It can't have been easy for her mother with all that negativity about her brother's ethics, either. She had to live there, too. He really was a selfish oaf, she felt like ringing him and telling him what she thought of him once and for all. As if reading her thoughts, Mary spoke up.

'There is no point in talking to him, he will listen to no one. Anyway, the damage is done now, he can't build any more. The banks won't look at him and he is up to his eyes in debt.'

'I can give you some money Mary, nobody has to know.' Mary smiled gratefully at her sister in law's kindness.

'My dad has given me money. It's in his name in the credit union, but he comes with me if I need to get any out. God forbid Michael finds out, as he would take it. No, I have it for the girls, for the little things that they need and their little activities after school. I tell Michael a pack of lies about how I pay for them and to be honest he doesn't even know half of what they are involved in.' Beth was so ashamed of Michael, he had such a beautiful wife and kids and he had no appreciation for them.

At that Mary's phone rang, it was Michael.

'I'll answer it, I'll say you are in the bathroom,' Beth said.

'I bet he is looking for his tea.' Beth threw her eyes to heaven as she said hello. He was looking for his tea and was not very happy that they were not back.

'Well Michael, Mary is in the bathroom. I am sure you don't want to rush her home so will I tell her that you will just fix yourself a sandwich tonight and for her not to worry about it. It's probably the best plan as the girls have met some friends here and I know you would hate to break up their fun.' She could sense this was not going down well with him. He made no reply so Beth continued as if nothing was wrong.

'I thought I might bring Mary over to the hotel for a drink afterwards, the kids can have a little play around. The hotel is very family friendly up until about nine. So, we will see you around ten.' More silence from his end.

'Is there anything else, or is it just about your tea you rang?'

'I don't think it's a good idea to have the girls up late,' he bellowed back.

'Oh, it's not often I am down, I have already told the girls and they are really excited, sure they wouldn't sleep if I brought them home. Anything else Michael, or will I let you fix that sandwich for yourself?'

'But.'

'Bye, Michael see you later.' With that Beth hung up and they both had a good laugh about it.

'He would hardly know where the fridge is. He might go over to your mother's and get her to make something for her,' Mary sighed.

'I can't imagine what it is like for you,' Beth said.

'I did a computer course this year. I am pretty good at it. I love organising things. I have looked up some jobs but to be honest I don't think I will be here. I don't know where to go. But staying here if we break up would be a nightmare. I don't mean to leave Ireland. But I want to leave Limerick, give the girls a fresh start.'

'You sound like you have already made up your mind,' Beth said tentatively.

'I think deep down I know I have to, it's just finding the courage,' Mary replied.

'Look I have moved to a lovely little village in Wicklow, its right by the sea and a short distance to Dublin. You could get work close to Dublin and live in the village. At least I would be there, so you would have some family,' Beth said.

'Gosh, Beth, it sounds lovely. I will think about it over Christmas and see how that goes. I have to decide to stay and get on with it or I have to make that step,' Mary sighed.

'Look whichever you take, just know I am in your corner,' Beth said as she leaned over and gave her a hug.

Chapter 28

Melancholy
Constance Marie Charpentier. Musee de Picardie, France.

The breakfast of corn flakes and toast lay cold on the tray. He had drunk the tea, it was a comfort to him. The food was a bigger chore. This was a busy time on the wards, when the rounds would start and the beds were made up. He could hear the clatter of heels in the corridor, they were coming in to him. They had told him he would have to start walking the corridor.

'Good morning Dan, we must get you to try walking a little today, the physio is waiting for you.' One of the nurses said rather loudly to him.

'I don't feel up to it today,' he replied curtly. He wanted to stay in the room. He felt safe there, he certainly didn't want to meet or chat with any Physio. He didn't want to talk to anyone.

'Up you get now Dan.' She was about fifty, with very glamorous hair and makeup. She always looked very happy, as if life was very good to her. She had a big laugh and chatted all the time. He wondered what it felt like to be so untroubled. He preferred the other nurse, she was quiet, without all the makeup and the loud laugh, and she seemed to understand a little more.

'Dan, just hold my arm, we don't have to talk to anyone, and we will be back in the room in an hour,' the quieter nurse said as if reading his thoughts. Yes, she did understand him more, he wished the other one would go away, but of course she didn't and she kept talking. His body ached so much, it was such a struggle. But his legs were working. If he just had the will to walk he knew he could.

'Here, we will put this robe on you,' the larger nurse instructed. He did what he was told. He held onto both and tried to walk, the sweat was on his brow, the pure effort just to walk. They kept talking to him, he blotted them out, they stopped to talk to a doctor.

The doctor looked about Dan's age and was very well turned out in a fitted suit. The loud nurse was smiling and chatting as she ran her fingers through her hair. The doctor cast his eye on Dan for a fleeting moment. Whatever he said to the nurses, they agreed with him.

'We will turn back now Dan and perhaps leave it until tomorrow. His room had become his sanctuary and his prison. They would make him sit in the chair now, even though he would have preferred to lie back in bed.

'Well done Dan, you are getting so much stronger, we will do the bed now and then give you a bit of peace.' The quiet nurse smiled at him and handed him a glass of tepid water. The other one was chattering about her big dinner out for her son who had graduated with loads of honours. The food would be fabulous, her outfit from Harvey Nichols was divine, and she was the luckiest mother in Dublin to have such a perfect family. The other nurse listened while giving Dan a knowing look. They made the bed, settled Dan, and allowed him the peace he was craving.

He liked to look out the window on days like this. It was a dark day with the clouds full of rain. A mist now with the promise of rain. He looked forward to the sound of the rain, it calmed him. He closed his eyes and his mind drifted, far away with the clouds where he could be alone. He must have dozed off, his eyes were heavy as he realised there was somebody in the room. It was Sive.

'Hi Dan,' she kissed him on the forehead. It made him feel like a child and a patient. He made no reply. Sive looked good but different. A little like when he knew her all those years ago. It suited her, earthy or something like that.

'I brought you a little food.' She took out a flask.

'It's a smoothie, I made it myself.' He reluctantly tasted it. It was sweet but good.

'I have a fresh muffin too, they taste really good, would you like some?' He shook his head.

'I have a bit of news actually Dan, I found a lovely house to rent out in Avara. It is close to the little coffee shop that I am working in now.' He looked at her and then he turned away, back to the window. The rain would come soon now, the sky was even heavier. Sive took a book from her bag, she had found it in the house with all the books that had been left by Jim. Dan had a great interest in nature. It was a David Attenborough book and it was about the deep rain forests. Dan glossed over it. Sive had hoped to tell him all about the house but it was clear he had no interest. She sat back and closed her eyes for a while, trying to figure out how she would get him to agree to come to Avara.

An hour passed and Dan seemed to dose off again, Sive looked at his face. His jawline was still as strong, but his face was now so much thinner. His hair was greyer than before. His robe was wrapped tightly around him and she fixed a blanket around his legs. The bruises were starting to fade on his face now and the swelling was coming down. It felt like a dream sometimes to see Dan here. Dan who was always on the go, always ready to crack a joke and see the lighter side of life. It seemed surreal to be wrapping a hospital blanket around him, so that he didn't get a chill. She sat back in the chair and tried to remain positive. There was no mention of how long he would be in here, and Christmas was only a week away now. Sive didn't really care, all she wanted was to be able to bring him home. She thought back to her visit in the nursing home. How Jim would probably never leave. But Dan had his whole life ahead of him, they had their whole life ahead.

The door opened and it was the tea lady. She placed a cup of tea and two plain biscuits on a plate for Dan. She said hello to Sive and handed her a cup, too.

'Thanks.' When she left, they had their tea in silence.

'Is there anything you need, that I can bring in for you?' At first, she thought he had not heard her, he was so distant and far away in his own world, but then he looked at her.

'No, but will you make sure nobody comes in to see me.'

'Oh, if that's what you want Dan, but what about your mother, and Tom is meant to come up tomorrow.'

'I don't mind Tom but not my Mother. I still can't deal with her.' She could see the anguish on his face and knew if she had to stand at the door to stop any visitors coming in she would if she thought it would help, but telling his mother she couldn't see her son for Christmas? She knew how it had felt.

'Is there anything else you need, I can pop up tomorrow after work.' At least he hadn't told her he wanted her to stay away. He must have read her thoughts, he reached for her hand and held it tightly.

'I am glad you are here now, I just can't face the rest of the world just yet, I need some more time. I hate being here, feeling so dependent on everyone, having the rest of my family pity me and watch them worrying, it's too much.' He let go of her hand then and as he turned his head Sive knew how broken he was. She looked at his fragile body and a surge of love hit her that almost overpowered her. She got up and very gently hugged her husband, he didn't try to stop her. In a strange way, they were more connected in that fleeting moment than they had been in the last few years of their marriage. He turned to her again, his eyes glassy with unshed tears.

'I hate it Sive, I hate waking up thinking about it all. The house, our life, everything we worked for. Gone.'

She wanted to tell him that it was ok, that the house was not important any more, having all the money they had was not important, just being well and being alive was what counted. But she was wise enough to know that Dan was not ready to listen to that yet, he needed time to grieve his loss and come to terms with what had happened. He was a proud man, and his dreams were gone for now. And Dan had always dreamed big. From the first time they met, he was dreaming of his future. He loved being in business, he seemed to get energy from it. Always chasing the next big deal. He loved flying first class, having the best of hotels. He loved the sea, surfing and boating. His boat was gone. Sive was dreading telling him that. Perhaps he knew, they didn't talk about stuff like that at all yet. The fact was that everything was gone.

Sive was surprised herself how she had stepped out of the affluent life they had led so easily. Yet she had left it behind without too much remorse. Something about her upbringing had helped her. Images of the sea shore, picnicking on the beach, laughing with her mother. They had not been rich, yet she knew they had been so happy. Even when her mother had died, she had never craved anything material, only the loss of her mother. Yet, she had had so much love from her mother in those first years that somehow it had sustained her. A fleeting image of her mother entered her thoughts, it happened more often now for some reason. Perhaps in some strange way she felt her presence, guiding her. She liked to think that anyway, to have someone watch over you was a very comforting thought. Holding her husband's hand again, she said a silent prayer, for help for him.

She went down to the cafeteria for a coffee and decided to call Mrs Gallagher.

'Well Sive, how is Dan today, any improvement?'

'It is taking longer I am afraid than any of us expected. The reason I am calling, is he has asked me to let you know that he does not want you to come up for a little while to visit with him. He needs some time to adjust himself.' There, she had said it. There was silence on the other end, which was a first with Mrs Gallagher.

'Look I wouldn't read too much into it, it's probably just a result of the accident, he is a bit lost in himself,' Sive said gently.

'Oh, but surely, he will want to see me for Christmas. I was planning on being there for Christmas Day,' Mrs Gallagher answered. Sive knew exactly how she felt, and it was horrible to be shut out.

'Try not to worry Mrs Gallagher, sure he is the same with me, it's obviously just a part of his recovery.' She thought it kinder to say that.

'Sive, will you let me know how he is doing, I need to know and those nurses tell you nothing,' Mrs Gallagher replied. Sive could hear the fear in her voice.

'Of course, I will, if there is any change at all I will call you, bye Mrs Gallagher.'

Chapter 29

Presence of the Past
Gunther Gerszo, Private Collection.

'Two lattes, two teas, two lemon drizzle, one coffee cake and one pecan slice. Would you all like some cream with your cakes ladies?' Sive asked.

'Yes please.' They all agreed.

'Excuse me I need two extra coffees and any chance of another two chairs, our friends have just joined us?' one woman asked.

'I'll see if I can locate two,' she replied, mentally thinking that she could try and grab two chairs in a minute as two people were leaving. It was mayhem. They would be opened right up to Christmas Eve. The Christmas music was on and the fairy lights twinkled in the windows. Ladies were meeting for their Christmas lunches. The smell of cinnamon and cranberries filled the coffee shop. Some people were a bit stressed as they were not as organised as they wanted to be, others lingered and caught up with their friends over lattes and muffins. Everyone seemed to indulge a little more than normal. The early morning time was busy, with people opting for the omellette or delicious homemade muesli with the creamiest yoghurt and honey drizzled over.

She was slowly getting Dan to sample some of the food. Hospital food was not too bad, but she was constantly trying to tempt him with delicious muffins, wraps and soups she brought up in a thermos. He was slowly recovering. He would remain in hospital for Christmas. The cottage wasn't nearly ready yet anyway. After Christmas, Sive knew she would have more time to work on it. She had hardly seen Beth, so she was delighted to see her walk in just as she was finishing her shift. They sat down and had a coffee together to catch up.

'Well I thought I would drop in. We seem to be like ships in the night passing each other.'

'Oh Beth, it has been busy, but I have so enjoyed it, I feel like I have attended a healthy cookery course. But tell me, any news with you?'

'There is something I wanted to ask you. I am trying to get that designer from Rome interested in showcasing in the store. Her designs are so beautiful. Mostly hand painted silks and intricate gold embroidery. She is very interested, she has her own shop in Rome where she works and exhibits and just after Christmas I am going over to meet with her. I would love you to come, your flights and hotel and everything will be covered, my PA was to come but her mother is very ill. I will be busy with a few meetings but there is so much to see in Rome you would not be bored.'

'Sounds fantastic it's exactly what I would love. I was there as a child with my parents, and I would love to go back,' Sive replied, jumping at the chance.

'I know you may be worried about leaving Dan, but it's only for a quick weekend. You could see him the Sunday evening,' Beth pointed out.

'Give me the dates and I will check if I can get the time off, I would love to go,' Sive added.

'OK, I have to run. Hey, I know you want to spend Christmas day with Dan but perhaps in the morning we can have breakfast together? I am heading over to Rose for about two.'

'Sounds good. I'll cook. Eggs Benedict, my speciality.'

'Deal done. It would probably be a plain old scrambled eggs and toast if it was me. Lovely. Bye.' Beth breezed out of the café.

Sive bought some muffins and chocolate cake to bring to the nursing home as she was heading to see Jim. She loaded the stuff, went home for a quick shower and change and headed up to the nursing home. She had become a regular visitor and she enjoyed it as much as he did. She had got to know a good few of the patients and even the owner had warmed to her. Today Marjorie asked if she could have a word with her. Sive noted she was smiling so felt it wasn't to give out to her.

'I believe you are an artist, I was wondering if you would consider giving some art classes to the patients. I know you get on quite well with them and we have a lot of easels and stuff in the store. A lady was to do it but it fell through last year. We haven't got around to getting someone else.' Marjorie added.

'I would love to do it, thank you so much. It would be a pleasure,' Sive said. They settled on a price per session that Sive was more than happy with, and she suggested that Sive come once a week for two hours and she would pay her accordingly. Sive was thrilled and told her so. They went to see the easels and Sive realised they had bought good quality brushes and paints as well. They had everything they needed to do the art class. They agreed on an afternoon when Sive was off for the day. She was already looking forward to it and was dying to tell Jim the good news.

'Jim is in bed today Sive, he was feeling a bit under the weather. The doctor has seen him and he just said to rest for today and we will see how he is tomorrow.'

'Oh, I will just pop in for a few minutes then, not to tire him out.'

Jim looked very frail in the bed, but his eyes lit up when he saw Sive.

'Did you get past Marjorie?' he asked, smiling.

'Jim, she is after giving me a job.' She filled him in and Jim was delighted he was going to see more of Sive. She made him a cup of tea and they tried out the home-made chocolate cake. Jim just ate a little, but it was delicious. He closed his eyes and Sive realised he was dosing off.

'I will leave you for now, Jim, but I will be back on Christmas Eve.' He opened his eyes, and it struck Sive how childlike and vulnerable he looked.

'Sive, will you bring me something from the garden at the cottage? Down in the corner I planted some Christmas roses and some gardenias. Perhaps they have died but if there is any of them there will you cut one and bring it to me? Gretta loved them.' Sive caught his hand and gave him a gentle hug.

'Of course I will. Rest now Jim, and I will see you soon.' She settled the covers over him and within a few minutes he was sleeping. Somehow Sive felt he was dreaming of Gretta, his garden and his beautiful flowers. When she was leaving she stopped and under Jim's instruction gave the muffins and the chocolate cake to the other patients. It was afternoon tea time so they were delighted and Sive cut up the cake in little pieces. Elizabeth was dancing with her invisible partner, her dainty feet tipping the floor like a ballerina. Some of the other patients were sitting chatting. Some were reading and others were lost in a world far from the confines of the day room, their white hair like a little halo on their delicate heads. Sive sat down with them and chatted. There was no doubt but they were well looked after in this nursing home, it was just the loneliness that seemed to emanate from some of them that tugged at her heart. A few had relatives or friends who visited regularly but some seemed to have very little contact from the outside world. One man looked only about sixty but he had Alzheimer's disease. She had seen his bewildered family come in to see him. Their loss was huge to watch, their father lost to them now, living in his own world.

'It's much better to look back and know I did the best I could,' Mary a wise woman of about ninety who liked to spend her time doing lace, told her.

'Life throws up all sorts in your path, you just have to cross it the best way that you can and not live your life regretting your errors. Learn from them, that is all we can do and hope we do a bit better the next time.' The lace cloth she was working on was very delicate, and slowly Mary was making progress with it.

'The hands are bad with the arthritis now, but in my younger days I could spend hours at night while the children were asleep, making my lace,' she explained to Sive.

'What did you make?'

'Christening gowns, wedding dresses, communion dresses and table cloths for the big houses.'

'Have you any left, I would love to see them?' Sive asked.

'Yes, sure nobody would be bothered with them now, but if you would like one I have a couple at home in some box, I will ask one of the lads to bring it in.'

'I would really love to see it, thanks Mary.' She stayed for a while watching Mary work. Despite her arthritic hands, she expertly did the delicate weaving.

'Lace is a little like life you see, you have to look after all the threads. When one thread becomes loose or frayed it puts a strain on the other threads. But with some care and love you can restore a piece of lace. It just takes time and patience. Just like life I suppose, yes, mending lace is like mending life.' Sive knew how wise her words were and she hugged her.

'You are a wise woman Mary.'

'Perhaps I am, but it only comes with age and learning through my mistakes, you just have to take the best from life and learn from everything else. Life is a mystery to us all, even now I don't understand so much about it. But I do know how there is beauty in life amidst pain. We just have to keep on searching for the good.' Mary looked like she was looking back into her own life as she worked her precious lace and Sive sat comfortably in the silence watching her work. She stayed for another hour chatting. She bid them goodbye then and promised to see them on Christmas Eve. She realised she was really looking forward to seeing them again, and starting the art classes in the new year was fantastic. The new year was busy now with work, the cottage and now her classes. She couldn't even think about the fact that Dan had said very little if anything about moving to Avara. She tried not to worry too much about it. But deep down she knew that she was drawn to this place and did not want to leave. Looking back, she knew she never felt that way before. She had loved their house but here in Avara, there was something else. She felt at peace there. Hopefully Dan would give it a chance. On the way home, she drove to the cottage, even the little bit of work she had done on it had made such a difference. Suddenly she thought of the flowers that Jim wanted, she hoped they were still there. It was raining hard so she waited for it to die down and then made her way out. There were so many brambles out of control it was hard to see anything, but suddenly down in the corner she saw a whisper of white and rose. Sive knew a little from her dad and knew that these were the Christmas roses. Winter flowers are of course rare but these tend to do well in the dappled sun in moist soil. Then under the beautiful hawthorn tree she could see tiny shoots of green waking up the cold canvass of winter. Tiny white flowers filled the damp still air with the delicate scent of a fragrance like honeysuckle. Sive made a mental note to bring in the flowers to Jim.

Later that night, she was awakened suddenly and could hear soft crying. For a few minutes, she had no idea what it was, then she realised it must be Beth. There was no one in the kitchen or sitting room area, the crying was coming from Beth's bedroom. Knocking softly, she called her name but there was no answer. She called a little louder and knocked harder on the door, but there was still no answer. She tried the door, starting to panic a little. Beth was fast asleep but crying and rocking herself like a baby. Sive tried to waken her, she looked so stressed, and Sive realised she was having a nightmare. Gently so as not to frighten her, Sive called her name. There was perspiration on Beth's face which was as white as snow. Slowly she started to awaken. She stared at Sive, without speaking, and as if coming into reality she awoke properly.

'Beth, I am so sorry to come into your room, but I could hear you crying and I was worried.'

'It's OK,' Beth replied, visibly trembling.

'Are you all right, you seemed to be having a nightmare?'

'Yes, that's all it was, I am fine now.' Sive thought she looked anything but fine.

'I will make some camomile tea for you.'

'Thanks, Sive.' As she busied herself in the kitchen, she felt this was no ordinary nightmare. There was something that didn't add up. Whatever it was hopefully she would tell her when she was ready. To share her troubles would surely help, and whatever she said, she was troubled. Denying it wasn't going to make it go away. Beth came in with her robe around her and they sat and drank the tea.

'Sorry, I know you must be worried.'

'You know if you want to talk Beth, I am a good listener,' Sive said gently.

'Sometime Sive, but not now, not yet.'

'Are you sick Beth, is there anything I should know?' Sive wondered what the hell was going on with her.

'No, I promise, nothing like that.' Beth drank her tea and looked away.

'Sometimes the past haunts the present, that's all. Things are always hard for people coming up to Christmas, if you have any troubles that you are carrying with you. They seem to surface most of all when we are meant to be joyous.' She looked at her friend then.

'Perhaps another time I will talk about it, but for now, I would prefer to leave it.' Sive knew she had no choice but to leave well alone.

'To be honest, I almost feel guilty being in good form with Dan being so low.'

'But Sive, he needs you now to be positive for both of you.'

'I suppose I didn't think of it like that.'

'I know myself when I am feeling down, it's good to have someone who is positive and can help lift your spirit. I suppose that's why I love going to see Rose, my landlady from my college days. Ever since I met her she has had that effect on me, she can see the brighter side of the crisis. It's a natural gift she has. Life has thrown up all sorts of crap to her, but she still puts on her bright lipstick and her colourful clothes and gets on with it. She has lifted many a day for me I can tell you, I always knew the day would be a little bit better when Rose was around, I owe her so much.' Beth suddenly looked far away, as if she was lost in another time. Sive was trying to stop herself asking what she was thinking about. But somehow, whatever it was, she felt Rose knew all about it. She got up and went over to the balcony and pulled back the big curtain. The dawn was coming in over the bay, and it looked ever so beautiful.

'Wow, what a sight, daybreak. It was worth getting up to see that. I think I will try painting it.

'I'll have to have more dreams to wake you up in the middle of the night, so,' Beth laughed, the stress of earlier melting away. They finished their tea and Beth went back to rest for a little while before her day began. Sive started painting. After a couple of hours, Beth was up and ready to go to the city. She was dressed in a silk dress in a rich blue with a matching cashmere wrap. Her hair was tied back and she wore a delicate layer of makeup. There was not a whisper of what had happened during the night. They had some coffee and chatted about what they were going to do for the day; whatever secrets lay with Beth, it was for another time.

Chapter 30

The Holy Family
Alte Pinakothek, Munich, Germany.

Christmas morning brought purple blue clouds full of thunder, and Sive wrapped herself tighter in her duvet. It was great to be off. Christmas Eve had been manic in the coffee shop and she had stayed late to help tidy up. Closing her eyes, she listened to the wind as it blew and whistled, her thoughts drifting between waking and sleeping. She had visited Jim the day before and they had spent a couple of hours chatting with the other patients.

'We have something for you,' Elizabeth had said smiling. It was wrapped in a beautiful gift wrap and tied with a piece of golden ribbon.

'For me?' Sive exclaimed.

'Please open it now,' Elizabeth said, eager to see Sive's face when she saw it. She opened the delicate gift wrap. It revealed the most exquisite piece of lace set in a beautiful frame.

'Oh, my goodness, is this your piece Mary?' Sive exclaimed.

'Yes, the girls saw it and came up with the idea, everyone chipped in to get it framed.' Sive looked at the girls she was referring too. Elizabeth, who today looked china-like with her long white hair flowing down her back. Bessy and Moira, who some days were lost in their own world, seemed brighter today, as if their future held more than they had anticipated. She held the picture close to her and could feel the tears prick her eyes.

'I will treasure it, thank you so much.' And indeed, she knew she would, she had come to care for the patients of the nursing home. As for Jim, with his wisdom and his stories, he had given her so much. This Christmas was so different to any other. The last Christmas they had spent at home and the next day they went skiing to Italy.

Now sleep was leaving her and she threw her robe around her and searched for her slippers. She got up and made a pot of coffee, pulling back the blinds in the living area, she looked over the bay. The sea was roaring and full of white waves, crashing against the rocks. The sky dappled with rushing gulls and dark blues. The view from the apartment brought you straight into nature, as if you were one with the earth and the sea. There was such peace in watching the rugged beauty of the sea when it was at its wildest. It was rather like watching a fire blaze in the hearth, you got lost in the motion of it. She decided to throw on some clothes and walk by the sea shore.

She had to struggle to stop the wind blowing her. It was exhilarating feeling the power of the wind almost catching her. When she walked in the direction of the wind it blew her so much that she had to run to keep up with it. It crashed against her face, leaving her skin damp from the salty sea droplets. There was hardly anyone around, except the odd dog walker who was struggling with the wind. Looking at the sky she could see the heavens darken. Suddenly out of nowhere there was a clap of thunder. She ran for shelter, but there was nowhere really to go, so she ran for home. Suddenly the sky was alight with the brilliance of lightening. She ran all the way to the apartment as the heavens opened and the rain came in torrents. She could barely see the keyhole with the rain running down her face. It had been terrifying, yet she had never felt so alive. She took off her shoes as she tiptoed into the living area.

'Oh, my God, were you out in that?' a sleepy looking Beth asked.

'Yes,' laughed Sive, 'I am soaking. I am going in to get changed.'

'Happy Christmas,' they both chorused as they hugged each other. After changing, Sive came back out to watch the storm. After a while the storm calmed and the water stopped crashing so much. Sive made some delicious eggs Benedict for both and they leisurely had their Christmas morning breakfast. They were going their separate ways today, Sive to the hospital and Beth was spending the day with Rose.

'I am going to move into the cottage next week Beth,' Sive said.

'I will miss you so much,' Beth replied with a touch of sadness.

'You have been such a good friend these past few months,' Sive said to Beth.

'I have loved having you to be honest and now that you are going to remain in Avara, I am thrilled.'

'Let's hope Dan is just as thrilled,' Sive said anxiously.

Rose opened the door and rushed to give Beth a massive hug. Her platinum blonde hair was piled high on her head. Her dress was crimson and had a fifties look to it. The smell of Christmas spices filled the air. The table was set with red, pink, green and orange and that was the theme throughout the rest of the kitchen and sitting room. Yes, it was mad and completely over done, with baubles of all descriptions hanging from the ceiling. The tree was a mirage of colours with flickering lights of every colour. Berried holly covered the mantel piece. Old fashioned tinsel covered every available picture frame. A fire burned in the hearth. As Rose gave Beth a large glass of mulled wine, Beth felt as she always did at Rose's, that she had come home. She sat at the kitchen table while Rose busied herself with the last bit of preparation.

'As usual you have gone to so much trouble,' exclaimed Beth.

'You know me Beth, I absolutely love Christmas day and later, my friends will come in for a few drinks and a few songs. I love that part too, some years we have stayed up until dawn. Will you stay this evening? You can have the guest room.'

'Thanks, Rose. I will but I will get a taxi back later, here I brought you some bits for today.' There was some gorgeous cheese, wine, perfume and a very expensive bottle of brandy.

'Oh, my goodness Gilbert will love this, he loves his little brandy in the evening while he is buried deep in his books.'

'What is he working on now?'

'Oh, some history book about the last world war. Sometimes he forgets whether it's day or night only I tell him to go to bed or to get up.'

'You seem so happy Rose,' Beth said smiling.

'I am, who would believe after all these years I would find the love of my life? We are as different as could be and yet we just go together. I was so used to being on my own, I had accepted that was my path, and then out of the blue, I meet Gilbert. We both knew what loneliness was. We both knew we could never be with anyone just for the sake of it, and here we are like two old peas in a pod.'

'You so deserve to be happy.'

'We all do Beth, we all do.'

Her partner was a lovely man who was as different to Rose as Beth was. But they had one thing in common, they both knew how special Rose was. It was wonderful to be in her company, it was like the room was brighter with Rose in it. After the Christmas dinner with all the trimmings and their tummy's full, Gilbert fell sleep in his chair while reading his book and Beth and Rose sat by the fire with their Irish coffees. There was never any pretence with Rose. Beth could totally be herself. Rose knew all there was to know about her past.

'I think Sive knows something to be honest, she is guessing, but it's getting hard to hide it.'

'Why do you want to hide it from her?' Rose enquired. Beth looked away as if to think.

'It's just been a secret so long it's hard to share it at this stage,' she answered.

'Perhaps it's time to share some of your secrets Beth, it may help you to heal a little bit more,' Rose spoke quietly. She could see the emotion building up in Beth, the emotion she normally hid from the world.

'I still think of him so much, how old he would be, what he would look like, sometimes I drive myself demented thinking.'

'To lose something so precious can take a lifetime to heal, but you have to let go, too. You have your life to live Beth and you are a young woman. We can't do anything about who has gone, we don't have that choice.'

'It's just lately, I keep having dreams. I am totally shaken afterwards, it takes a while to find reality and the fact that it is now long ago in my past.' Rose held her hands and whispered as if to a child.

'Still, it's not that long ago, Beth. And perhaps the amount of years makes no difference, healing is a strange thing. You almost have to allow yourself permission to heal before it can,' Rose replied.

'Perhaps you are right, I am tired hiding the past all the time, it's just that once you start it's hard to change.'

Chapter 31

Harmony in My Head
Amy Wheeler. Shoshana Wayne Gallery, Santa Monica, CA, USA.

The foyer was quiet for a change. Anybody who could go home was gone. The Christmas tree looked wilted and tired with lots of the baubles and tinsel missing. Sive made her way down the now familiar corridor to the stairs which led to Dan's room. There was very few staff on. A man pushing a drip attached to him on a stand was slowly walking down the corridor.

'Happy Christmas,' Sive smiled.

'Happy Christmas,' he replied. Sive noticed the sickly look to his eyes. He didn't look like he should be even walking. Probably had to get out of the room for a little while. It was so hard being in hospital over Christmas, but so many had no choice. All the years Sive had a normal Christmas, she never realised how lucky she was. Everything was taken for granted. But here she was visiting her husband, who was too unwell in so many ways to leave hospital over Christmas. Wanting to make it special somehow, she had come armed with goodies and hopefully some gifts that he might like. Gently opening the door, all was quiet in his room. Dan was lying in his bed staring at the window as he usually did. He didn't turn around when Sive came into the room.

'Hi love.' Sive made her way over to him, tentatively giving him a kiss on the cheek. He seemed different today somehow even more distant than usual. She tidied the bed and helped him to sit out onto the chair. She noted how thin he had got. His arms seemed to have lost their muscle. He was still so weak but he was not attached to anything now he was getting better; his body was anyway. She tried not to look at his face because that showed a different story. Dan seemed to be broken and she had no idea how to help him.

'I brought some nice things to eat, are you hungry at all? I also have some books and a diary, I thought you might like it while you are in here.' She left the books on his locker.

'Thanks,' he replied, without looking at them. She was about to tell him about her morning on the beach but decided against it. His eyes were closed again now. If only she knew how to help the turmoil that seemed to be behind his eyes. She took out her book and began to read.

'I am here if you want me Dan,' she said quietly. His eyes were closed and he was drifting off to sleep. It was hard to concentrate on the book, she could feel herself get increasingly worried about him, please God he wasn't getting worse, eventually she got up. He was dozing but not asleep.

'I am just going for a little walk Dan, I will be back soon.' She smiled at him, a big positive smile that she didn't feel. She walked down the corridor and back to the foyer. 'Where is there to go in a hospital on Christmas day?' she wondered. Eventually she found a little chapel. It was so peaceful in there with the candles lit. Just a few ordinary chairs with a simple altar. She sat and watched the flickering flames. Her mother had prayed, to whom she wasn't sure. But never in a chapel, she preferred to pray on the wilds of the beaches of Clare. It was her way of connecting with the earth.

Sive knelt near the small crib that had been placed near the altar. Closing her eyes, she tried to pray.

'Please God, let Dan get better, please.' She could feel the tears on her cheeks, it was a release to allow them to fall. She sat back and closed her eyes and allowed the peace of the room to curb the turmoil that she was feeling. Seeing his anguish was hard to bare at times. If only she could reach him and pull him out of the darkness that he seemed to be in. He seemed so low today. But it was the distance, the aloneness of where he was. She wanted to say so much to him. That it all didn't matter, she did not care about the house, they had a life to live and she needed him to want to live it with her. She put her head in her hands and cried and prayed at the same time.

Afterwards her head felt better, the turmoil and the worry of Dan had subsided a little. She made her way back to his room. It was as if he hadn't moved. She went over to him and knelt on the floor beside him, grabbing his hands.

'Try to get well Dan, please, I need you so much, I love you, please come back to me, and I am so sorry, so sorry for not being there when you needed me most.' She could feel the pain physically trying to strangle her. She put her head down on his knee and sobbed and sobbed. Dan put his hand on her head as if she was a baby and tried to soothe her.

'It's ok love, it's not your fault.' His voice was a whisper. Sive looked up at him, searching his face for the answer. Did he believe that or was he just saying it? Did he blame her?

'It's not your fault.' His voice was breaking and barely recognisable. But Sive recognised the truth in it. Dan didn't lie to her. In that instant, she knew he didn't blame her.

'Dan, if I could turn back the clock, I would have been there for you, but I can't,' she cried.

'Hush, hush, it would not have changed things,' he said.

'But I was so lost in my own stupid world, I had no idea you were so worried about everything, Dan I didn't want to know.'

'As you said, we can't turn back the clock, it's just...'

'What Dan, it's just what?'

'It so fucking empty, how could I have fucked up so much, I feel such a fucking failure, I have failed you, my family, everyone but most of all myself,' he cried.

'Stop Dan, you have not failed everyone.'

'But can't you see, its wrecking my head, I don't know who I am any more, everything I seem to know or believed in had shifted. I got it wrong Sive, I got it all so fucking wrong.' He put his head in his hands.

'I never should have taken the risk, I had too much to prove, always trying to prove…'

'But it doesn't matter, none of it matters,' she cried.' She knew she had to break through to him.

'We have nothing Sive, everything is gone, we don't even have a home,' he replied.

'We may not have any money, but we still have our marriage, you are alive, your injuries are healing, we can build a new life, a better life.' Dan shook his head and for a while neither of them spoke.

'I don't know how to live a different life Sive, I don't know if I have the will to.'

'Look at me Dan, yes you do. I will help you, we are together in this, you are not alone. Let me help you Dan, just come back to me please.' Dan looked at his wife, his face grey and tired, his eyes holding the pain that he felt.

'I'll try Sive, I owe it to you to try.'

'You owe it to yourself, too, Dan.' She cried now with a sense of release, release from the guilt she was unknowingly carrying inside.

'I need to tell you something.' Dan looked gravely serious.

'What, what do you need to tell me?' she said worriedly.

'No more lies, or cover up,' he added. Sive looked at him anxiously.

'Sive, when I was sixteen I tried to kill myself.'

'What?' Sive replied, aghast.

'I know I never told you. I should of,' he replied.

'It's quite a big thing to never have told me. Why, had something happened? Why did you try to do such a thing?'

'I guess I had a breakdown,' Dan replied, almost in a whisper.

'A breakdown, but I never knew, you never said you were ill. Other than the glandular fever...'

'That's it. I never had glandular fever. I had a breakdown, had treatment privately and when I came home to recover, my mother insisted that I tell nobody and she persuaded my father, who was the only other person who knew, to pretend I had glandular fever,' he explained.

'But that was ludicrous,' Sive replied.

'I know. Truth was I think she was ashamed to tell anyone the truth and she then piled that shame on me. I did recover but I was now burdened with a heavy secret that I felt terribly ashamed of.' Dan said, almost silently.

'Oh Dan, why on earth did you not tell me?'

'It was the way I was brought up Sive, nothing to do with you. I was shamed of my past. Now I know I have to be honest with you if I have any chance of ever recovering, and maybe one day leaving that shame behind.' Dan explained.

'But Dan how could she do that, what a dreadful thing to do,' Sive said, shocked.

'She didn't know how to handle it, it frightened her. Somehow I could forgive her for the past but if she continues to lie now I can't forgive her,' Dan said, the anger evident in his voice.

'Is that why you asked me to keep her away?'

'Yes, I can't believe she is trying to cover this up again. At first, I felt so ashamed, but I am slowly starting to realise that if I don't stop this vicious circle of shame and be honest with myself, I can never get well. The only thing I have now is the truth.'

'I knew sometimes you seemed a little lost over the years, but I had no idea what it was, I knew you would talk about it if you needed to. I just wish it hadn't taken all this trauma for you to tell me,' Sive said sadly.

'I know, but hindsight is a strange thing. When you are living that lie it seems easier to stay in the lie. Being honest is not always easy,' Dan said.

'That night on the beach, were you going to throw yourself in?' Sive knew she had to know; her heart missed a beat waiting for him to answer.

'At first yes, I did think about it, but I was on the way back to you Sive when I had the accident. I wanted to come clean. I remember I wanted you to know everything. But something so strange happened that night.' Dan tried to remember.

'What do you mean, strange?' This was a rollercoaster of emotion. Sive tried not to sound too shocked.

'I fell and almost drowned. I thought I was dead but someone was pulling me out. At first, I thought it was you, she looked like you but a little older. It's only now when I have time to think about it, she looked like the photo of your mother that you have,' Dan said warily.

'What are you saying?' Sive asked in amazement.

'Look, I know its sounds cracked and maybe it was some weird hallucination, but I thought your mother saved me that night, like a ghost in the water. I don't want to frighten you Sive, but I want to try to tell you everything now. If I don't I have no hope. We have no hope,' he added. Sive was silent for a few moments, allowing this news to be absorbed.

'It's strange you say that, I keep hearing my mother's voice as if she is guiding me. At first, I thought I was imagining it. But at times it seems so real,' Sive added.

'I don't know, it seemed so real that night on the beach, but sure if we told anyone they would say that we were losing it,' Dan grinned.

'Your mother would probably think I have you on magic mushrooms or something.' They both laughed. It felt good. They stayed like that for a while until they were both calmer and somehow closer. They watched the rain lash at the window. Sive got up and washed her face.

'All this talk of ghosts is making me peckish, we could have some of that chocolate cake and coffee you brought?' Dan suggested. Sive looked at him, knowing how hard he was trying. He looked frail and tired, but there was a tiny hint of the old Dan there. She kissed him again on the cheek and set about opening the flask.

She stayed until late. He opened the books she had brought him and the diary.

'Sorry I have nothing for you.'

'You have given me so much since I met you Dan, and I don't mean just material things. You have loved me. Just get better, I do need you so much. I will go now but I will come back tomorrow.' He looked so tired now, it had been an emotional Christmas day, but Sive felt they had made some small, very important steps back to each other.

Chapter 32

The Persistence of Memory
Salvador Dali. Museum of Modern Art, NY, USA

She could hear the crying again, it was the middle of the night. Beth was weeping in her room. Sive couldn't leave her, she knocked but there was no answer. She opened the door and when she walked in she realised Beth was asleep. She must be dreaming again. Not knowing what was the best thing to do she gently called her name. Beth opened her eyes, the tears were streaming down her face.

'Beth, you must tell me, I want to help you, are you sick?'

'Please, Sive, leave it,' Beth cried.

'I wish I could but as your friend, I beg you to tell me. Perhaps I can help, even in some small way.'

Beth fell to pieces and cried as if her heart would break. Even though it had happened a long time ago, the pain was as real as if it was today. Her face took on the same haunted look that Sive had seen the other day. Perhaps she had rushed her, she wasn't ready to talk about whatever was troubling her. Her pain was physical. She wrapped her arms around her friend and cradled her. When Beth was worn out from crying she lay back on the bed and Sive put a blanket over her. She made some tea and turned the light down. The last thing she had wanted to do was upset Beth, perhaps she had pushed her too much. Beth came out to the table in her dressing gown, her flame hair fanning her pale face. She sipped the tea.

'Okay, I will tell you my story,' she said. Sive put a shawl over her friend and sat down to listen to her.

'When I was eighteen, my first year in college, I got pregnant. It was the nineties. I knew my parents would not welcome me with open arms. They may have closed the Magdalene launderettes by then, but there was absolutely no way I could go home.'

'But surely, they would have been upset, but they would have supported you?' Sive asked, shocked at the revelation.

'They would have done nothing of the sort,' Beth replied with bitterness.

'To bring that kind of shame into the family was as bad as any crime could be. They had been very clear about it. So, I wrote a letter home to say that I would not be home for the next few months as the study was difficult and I needed time to catch up. They never even questioned it.

'In the end, I decided to disappear from Dublin. Afterwards I would take the baby and start again and never set foot in my family home. I had some money in the bank that was meant to keep me in college for the year. I had been very diligent so far so I took the money out, I wrote Rose a note, saying how sorry I was for leaving, and I took the first bus out of Dublin. It was going to Donegal. I rented the cheapest room I could find and tried to figure out what I would do once the baby was born. Who would mind it if I was to work? I got a job in a small vegetable shop. It was long hours, but the family that owned the shop were kind to me. Out of the blue Rose had somehow found me. She had suspected what was wrong. She stayed with me in the last few days coming up to the birth. My baby was born.' The tears were flowing down Beth's face.

'Oh, Beth what happened, where is your baby?' Sive cried.

'I heard a cry, my baby gave its first cry. Then I waited. I knew. There had only been one cry. I screamed to see the baby. Rose was crying.'

'No, Beth,' Sive cried.

'He was gone.' Beth was staring into space, as if she was lost to herself.

'He died, he took one breath and left me, before I could even try to hold the life in him. I can still hear that one cry, from my beautiful baby.'

'Oh Beth!' Sive tried to comfort her.

'It haunts my nights still.' Sive knelt on her knees in front of her stricken friend. Now she knew what was in her friend's nightmares, how alone she must have felt.

'I am so sorry Beth, thank goodness Rose managed to find you, I hate to think of you being alone.'

'I had Rose holding my hand during the birth but the pain of birth was nothing to the insurmountable pain of the loss of my son,' Beth stated, with pain in her voice. They both sat in silence for a while until the rawness of what Beth said was over them. After a while, Sive got up to put the kettle on, they needed a cup of strong tea. She handed Beth a cup, she seemed a little calmer now, but the sadness was almost tangible.

'All these years, his memory is all I have, it is so sacred and precious to me, that I think subconsciously I was afraid to share it as it could somehow damage or weaken the only connection I had. Rose knew of course, and I always knew I could talk to her about it. And Christmas is always harder. But lately, I keep thinking of him, the memory is so strong, Sive, I can't let go.' Suddenly, her voice broke.

'I need to let go, Sive, somehow I need to allow him to rest in peace and me to live in peace.' Her heart was breaking reliving it. Somehow, Sive knew he must have had a name and as if reading her thoughts, Beth looked at her, with all the brokenness of the past eighteen years etched on her face.

'Baby James, my beautiful little baby James.' Her voice was now a whisper. 'He was perfect, my perfect little gift, stolen from me, before I could even hold him,' Sive hugged her friend as they both cried for all the lost years and memories that had never been.

'How does it feel to talk about it?' Sive asked gently.

'It's strange, I never thought I could talk about it, only to Rose of course. But it's good to remember too, remember stuff that is hidden far in my memory. As painful as it is to remember, it feels good too.'

'Why do you think you are having the dreams now?' Sive asked curiously.

'It's been eighteen years now and I have only talked to one person about it. I have lived so long on my own, it was difficult to hide the fact that sometimes I lose sleep over what happened. I now know it has been good for me, I knew you were wondering what I was hiding.'

'I thought perhaps you were having an affair or something,' Sive smiled.

'No chance of that, relationships and I have not really worked out. I don't know if I will ever have a serious relationship,' Beth replied with a hint of sadness.

'Because of the past?'

'Perhaps, and due to my childhood. I wasn't exactly exposed to a happy marriage. I have met some men of course but as soon as it seems to be getting serious, I want out. I can't imagine myself changing.' They watched the dawn come in over hot buttered toast and more tea. It was a beautiful morning.

'How lucky you are to have such a glorious view of the sea,' Sive said.

'I know, there have been nights where the sleep left me and I have watched the light come in on the crashing waves. It is beautiful and I just love the apartment. I knew it was home as soon as I moved in. I know now I had never felt totally at home anywhere before. Home is not always where you are from or born. It can be a collection of things and of people of course. Here, watching the gulls and the white foam floating up on the rocks. Knowing I have people like you and Rose who care about me. Even neighbours from home who will always know me and have always showed me kindness. That's home. Not the aloneness I felt in the house I was reared in, that to me was never home, not where I belonged.

Sive lay down on the couch and pulled the blanket over her. At her own home with her father, she had always felt she belonged. The sounds of the sea now brought her back to Clare, back to the wildness of the beautiful west.

It was late morning when she awoke. Beth was up having some home-made muesli and yoghurt, she was dressed beautifully in a very fine pale pink knitted dress that looked amazing on her. Her red hair was loosely knotted behind her head and her light make up on her creamy pale complexion immaculate.

'My God, how do you do it? I look wrecked,' Sive exclaimed.

'Years of practice,' Beth laughed.

'But you always look so well turned out, even after last night with very little sleep.'

'I know. I feel ok now to be honest. I have had lots of nights that I have lost sleep but I will make up for it tonight. Luckily, I do love my life. I may be on my own but I am not lonely, I am sad at times because of the past, but I have never wished to be married or in a different situation. Speaking of being lonely, my sister in law has been in touch. She is leaving my brother. I have told her that I will look for somewhere for her to stay. I wanted her to stay here, but she needs a place for the girls and herself. She is moving to Avara for a little while anyway. She needs to get away until she figures out what she is going to do.'

'It can't be easy, trying to start again. At least I had no children to worry about,' Sive said.

'By the way, I have the tickets booked for Rome in two days' time, are you still OK to go?'

'You bet. I have to work tomorrow and then I will go see Dan, hopefully he will be ok while I am gone.'

'He will I am sure, and a change of scenery will do you good.'

Chapter 33

The Enigma of a Day.
Giorgio de Chirico. Museum of Modern Art, NY. USA.

The smell of hazelnut and calypso cake coming out of the oven met Sive's senses. Kaitlin looked up and gave a smile of instant relief.

'Thank God you are here, I slept it out for the first time since I opened the coffee shop. Luke had a temperature last night, so I was up all night with him.'

'Is he ok now?' Sive asked, concerned.

'He's better, but I hated leaving him with the au pair, I rang my Mum and she is on the way up.'

'You should of rang me, I could have opened up for you and started the cooking, you have showed me so much, I think I would be fine,' Sive replied.

'To be honest, I didn't think of that, poor Mum, she is forever rescuing me.'

'For what it's worth, I think you are amazing, you can't do everything though, and I am sure your Mum is only too happy to help.' Sive had met her mother, she was one of those really motherly types who completely adored her grandson.

Everyone in Avara seemed to have very little else to do but meet up for coffee and cake or lunch. The cakes were going down a treat, served with a big dollop of clotted cream. Sive had hardly time to think, as she served armfuls of plates of quiches, salads, cakes and lattes. Everyone seemed to be in a good mood, and they had the place full most of the morning and right up till after lunch. Kaitlin made up some fresh fruit and natural yoghurt smoothies for the staff to keep them going. Once the lunchtime rush was over, Sive grabbed salad and some soup. They had a little area out the back to chill when they could.

'I have never eaten so healthily since I came to work here. I always thought I was relatively healthy, but this has been like going on a nutrition course.'

'Healthy body, healthy mind,' replied Kaitlin as she munched down a pita bread with hummus and grilled veggies. 'I worked in some restaurants before and sometimes the food for staff is so crap and unhealthy. I said if I ever have staff, they can have a healthy choice.'

'Your food is delicious too,' Sive replied.

'It does help, whatever you are going through, look after your health and you do have more energy to deal with everything else.'

'How is Luke?' Sive asked.

'Great, gone off with my Mum, the au pair is not really working out to be honest, she seems to be more interested in her social life than Luke. Her idea of looking after him is turning on the TV while she can go on Facebook. I may have a rethink.'

'I can do more hours if you want, just let me know if you want me to.'

'That would be great, as soon as the Christmas period is over I am closing for two days to repaint and then I might take some time off to figure things out. By the way, when the painting is done would you like to display some of your art for sale on the wall? I was thinking of just doing white wash as the stone looks great just white, your art would look super on them and hopefully you might sell some with the tourists.'

That would be great.'

'Are you going up to see Jim this evening, you normally go Tuesdays, don't you?' Kaitlin asked.

'Yes, just going for a quick shower and then I will pop up.'

'Here, I have some extra cakes, bring some orange and ginger cake for his tea.'

'Ah thank you Kaitlin, that would be lovely.'

At last the coffee shop was calming down when the door opened and in walked Mrs Gallagher.

'I need to speak with you Sive.'

'This is not a good time, you can see I am working,' Sive replied curtly.

'Well, if you had the good manners to answer your phone I could have made a different arrangement.' Sive was about to tell her what she thought of her when Kaitlin intervened.

'You can use the small office out the back Sive. I will bring you some coffee.'

'Tea will suffice. Please make sure it is served in a proper cup,' Mrs Gallagher demanded.

'Of course,' said Kaitlin, secretly winking at Sive in support.

'Very well, follow me.' Sive brought her into the office. Kaitlin arrived in with two spotless tea cups.

'That's fine for now waitress, you can go.' Sive looked up to see Kaitlin burst into giggles, and doing a bad job of hiding them from Mrs Gallagher.

'So, what brings you here that is so urgent?' Sive asked. Mrs Gallagher took a sip of tea then settled herself in, eye balling Sive.

'We need to get Dan home. He will be out of hospital soon. I want him to come home to Thornback. He will gain strength quicker there.' Sive was surprised that this could be an option at all.

'Have you spoken to Dan?' As far as Sive knew Dan had not spoken to his mother.

'No, he is still resting. He just does not want to worry me, that is the only reason he asked me to stay away from the hospital for a little while. My Dan will always worry about me, bless him. I am going to set up the spare room for him to recuperate. You can have the room beside it. I know once he is home he will get much better.'

'Hold on, Dan knows nothing about this I assume?'

'Well I want you to mention it to him, let him know it's the best for him? Well, it is Sive? Where else can he go?' Mrs Gallagher asked.

'I have the cottage all ready as you know?' Sive replied quickly.

'You are hardly going to drag him away from his home to stay in some old rented cottage in Avara. Seriously Sive, that will not do. I know you are trying, but your place for now is at Dan's side. You can hand in your notice and move up to Thornback. I have a lot of contacts, I can get you a little job in an office. Something more suitable. All those apparatuses are off him now. The physio can visit him and the doctor in the village is a very good friend, if I need him ten times a day he will come and attend to Dan. I have often had him over with his wife for Sunday lunch.' Sive could not believe Mrs Gallagher. She was utterly unbelievable.

'And what about the psychiatrist, will he come at your beck and call too, Mrs Gallagher? Do you have a hotline to the psychiatric department too?'

'There is no need for your impertinence. Dan will not need any of that once I get him home. I know my son better than anyone.'

'What do you want to do, have my blessing so you can take him out of the hospital and pretend none of this has happened? Over my dead body, you will. Dan is a grown man, you cannot decide what is best for him.' She wanted to add, 'like you did all those years ago, when you pretended he had glandular fever.' It made her so angry to think of it.

'I will have a chat with my son, he needs to come home to Thornback,' Mrs Gallagher said bluntly. Sive had heard enough.

'I think that is the last thing he needs, but it's Dan's decision where he is going,' Sive replied.

'I assure you, Dan is going back to Thornback one way or another,' Mrs Gallagher retorted.

'Please leave Mrs Gallagher, and please do not call to my place of work again.'

'I will see you in Thornback, Sive, there will be no need to visit you here. Good day now, I will let you back to your washing up.' With that Mrs Gallagher downed her tea and walked out, but not before having a word with Kaitlin.

'Waitress, this is a nice tea shop, I will recommend it to my Ladies Club. They may use my name when they book so please look after them and make sure all the cutlery is clean. Mrs Gallagher of Thornback Farm. I have my name to look after, I do not recommend places easily. But this looks very clean and your cakes look good. A nice apple tart would not go astray though. I have my own secret recipe but unfortunately, I must protect it and keep it in the family. Yes, tell the owner I was very impressed. Sive has my number if she would like a little advice. Have a good day now girls, keep busy now, no slouching.' With that she was gone.

Kaitlin looked after her, dumbstruck. The anger Sive had felt turned to laughter at seeing Kaitlin stare after her. It was not every day you had the likes of Mrs Gallagher in your café.

'What was that?' Kaitlin said, aghast.

'That is my mother in law, not quite like anyone else you will ever meet,' Sive replied.

'She is gas, I love her hat, I thought she just dropped in on the way to the races,' Kaitlin grinned.

'That's Mrs Gallagher's attire most days,' Sive informed her.

'Certainly unique,' Kaitlin added with a grin.

The nursing home was quiet when Sive got there. Jim was sitting in the day room with the other patients playing cards. He looked up, delighted to see Sive.

'Keep playing your game, I might learn some tricks from you,' Sive smiled. Elizabeth was sitting near them on her own. She was paler than before and seemed to have lost weight. She had a blue dress on with red butterflies printed on it. She was desperately trying to take the butterflies off. She was muttering something to herself repeatedly. It started to sound like a chant. Sive went over to her.

'Hi Elizabeth, it's me Sive.' When she looked up she didn't recognise Sive. Her frail white hair was pinned up with its usual silver combs, and Sive could smell the familiar scent of lavender cologne coming from her. She had a paisley scarf around her neck.

'Elizabeth, would you like me to help you with your crochet.' Despite her arthritis, Elizabeth had managed to crochet a beautiful blanket with soft lemons and blues for her grandson, who lived in London.

'I am far too busy, I have to prune my roses before tea and then the cake sale, I must make some sponges for the cake sale.' Jim looked over at Sive and beckoned her over to him.

'Poor Elizabeth, her dementia seems to have become worse over Christmas. She has been unwell the last few days.' Sive watched Elizabeth as her delicate little body sank into a chair. Her head was bent and she was back trying to catch the butterflies.

'Her son is a surgeon and as far as I know that is all the family she has. He lives in London. She was hoping to see her grandson for Christmas, but just her son arrived over for a few hours. She was very disappointed.' Sive looked over at Elizabeth, her hands not showing their usual pink nail varnish that she loved. Her face normally had a touch of powder and pink lipstick but was now bare. Her blue eyes lost and empty, there was no dancing or looking for music. In her delicate body and her silver hair, she reminded Sive of a little fairy, but today her wings had been damaged and her usual dancing feet were quiet.

The tea was coming around and Sive divided up the cake. She watched as Elizabeth barely touched it. Her mind was far away, lost in another time for now.

'So how is Dan?' Jim asked.

'A little better. Sometimes it's hard to know if I am saying the right things to help him get well.' Jim looked straight at Sive and held her eyes. He could see the worry in them.

'Only he can get himself where he wants to go, you can only be there for him and help him on his journey to recovery.'

'How come you are so wise?' smiled Sive.

'You don't get to be almost ninety without picking up a few tips along the way.'

'Looking back on your life, what was the best thing about it?' Jim sat back and his eyes shone as he remembered the past.

'So many things really. Love, friends and good times. But perhaps the knowledge to appreciate what I had and not to be thinking the grass is always greener. Happiness is within you, it is not something you can create or buy. But how about you my dear, what does happiness mean to you?' Sive smiled and thought about it for a while.

'When I was young it was just being free, the beach, painting. I was happy, but my Mum dying was hard. I was lucky because Dad was such a good father, although we missed her terribly, I had a happy childhood. As I got older, I was a little bit lost I think, then meeting Dan, his road seemed to be my road. Now I look back on our life together and I must question lots of things, perhaps I forgot my own road? Since Dan's accident I have had to question a lot about my life. I thought I had accepted my mother dying so young, but in the past few months it has haunted my dreams and at times I feel I am going mad because I can almost hear her.'

'Losing your Mum was part of the void you felt when you were young. Meeting Dan helped, but your loss is still there. Your father did the very best he could, but it's hard to heal the loss of a parent so young.'

'I spent years thinking I had dealt with her death so well, but now I just wish she was here to talk to, I really do.' They sat in silence for a while, a silence that only two good friends can feel comfortable with. Sive felt better afterwards, talking had helped her.

'I am not sure where that came from Jim, I think seeing Elizabeth so alone, it's not right that she should feel this way. We are great in Ireland at preserving our heritage, but perhaps we should care about our elderly a little more.' Jim shook his head and smiled.

'Some cultures see us as wise men and women, but in Ireland it is a different story.' Sive stayed for another hour and chatted to the other patients; it had become part of her visit now. Some looked happy and content, others looked lost and a little forgotten. It was almost supper time when she left and she promised to see them soon when she would start her art workshops. On impulse, she rang her dad.

'Hi Dad, how are you?'

'Good, I was thinking of coming up to give you a hand with the cottage.'

'Thank would be brilliant, Dad, especially the garden.'

'I'm heading out for dinner actually'

'Oh lovely, with your farmer's market friends, the cult,' Sive laughed.

'Em... with Ruby actually. Do you remember her?' Sive was taken aback.

'Yes of course, she seems nice, have a lovely time.'

'Are you ok Sive?' Sive regained her composure.

'Yes Dad, just tired. I will chat with you when you come up.'

'When are you in Rome?'

'We fly out tomorrow.'

Chapter 34

Madonna di Loreto
Cavalleti Chapel Of the church of Saint 'Agostino. Rome.

'Two large gin and tonics please.' Beth sat back in the comfort of first class.

'Would you like some ice?' the air hostess asked politely.

'Yes, please.' She handed one drink to Beth and the other to Sive and told them she would be back shortly if there was anything else they needed.

'Do you always fly first class Beth?' Sive asked as she took a long sip of her drink.

'Yes, my boss is good that way, I have an excellent expense account that is going to be used to its maximum for these few days.' Beth replied with a grin.

'When I was there as a child, we had travelled by boat to France, then by train to Italy, and I think a bus too until we made it to Rome,' Sive remembered.

'Can you remember much about it?'

'I remember the streets and the food. I think I fell in love with pasta on my first day in Italy. I remember the rich taste of olive oil on the tomatoes and the Italian accent. My mother loved Rome, she loved the little streets, the history, the cafés and the art. When Dan and myself toured Europe, I didn't want to go to Rome. I had too many memories of my mother but now I feel a little closer to her knowing I am going there.'

'You were very close to your mother?'

'It's odd but lately I feel like she is guiding me. I know this sounds a bit mad. The day that I was told that Dan did not want to see me I thought I heard her voice trying to soothe me. It sounds weird but I wasn't frightened. Maybe it was just lack of sleep.'

'Possibly,' Beth agreed.

'Then Dan told me that he thought he saw something in the water, that night on the strand. At first, he thought it was me but he said it was like an older version of me. If you look at my mother she does look like me. It was like a vision guiding him out of the water. Perhaps my mother did help him that night.'

'Sive, are you telling me that you think the ghost of your mother saved Dan that night?'

'I know it sounds ridiculous but I don't know, who knows really, Beth? I could only ever tell you this, anyone else would think Dan and myself were mad to be talking about visions and the like.'

'And as your friend I can, too, but that does not mean I love you any less.' They both laughed and clinked their glasses.

'Seriously Sive, do you believe it even a little bit or have you both read too many ghost stories.'

'Maybe I just want to believe it. The first time it happened, I was even a little spooked, but now I'm not. Do I believe it? It sounds too ludicrous, but who really knows?'

'Okay I think I need another drink after that little revelation,' Beth signalled for service.

'Two glasses of prosecco please,' she ordered from the hostess.

'We will be falling out of the plane at this rate, we have only just taken off.' Sive grinned.

'To Rome,' Beth said.

'To friendship,' Sive replied, smiling.

A car was waiting to take them to their hotel, which was not far from the Spanish Steps. Sive was enthralled by the ancient streets. There was something hauntingly beautiful about Rome at dusk. It did look every bit as magical as she remembered. She felt like she was in ancient Rome as they arrived at their hotel. Beautiful tapestries and art hung on the walls. They each had their own exquisite bedroom with large marble bathrooms. Sive's phone rang in her room. It was Beth.

'Meet me in an hour for dinner. I have it booked downstairs.'

'Absolutely. See you soon, going to hop into this big bath first, I feel like Cleopatra,' Sive laughed.

'Wow, the food is fabulous, it's so filling though, I think I need a little walk to let it settle. Are you up for one?' Beth asked.

'I have my walking shoes on,' Sive replied.

They walked down the Spanish Steps and then over towards the Trevi Fountain.

'Legend has it that if you toss a coin into the beautiful fountain that you will return to Rome,' Sive said. They both tossed in their coins, marvelling at the beauty that was Rome. They found a little café in full view of the fountain and had a liqueur and watched the world go by.

'Excuse me beautiful ladies, but a drink from the two gentlemen over there. They want to know can they join you?' Beth and Sive looked over at them.

'They look a bit dodgy,' Sive said.

'A bit... let's get out of here,' Beth grinned. They left as quickly as possible, laughing as Beth stumbled and almost fell.

'Come on, in here looks lovely,' Sive said, pointing to a little tavern.

'Two gin and tonics please,' Beth ordered.

'It's so strange, I have not had to run away from a man for many years,' Sive grinned.

'You love Dan, though. Could you ever see yourself with anyone else?' Beth asked.

'If I have learned anything from the past few months, it's that I really do love Dan, but I depended on him far too much. I never want to do that again.' Sive said

'How about you, can you ever see yourself settling with someone? Settling down properly.'

'I don't know Sive. Maybe I just never met that man.' Beth replied, with a touch of poignancy.

'What about Tom?' Sive suggested quietly.

'What about him?' Beth asked.

'Well to me he seems smitten with you,' Sive replied as she sipped her drink.

'There is something about Tom, but our lives are so different. How on earth could that work? He is a farmer, no it could never work.' Beth replied shaking her head.

'Oh! can you imagine Mrs Gallagher's reaction. She would accuse me of putting a spell on Tom to bewitch him. She is convinced that I have some witch power. Sure, how else did I get Dan to fall for me, when she had the perfect girl picked out for him,' Sive laughed.

'Are you serious?' Beth grinned.

'Oh yes, a lovely trainee solicitor, and her father is the local bank manager. A very good friend of Thornback Farm, according to Mrs Gallagher.'

'Come on you, I need to get some rest' Beth sighed.

'Me too, I want to explore Rome a bit tomorrow,' Sive replied with a yawn.

Back in her hotel Room, Sive fell asleep within minutes. But within an hour she was awake, a voice had awoken her.

'Look my little Sive, see the beauty that is Rome.'

It struck her that she had never fully let her mother go, maybe that was why she felt her so close.

The next morning it seemed ludicrous that she heard her mother. As she walked down the Spanish Steps, she remembered her mother and father laughing and teasing each other. Sive knew even then that they loved each other very much. She had arranged to meet Beth for lunch.

'How did you hear about this place Beth, it's like a hidden gem?'

'My designer told me about it, the food is meant to be delicious,' Beth said as she ordered two glasses of prosecco. It was bustling with mostly Italians.

'I signed my designer, and she is even more talented than I thought. Her designs are impeccable. I have got so many ideas for the design studio from walking around the boutiques here in Rome. I think our clients will love her designs. Her name is Floriana. She has a boutique in Milan, too, but this will be her first city outside of Italy to showcase and sell her work. It's days like these that I absolutely adore my job. How are you, you are not lonely on your own?'

'I have fallen in love with Rome again,' Sive didn't say anything about her dream last night. She did not want Beth thinking she had lost the plot altogether. Maybe it was the gin anyway. It was not something she could explain to anyone, and what else could it be?

'Coming away has given me some perspective. If my mother thought me anything it was to grab each day and treat it as a precious gift.'

'Okay let's enjoy the rest of the afternoon, more prosecco to begin with,' Beth laughed.

Chapter 35

Portrait of a Child Holding a Rattle
Niels Rode. Private Collection.

The sale was in full swing. Everybody in work seemed to be looking for a piece of her.

'Excuse me I was just wondering if I could possibly try this on?' The customer was in her late twenties, with blonde hair and blue eyes, and beside her was an expensive looking white buggy with a baby sleeping peacefully in it. Beth's eyes fell on the sleeping baby, he looked only a few weeks old. There was a soft blue and cream blanket covering the buggy and a soft blue hat on the baby.

'He's gone asleep for a few minutes so I thought I might try this on?' The woman was holding up a cream lace blouse looking enquiringly at Beth. Beth would normally swing into sales mode, but her eyes remained on the baby, she took in every curve on his mouth, the way his rosy cheeks looked, his little mouth, hands stretched in a deep sleep. She was rooted to the spot, there was a waft of baby lotion that seemed to overpower her. The customer looked perplexed.

'Everything ok?' Another assistant came over and smiled at the customer. Beth never moved.

'Hello, would you like to try that on? It's such a beautiful piece, so delicate and feminine.' The interlude gave Beth a chance to gather herself.

'Amy, I will let you take over here, I must dash to the office.' Amy helped the customer to the dressing room while Beth escaped, her heart beating rapidly. Once safe from prying eyes she locked the door and breathed deeply. What the hell had come over her? Beth felt frightened by how powerful the feelings were. It was as if she was back all those years ago, it was eighteen years, how on earth could this happen now? The baby had looked so peaceful, Beth knew she had been rooted to the spot. She put her head in her hands.

'Help me to move on now, it's time,' she whispered. She stayed like that for a while. There was a gentle tap on the door.

'Who is it?' she said more sharply than she intended.

'It's just me, Amy, I have a cup of tea for you, you looked like you needed it.' Beth opened the door and Amy came in with a tray and a pot of tea and a biscuit.

'Are you okay, you looked like you were going to pass out,' Amy gently asked.

'I'm fine, just a bit stressed with the sale,' she lied.

'It's going really well, everyone wants to find a bargain, even if it is designer clothes,' Amy said lightly.

'Thanks for the tea, and for rescuing me earlier, I'm fine now honest,' Beth replied.

'No problem, I will get back on the floor, the lunchtimes are starting with the girls.' Beth felt grateful for Amy's professionalism. If she thought it was strange to see her boss go into shock staring at a baby boy in a buggy, she didn't comment. She just took over. Before leaving work, she rang Rose. She still felt a bit shaken after what had happened.

'Would you mind if I called out on my way home Rose?' Beth asked her friend.

'Call any time Beth, you know that, I will have the kettle on, see you soon. Beth never remembered ringing Rose and being told that it was inconvenient to call. She always made her feel so welcome. Like so many times before she wondered what she would have done without her?'

There was a very welcoming smell of essential oils when she arrived.

'What's that burning, Rose, its lovely?' She handed Rose some flowers she had bought on Grafton street.

'Essential oil of rose and ylang ylang, come on into the kitchen, the flowers are beautiful, but there is no need to be bringing me anything pet, I am just delighted to see you, I have the kettle on.' They sat down and Beth made a pot of tea and some cream slices to go with it. Beth told her what happened in the shop today, and about telling Sive.

'It's probably just talking about it with Sive, its bringing back all the memories love,' Rose said soothingly.

'I was just shocked at how powerless I felt, how much emotion I felt.' Rose took Beth's hand, and looked right at her. Every mother has a bond to their baby. It will always be there. Whether your baby grows up and becomes an adult or if it passes away at birth, your bond will always be there. Your little baby has been on your mind so much lately, it's not that surprising about what happened. Just go with it, it doesn't mean it's going to happen again so don't let it frighten you,' she added wisely.

'I know you are right, it's just so long now, I am tired Rose, tired from thinking about what might have been. Every year is another year of wondering, I must move on. I haven't been to the grave all these years. I was thinking of going at the weekend.'

'Would you like me to come with you?'

'No, but thanks Rose. I need to go alone.'

Chapter 36

Waterlillies:The Clouds
Claude Monet. Musee de L'Orangererie, Paris, France.

His room had not changed except for the cards and few belongings he had. He felt safe in the room, away from questions and people. Talking to anyone was draining. The unread books lay on his dresser. There was a routine to the day. He would awaken to the sound of clatter of the breakfast trays. He ordered the same breakfast every day.

'Just the cornflakes, Dan, and the tea, I will leave you some toast just in case.' He barely touched any. He liked the tea, it soothed his head in the morning. Sometimes the smell of lunch coming around made him feel queasy. On these days, he refused any. Probably the medication, he thought. The evening meal was normally a light salad or a sandwich. He would try to eat this and more tea. He could feel his body healing, he had more strength now. The persistence of the physio meant he could walk with a cane. The physio was hopeful that with a lot of work he might be able to get rid of the cane. The headaches were fewer. Yes, the healing process was happening. He should be grateful, thrilled that his body was getting better. He could get back to living again. Yet the thought filled him with dread. He wanted to stay cocooned in these blue grey walls, facing reality some other day. From the last visit of the consultant, his time was coming to leave. The consultant told him with a big smile on his face.

'Yes, the X-rays look good, you can go home soon,' he said cheerfully.

'What if you have no bloody home to go to?' he had felt liked screaming at him.

'What if the bloody bank has taken your home?' It was simpler when he could stay in hospital, when he had no choice. Soon he would have no choice but to leave it. His head hurt when he thought about it. Everything was gone. He tried to brave it out when Sive came in, but it was eating him up.

'You can start again,' his father had said. He didn't want to start again, he never wanted to start again. He knew they meant well but it was hard to listen to. Perhaps if his father had lost the farm he would know how it felt.

'Just start again.' How would he feel? Not so easy, Dan bet. Fear that felt like terror invaded him when he thought about leaving. What were his choices? Sive wanted him to move to some bloody rundown cottage in the arse hole of Wicklow and his mother wanted him and Sive to come live at home back in Thornback. What a bloody choice. He felt like running so far away that nobody could ever find him. Sive, she was trying so hard. Working in a café and giving painting lessons. He was proud of her though, how she had coped with the loss. She seemed to love the life they had led so much, he could not have dreamed of her adjusting so well. But then he thought of her before he met her. It was her simplicity that had drawn him. She never craved material possessions, but she indulged him in his dreams.

'I want a big business, with the best office in town.'
'You should have your dreams Dan, I hope you do.'
'But I want you to be part of them, to help make them happen.'
'I will love you as a rich man or a pauper.'

And she had kept her word, he had lost everything but not Sive, but somehow, he feared, he was not ready to go back there. That was the frightening thing. But if he had to leave the hospital, how could he pretend to be a husband again? His mind was in turmoil. There was a knock on the door and it was Milo, Sive's Dad.

'Just up in the big smoke today and I thought I would come see you first, to see how you are doing,' he said smiling.

'Come in, Milo,' Dan replied quickly.

'Well how are you, I believe you will be leaving hospital soon,' he said with optimism.

'Yes, that's what I have been told anyway,' Dan replied quietly.

'Do you feel ready Dan?' Dan admired his intuition.

'I feel lost, totally lost.' Milo looked over his glasses at him. Slowly he took off the glasses and crossed his legs the opposite way.

'I feel like walking out on my life, running away from everything I know. I know I must sound selfish and cowardly, I am married to your daughter for Christ's sake. I just feel so tormented, that I feel like running,' he said, his voice full of anguish. Milo was quiet while he considered what Dan was saying.

'For what it's worth, I don't think you are cowardly, you have been through a very traumatic time, its only human to want to run. But you must be open with Sive about how you feel. She is trying so hard, maybe she can help you,' Milo suggested.

'How the hell can she help me, I want to run away Milo, and Sive wants me to play happy families off the coast of Wicklow.'

'I think you just need some time out Dan, to come to terms with what has happened, that's all,' Milo suggested.

'But how am I going to do that, I am going to be discharged shortly and where the hell am I going to go and how do I tell Sive that I need time away from her?'

'Dan, is that what you really want? What do you want? Sive is your wife.'

'But I am still struggling Milo, I feel if I could be on my own for a little while, I could get some clarity. I know that sounds terrible, Sive is your daughter and I love her more than anything, but I have to find my way out of this first, I cannot be a husband when I am still struggling at living,' Dan replied, his voice hoarse with the emotion of it.

'Sive is your wife Dan, maybe she can help you out of this?' Milo suggested.

'Right now, I can't be who she wants and needs me to be, I need to figure out my life and I need to do it by myself,' Dan replied.

'You can't just decide when you want to be married and when you don't. Sive has been through a lot, too. She is expecting her husband home. You still need recuperation, too. Who is going to do that?' Milo asked.

'I don't know Milo, I feel I am going crazy here thinking about things.' Milo looked at his son in law, he was a shadow of the man that he had been. His black hair had thinned and had turned grey almost in the couple of months. His pallor was so pale and his eyes were frightened. He could be angry with him for not just getting on with it, and not being a husband to his daughter, but that wasn't his way. The man was crying out for help, and crucifying him with guilt was going to do no good.

'Let me think about it Dan and see can I help, but you do need to talk to Sive and let her know. She deserves the truth. No more lies Dan. Promise me.'

'I will tell Sive, the truth is the very least she deserves, if I had been truthful about the bloody mess I was in, it may not have got as bad,' Dan replied regretfully.

'The future is what is important now,' Dan agreed with Milo but he knew deep inside that he had to deal with the past and accept it before he could ever move on and have any sort of future. And he also knew he had to do this alone. He would have to tell Sive, she had to know.

Chapter 37

Forget it! Forget me!
Roy Lichtenstein, Rose Art Museum, Waltham, MA, USA.

Jim was looking frailer today. He normally would be sitting out now but he was in bed. They chatted as usual but Sive could see he was weaker than her last visit.

'How is Dan?' he enquired.

'I am meeting with him and the doctor this afternoon. He has turned the corner, and hopefully he will be home soon.' Sive found it hard to imagine him home; it was strange how accustomed they both had come to living apart, even if one of them had no choice and was in hospital. As if reading her thoughts Jim said, 'How does he feel about moving to Avara?'

'To be honest we haven't discussed it much, I am hoping today we will know when he is going to be out,' Sive replied.

'I see. It will be hard for him and you Sive, he has had to come a long way. Just give it time and things have a way of working themselves out.' Sive smiled at him, it was a funny thing, Jim often knew instinctively what to say.

'I know it will be difficult for him to adjust to normal life after being in hospital all this time. I am worried but you're right, I am sure it will be fine when he is home and in the cottage. I hope he comes to love it as much as I do. By the way, your daffodils are about to burst into bloom, Jim.'

'You must bring me some.' Jim settled back against his pillow and Sive could see how tired he was.

'Would you like me to read to you Jim, or would you just like to sleep?'

'Perhaps a little poem, thank you, Sive.' She picked up one of his favourite books and began to read from Seamus Heaney. As she finished the poem, she lowered her voice. Jim was almost asleep.

'Rest now and I will see you soon.' She tucked the blankets around his shoulder and tidied his bed and side table. It was funny how important

Jim had become to her, he always seemed to know what to say to her to ease her mind.

Give it time he had said. Sive knew he was right.

On the way, she stopped at the day room. There was a new couple after arriving into the nursing home. She was suffering severe dementia and he looked totally exhausted. He was trying to get her to stay still for a while. Sive could see the stress on his face.

'It's all a bit strange here for my Ellie,' he said. Sive smiled at him and introduced herself.

'I am sure everyone feels a little like that at first. It's lovely to meet you.' He got up to explain to Ellie that she could not go outside.

'I must go, hens to be fed, weeds to be picked, just because it's raining does not mean chores cannot be done. Where is my coat?' Sive's heart went out to him. How lucky Ellie was to have a man care about her so much. Even now when he needed care himself, he felt responsible for his wife. She could see how difficult it must be for him. He needed a break, too. She wondered how he had managed up until now, had he family who helped, or was he alone in the world like so many. She made her goodbyes and promised to see everyone soon.

She stopped off at the house on the way home. She had made some of the blueberry muffins that Dan had started eating. The house looked so cosy and welcoming. The late morning sunshine had filled the kitchen with a yellow spring glow. She made a cup of tea and tried to imagine having Dan here with her. Truth was she had got used to being on her own. The first night she had stayed in the house she thought she would be afraid, but it was if she had just decided not to be afraid. She had locked the doors, got into her snug bedroom with the white wash floor and the soft green on the walls. Her precious paintings hung on the walls. That first night she had slept soundly, only to be awoken by a nesting starling above her window. From that day, she knew she had found her haven. She just hoped Dan would like it too.

The hospital was busy with visiting time. She had become friendly with lots of the nurses and some of the patients. Dan was not in his room, so she picked up a newspaper. He could be gone for an x-ray or something. He arrived back after about half an hour. He was walking on his own now with a nurse at his side just helping a little bit.

He looked a little worried when he saw Sive and she caught the change in his face. The nurse settled him in his chair and then left them.

'Could you close the door Sive.' Sive got up and did as he asked. She could feel tension in the air.

'They are letting me home soon.' Dan told her the news that most people would be so thrilled to say, yet Dan looked very apprehensive.

'That's wonderful, Dan.' It felt almost surreal to be saying the words. She went over and hugged him. Sive instinctively knew though that all was not well. She tried to figure out what was going on. Perhaps Dan had decided they should move to Thornback after all. His mother had been quite insistent, but it was hard to imagine Dan wanting to move in with her. But there was something up.

'Sive, they say I can probably go home in about a week. I feel a lot better, but I know I have a long road ahead of me. I have thought about this long and hard. I know how much you have done with the cottage and trying to find a home for us, but Sive I am so sorry, but I am not moving to Avara.' She looked at him. Had he just said what she thought he said? The strain was physical on his face. So, this is what was worrying him. He had decided they would not live there.

'Could you not give it a chance, it's such a special place and my job is there. It may not be much, but with the art class and my waitressing job, things are looking up Dan. What about me? I want to live there. I certainly don't want to move to Thornback Farm. I cannot believe you do, either,' Sive replied incredulously.

'I have no intention of moving anywhere near Thornback,' Dan replied.

'Well where is it that you want us to go?' Sive said exasperated.

'That's the thing Sive, this is so difficult to say, but for now, I don't want us to go anywhere.' Dan said struggling to find the words that he needed to say.

'I don't follow you, you are being discharged?' Sive asked, perplexed.

'Sive I know how far you have come and I am so proud of you, but I need to live on my own, for a while at least.' Sive looked at him, totally confused. What was he saying, or trying to say. Then as if someone was speaking for her she quietly asked.

'Dan, are you leaving me?'

Chapter 38

Nevermore
Courtauld Institute of Art Gallery, London.

'Sive I just need some time out, time on my own to figure out my life.' In disbelief, she could hear her own voice only holding it together.

'Most couples would do this together, we are married the last time I checked. What the hell, now you want out. Are you for real?' Sive could hardly believe what she was hearing.

'Sive, please try to understand. I know I am better but I have no idea who or what I am anymore,' Dan replied pleadingly.

'You are my husband in case you have forgotten,' Sive replied curtly.

'Well, that's just it, I don't think I can be that right now, I can barely get through the day, I don't know how to be anything to anyone,' Dan replied sadly.

'I don't understand, what are you saying, Dan?'

'I do need to be with someone just to fully recover, so I have asked Tom to move in with me for a little while, he is going to rent an apartment in town.'

'What?' Sive replied, aghast.

'I know it seems impossible to understand Sive, but I need to be on my own to figure things out. Truth is I need to learn a new way to live. I have lived a certain way for so long, I am terrified of trying to live any other, but I know I must. I thought if I was successful then that was all that mattered. But look at what I've done, I hid everything from you because I was too ashamed to tell you I had made a mistake. My risk did not pay off, I was so ashamed it almost killed me. I cannot live like that any more, shame cannot rule my life. The fear of failure, the fear of not being successful, the fear of losing you. Yes Sive, I know I am asking for time out, but if I don't I really will lose any chance of us ever being happy.'

'You are the one signing out of this relationship Dan, not me. I have been here all the way through. It is you that wants out, so do not tell me you are afraid of losing me,' Sive replied, tears rolling down her face.

'Sive, please try to understand. I need time to figure all this out in my head.' Sive could see the strain on his face. Not for the first time she wondered how on earth she had not noticed how he was falling apart before the accident, how was she so unaware? As if reading her thoughts, he held her hand and told her to sit next to him.

'I was very good at hiding everything Sive, you are not to blame, I know that now. At first I just wanted to blame anyone, you, the banks, Brexit, take your pick. The hardest part was admitting to myself that I had failed, I had let myself down.'

'But you did the best you could Dan.'

'But I should have told you, I should have told you that I was sick before. You had a right to know. And I lied to you about our house. I can't forgive myself for that. Not yet. I signed away our home and tricked you to do it, too.'

'You were desperate, I suppose,' Sive said, a little more calmly.

'It's not an excuse, it was wrong in every way. I should have told you the truth about everything.'

'I know now you were just trying to protect me, but you don't need to protect me Dan, I'm your wife, not a child.'

'I know, that was my mistake, not trusting you.'

'When are you discharged?'

'In a few days, it will give me time to come to terms with everything.'

'So, that's it, you are not coming home with me,' Sive replied matter of factly.

'Please forgive me,' he replied, tears now in his own eyes. She was bewildered, what was he trying to say to her? Then she noticed the fear in his face. He looked like he could crumble at any time. Whatever was going on she knew she couldn't press him for any answers. Truth was he had no answers. He was just struggling to be. She wanted to walk out the door and bang it loudly, but she could see he was struggling for his life. Her heart broke as she watched her handsome, charismatic, full of life husband crumble into heart wrenching sobs.

'I am so sorry Sive, you don't deserve this. For what it's worth, I know I still love you, after that I just don't know,' he said softly.

'Okay, Dan. Do what you must do.' She put her arms around him and they held each other for a long time, gaining strength from just being together. Sive realised how far he still had to go to really recover. It was enough for now. She hugged him and finally, with her heart breaking, she walked away and closed the door.

As she was walking down the corridor, the psychiatrist that was looking after Dan was walking up. She stopped in recognition. Sive was barely holding herself together.

'Are you okay?' Sive shook her head. The psychiatrist pointed to two seats in a corner.

'Here, sit for a moment.' Sive filled her in on the latest with Dan.

'He must accept eventually that his old life is over, but he has had such a dramatic change to his life path he is bound to struggle with the next step. Perhaps he just needs time to adjust.' Jim's words came back to Sive. *'Just give it time'.* Perhaps she thought she was asking way too much. She knew she had to step back and allow Dan to heal.

It was a lonely drive back to Avara. She had put so much thought into how things would go when Dan was released from hospital, but she had never thought that he would not be coming home to her. Well, that was it. She could not see into the future. Her mind was racing with confusion, anger and pure sorrow. But she knew she would not fall apart. Whatever was to be, would be, and this terrible feeling would pass.

Avara came into sight. Sive stopped off at the pier and went for a walk to clear her head. The darkness of winter was lifting. Spring was on its way, the sea air lifting her spirits. Afterwards she went home, it was good to be back at the house. It felt like a warm cosy blanket around her, protecting her. After a coffee, she took herself outside, the garden was starting to take shape, the first of the daffodils were up, their yellow flowers giving a burst of spring to the garden. She picked a few of the best ones and went back inside and made a small bouquet of them. Without thinking much about it she decided to bring them up to Jim. She knew he would love them and she wanted him to see the first ones.

Driving up to the nursing home, she thought about how important Jim had become to her. She knew the code now to the home. Marjorie was deep in conversation with a relative when she arrived. She said hello and Sive went to walk down to see Jim.

'Sive hold on there for a minute.' The owner excused herself from the relative.

'Sive, I was just about to ring you. It's Jim, I'm afraid he took a turn, he is very ill.'

Chapter 39

The Meeting at the Golden Gate
Giotta. Capella degli Scrovegni, Padau, Italy.

'Is it ok to come in?' Sive asked.

'Of course, I'm just finished.' The nurse checked her chart and left. Jim was propped up in bed. He smiled when he saw Sive, arms full of daffodils.

'You remembered, how very kind of you.' Sive arranged the daffodils in a vase and put them on his dresser beside his precious photographs.

'What is it about daffodils, Sive? You plant them in the late autumn and almost forget them until the earth throws up the precious flowers in the spring, giving you a new-found hope from the brown earth. And the yellow is the deepest kind, it signals life beginning again,' he said.

'How are you Jim?' Sive was taken aback by how much the turn had taken out of him. He looked very shaken, and a sudden fear for him grabbed Sive.

'To be honest Sive, somehow I feel my time is soon.' Sive grabbed his hand. Even though he looked shaken, he looked at peace. She could feel the emotion grabbing her and prayed she would not cry.

'Don't be sad for me Sive, to be honest I am ready to leave soon. There is a time to live and a time to die. And my time is coming. The natural cycle of life. I am not afraid, and my dearest wife will be waiting for me. These past few months have been so rich since you have come in to my life. You have made an old man very happy. At first, I wondered how long I could live in here, because silently my heart was broken when Gretta passed. But when you are at your lowest, God sends something to help you through it, and I believe Sive he sent you. You have brought great joy in here and not only to me.' Sive could feel her voice become choked. When Monica had said he had had a turn she never said he was this bad. She realised how much she had come to care for Jim and the thought of losing him was crushing her.

'I'm not ready to let you go Jim,' Sive said softly.

'Yes, you are Sive, you are so much stronger than you sometimes realise. But you have something much deeper than strength to carry you through. There is a great depth to you Sive, life may throw many things at you but because you handle them with courage and integrity, you will always come shining through. Promise me you will start believing in yourself Sive, because once you are true to yourself, everything else will slot into place.' Sive couldn't help it, the hot salt tears were coming down her face. She had not slept much the previous night and suddenly she felt exhausted. She put her head down beside the bed and Jim touched her hair. She stayed in that position, savouring what she knew may be one of the last moments with her precious friend. She must have fallen asleep. When she awoke, her head hurt from falling asleep in that position. She straightened herself up. The evening was after drawing in. She got up to pull the curtains and put on the bedside lamp. She looked at Jim, who was in the deepest of a sleep. She kissed his forehead, tidied the room a little and left. The other patients were in the day room. Elizabeth was sitting on her own. Sive went up to her.

'Are you ok, Elizabeth?' Elizabeth searched Sive's face as if for answers, her eyes distant and lost.

'Who are you?' There was no acknowledgement of Sive, just a fear in Elizabeth's voice that was palpable.

'It's me. Sive. There is no need to be afraid.' Elizabeth wrapped her cardigan tighter around her and gently rocked to and fro.

'Elizabeth's not herself today, Sive,' Amy, who was one of the carers, added. Sive looked at the frail little lady, her hair white like snow and as soft as a baby's. She tried to imagine her young and dancing in the dance halls of long ago. It was easy to forget that all the patients were young once, that they had had agile bodies that didn't need care every day. They had loved and lived as much as anyone. Elizabeth was now staring into space. Sive liked to think she was back in her youth, with her hair flowing, in a beautiful dress, her pearls around her neck, her face full of laughter as she became the dancing queen.

A couple of hours passed and she realised how long she had spent in the nursing home. It was strange but she was happy there. She got so much back from talking to the people. Marjorie didn't mind her being there anymore, happy that she wasn't the health inspector doing some undercover reporting. She got a cup of tea and was about to head for home when Marjorie came down to her; her perfume and the scent of hairspray always signalled her arrival.

'Sive, can I speak with you?' Sive wondered was she going to tell her to go, she had been there so long.

'Sive, it's Jim. I'm afraid the nurse has called me on the intercom. Jim has got much weaker. He's dying, Sive. Would you like to go and see him, I just thought I would ask you, as you are still here. Jim has no immediate family to call,' she said.

Sive knew she must be used to death, people mostly stayed here until they died. It was a waiting game really. Jim had been right, and his time had come. She wondered how it must affect the other patients, being so close to people dying. She wanted to protect them from feeling frightened, feeling alone.

'Thank you, yes I would like to go back in if that's ok,' she replied quietly.

'They are just making him more comfortable. Finish your tea, I will call you in a few minutes.'

As he slipped into a much deeper sleep, Sive held his hand. She did not want to leave him. She read his poetry to him. After a few heavy breaths, a serene look came over his face. Perhaps it was Gretta coming to meet him, Sive liked to think that it was. She closed her eyes and imagined his hand, his joining hers forever on their journey, never to be broken.

Jim took his last breath and was gone.

Chapter 40

Sunflowers
Vincent van Gogh. National Gallery, London.

Everything looked the same as it did since morning. Everything was the same except that Jim was dead. Even though he had never been in the house when she was there, since she had known him the memories of him and Gretta were instilled in the house. It was as if the house held his memory and knew he was gone. She tried to imagine Jim and Gretta living there. She imagined them both reading by the fire, sipping tea from china cups while the dogs gently snored on the mat. Perhaps they would have discussed the poetry they were reading or the state of the government. They would have had many friends over for lively discussions about the war and Ireland's past. There would have been laughter and song. There had also been sadness and heartbreak. Jim had told her how they had longed for a child but alas, it was only them.

'*The cottage helped somehow, when Gretta was at her lowest, she retreated into the cottage and somehow it helped her.*' Jim had told Sive. But most of all there had been love, a love so pure it would last beyond death. The memory of their love would remain within the clay walls of the house protecting it. Sive felt privileged to be living in it.

Suddenly, a thought struck her, what would happen now? She had a lease agreement with the landlord, that being Jim, but what happened now he was dead? She felt cold suddenly. She couldn't think of losing her home. Once in twelve months was enough. She may not own it but it felt as much like home as any house ever could.

Jim was gone, her friend that had meant so much to her in such a short space of time. For the first time since she moved into the house she felt lonely. But she was alone, except for the quiet of the night and the soft hum of a distant car, she was alone.

In work the next morning she couldn't concentrate, all she could think about was Jim.

'I asked for a green tea, not a coffee, and is there any sign of my organic porridge, I ordered it with my tea?' the customer huffed at Sive. Sive apologised and went about fixing the order. Her mind was all over the place. Kaitlin arrived and on hearing about Jim insisted that Sive take the day off.

'I owe you a couple of days anyway, and now is as good a time as any.'

'Thanks, my head is all over the place,' Sive replied.

'You need to look after yourself Sive, you have been through a lot this last few months, worrying about everyone else, don't forget about yourself,' Kaitlin replied.

'Thanks for caring Kaitlin, it means a lot.' As she was about to head for home, the nursing home rang, it was Marjorie.

'Sive, I have just been informed that Jim has requested that you organise the funeral, it's by his solicitor's request.' Sive was as shocked as Marjorie sounded to be. She agreed to call up in a couple of hours to discuss it.

Marjorie was clearly not happy with this arrangement. Sive wondered why Jim had asked her, he must have requested it recently. He probably knew that if it was left to Marjorie it would be done and dusted with as little thought as possible.

Beth called to the house when Sive was just getting changed.

'Beth come on in, I will be with you in a minute,' Sive shouted to her from the bedroom.

'I'm so sorry to hear about Jim, I know he meant a great deal to you.' Beth had met him at a carol service in the nursing home Sive had organised over Christmas. They had had a lovely evening in the home with mulled wine, mince pies and lots of beautiful singing. Jim was quite the baritone and had given a beautiful rendition of White Christmas. Sive appeared looking a little paler than usual.

'Not much sleep for you last night by the look on your face, come on, I will make you a coffee.' While they were having their coffee, Sive looked out into the garden.

'Look Beth, Jim's daffodils, they all seem to have come into bloom since yesterday.' The garden looked like a light had been switched on, with the soft yellows of the flowers blending together into a collage of sunshine.

'I know it may seem silly, but it feels like a sign,' Sive said softly.

'It's not silly at all Sive, and I am sure if Jim could send a sign he would be quite happy with one as glorious looking as a host of daffodils.' They sat for a while and chatted. Not for the first time, Sive was very grateful to have Beth. Yes, she had felt terribly lonely the night before, but today, she was deeply saddened to realise that Jim was gone, but she also felt very lucky to have met him, and somehow the raw isolation she had felt the night before had passed. She decided to confide in Beth about Dan's latest revelation.

'Dan is not coming home. Well he is leaving the hospital. But he needs some time out.'

'What, are you serious?'

'Very, him and Tom are going to rent an apartment in Wicklow town. Tom is going to stay with him to help him recuperate,' Sive said.

'Oh Sive, how do you feel about it? What does it mean?' Beth asked, astonished.

'I don't know, really. Are we splitting up? I don't know. Part of me is angry with him and the other feels numb. He is not well I know that, he still has a long way to go. Maybe this is it, the beginning of the end. I suppose it hasn't really sunk in.'

'How do feel about him, do you still love him?' Beth asked gently.

'I love what we had, but if I am not who he wants when he is sick, what does that say about us? Yes, I love him. But that doesn't mean we have a marriage.' Sive replied sadly.

'You were so happy Sive, maybe you can be again.' Beth replied wistfully.

'Time will tell.' They chatted for a little while and then Beth went off. Sive left the cottage and headed for the nursing home. When she got there, the solicitor had just arrived.

'Are you Sive?'

'Yes.'

'I am Jim's solicitor, Billy Doyle.'

'Oh, pleased to meet you, I understand Jim has asked me to organise the funeral.'

'Yes, there is an ample budget provided for what he would like,' he stated.

'I see.'

'I have left all the details with the nursing home. They will inform you and send the invoices to my office.' He gave her a card.

'Thank you,' Sive replied.

'Could you also meet me in my office in town next Thursday? I will have a reading about Jim's will,' he asked.

'Really, I don't think I have any place in being there,' Sive said, surprised.

'Well your name is mentioned,' he replied, looking up over his glasses at her.

'Oh, why?' Sive asked confused.

'I am not at liberty to discuss it here, if you could meet me at my office please.'

'Okay then.' Sive agreed to go in. Another visit to a solicitor's office. Maybe she could chat to him about the house. Her lease should hold for at least the length agreed.

Marjorie didn't look very happy about the fact that Sive was to be in attendance of the will reading. She informed Sive that Jim was now in the morgue. Sive asked her if she could visit Jim's room. With bad grace, she said yes. She was taken aback when she walked in. There was so sign Jim had ever been there, and two cleaners were giving it a good going over. The bed was freshly made, the dresser had none of Jim's beloved photographs and his precious books were all piled into a big plastic box. How quickly life goes on Sive thought, with a can of Mr Sheen and a few boxes, all memories of Jim had been moved out. She touched the bed, trying to imagine Jim there, but he was gone, all trace of him. It was as if he had never been there. She had tried to imagine his presence, his silver-grey hair, his elegant voice, but it was gone.

'Where are all his belongings going?' she asked the cleaners. They shrugged their shoulders.

'Depends what Marjorie says.' Sive made a mental note to ask her. She didn't want his beautiful books and photographs being thrown out. She walked down to the day room. She said hello to all and sat beside Elizabeth. There was no more dancing. Sive brushed her white silky hair with the pearl brush that Elizabeth kept on her lap. It seemed to soothe her. She brushed it as gently as she would a two-year-old. It was strange how childlike the aged can become in their remaining days. Elizabeth was barely aware she was there. She went in search of Marjorie before she left.

'Well I better give you the note from the solicitor.'

'Yes, I was very shocked to be honest.' Marjorie looked at her and Sive could see annoyance spread across her face, but quickly she recovered.

'Ok these are the instructions from the solicitor.' She almost threw them at Sive.

'Thank you, I will have a read through and see what I can do,' Sive replied.

'Very well, will you be up for your art workshop on Friday?' Marjorie asked.

'Of course, I am looking forward to. I will be in touch as soon as I look at this. By the way, what's happening with Jim's belongings from the room?' Sive enquired cautiously.

'I have no idea, hopefully they are mentioned in the will, if not the charity shop most probably.'

'Do you mind if I take a photograph and a poetry book. If anyone is looking for them I will return them.'

'Suit yourself, they are down in the room still, there is nobody to take them.' Sive went back down. She felt like she was almost disrespecting Jim, going through his stuff. She found the photograph and his precious poetry book. She left the rest, for whatever they might do with them. With his precious stuff tucked safely under her arm, she left the home to arrange Jim's funeral.

Chapter 41

The Pillars of Society
George Grosz. Nationalgalerie, Berlin, Germany

Mrs Gallagher had not taken the news very well that Dan and Tom were both moving into an apartment in town for a while.

'What on earth would you do that for? I do believe I am hearing things. What about Sive, has he forgotten he is married? And as for you, what about the farm? Have you both lost your mind?'

'No mother I have not lost my mind, and thankfully Dan hasn't either. He is still trying to get himself together and he needs a bit of space on his own to get his head right, and I am going to look after him until he is well.'

'Well there is a lot more space in Thornback if SPACE is what he needs, he is hardly going to get that in town is he?'

'Mother, stop!' Tom demanded.

'What? This is ridiculous, he has a wife to look after him and a home here, if he doesn't want to go to that cottage, I can understand. They can both come here, I have the room arranged. We will all be here to look after him, give him time to recuperate. He can have all the space he wants in Thornback. We can just tell everyone he was too physically weak for Sive to manage alone, so they are moving home to Thornback for a while,' she added.

'It's nothing to do with the cottage, he needs time away from everything and everyone.' Tom implored.

'Don't be ridiculous, he needs his family around him. Once he is home I know he will be as good as new in no time.'

'Can you both stop talking about me as if I am not here?' Dan said, his voice raised.

'And what about Sive, how come she is not moving into this, this flat in town?' She said the word flat with distaste.

'Dan has asked me and if this is what he wants then I am only too happy to help.'

'And what about the farm, who is going to keep an eye on things when you are sitting off in a flat in town, may I ask you? Or perhaps you have some fancy answer for that, too? Why don't we all take a holiday in town and get a flat, stay in flatland on our summer holidays?' she said with a note of sarcasm.

'You are being ridiculous, Mother.' Tom said irritated.

'I want to know how you will manage the farm?'

'I will come and go from the apartment, and I will hire on some farm relief hands as I need too.' It was all a bit too much for Mrs Gallagher.

'I have no idea what I am going to tell anyone, how do I explain you are both camping out in a flat in town.' Dan got up from the chair he was resting on and turned towards his mother.

'First, it is an apartment, not a flat, and I have no idea, nor do I care, what you tell anyone. Say whatever you have to, Mother, but this is what is happening, I am moving in this evening.'

'Dan, see sense will you, for goodness sake you know it is best if you come home, I can look after you.' Dan shook his head in frustration and paced up and down the room with the aid of a crutch. Then he turned towards his mother and spoke, his voice full of bitterness.

'Like you did when I was sixteen? You made sure you knew what was best for me then.' Tom looked from his Mother to Dan. He sensed the change in the atmosphere. This was the first time Dan had not stopped his mother from visiting since before Christmas and it was not going well.

'What do you mean, Dan? Do you mean when you were sick and you had glandular fever?' Tom asked confused.

'That's right Tom, the glandular fever. That is what I had, wasn't it Mother?' Mrs Gallagher looked like she had been slapped in the face. There was a silence that was tangible.

'What's going on, are you okay, Mam?' Tom asked, looking from his mother to Dan.

'Do you want to tell him?' Dan spat at her. Tom looked at his mother. The anguish on her face was evident.

'Will someone tell me what the hell is going on?'

'Tell him Mam, because I will if you won't.'

'Leave it Dan, leave it in the past,' she begged.

'That's the problem just because it happened in the past it doesn't mean I have forgotten it.'

'Will someone please tell me what the hell is going on?' Dan looked at his brother.

'Fine I will tell him, he has a right to know what the hell was going on at Thornback over twenty years ago. Dan, I never had glandular fever, I took a load of pills and almost died. I planned it. I took a load of sleeping pills that Mam had and took them all at once. Dad found me just in time in the barn. You were away at boarding school. But mother decided to keep it a secret and lie about it and tell everyone I had glandular fever.' Mrs Gallagher gave a little cry as if she was wounded. Tom looked at her.

'Is this true?'

She shook her head in despair.

'Is it true, Mam?'

'Tell him, tell him the truth,' Dan replied, his voice raised. Tell him how you brought me to England to a hospital, God forbid anyone find out the truth. Tom shut the door.'

Mrs Gallagher was visibly shaking, all the fight had suddenly gone out of her.

'Why for God's sake, why?' Tom shouted.

'Shame, that's why Tom. SHAME. She was ashamed to tell anyone so she lied and made me keep it a secret all these years. Even from you. She thought it would go away and it did for a while but it came back and almost killed me.' He was shouting now and Mrs Gallagher had tears flowing down her face.

'I am done with feeling ashamed. Stay out of my life if you still feel ashamed of me, I am dead to you if you cannot accept who I am,' Dan said to her. Mrs Gallagher was inconsolable.

'I thought it was for the best.'

'For the best, just like now. Get out, Mam. Please bring her home Tom. Now you know.'

'But I wanted you to have a fresh start without what happened hanging over you.'

'You wanted to erase it, like it had never happened. But it did. That's the bloody problem. You thought by shoving me into some hospital in England and not telling anyone, that when I came home, we could pretend it never happened. Well, get it into your head. It did happen. I was sixteen for Christ's sake. You landed me with a life time of shame so you could save face. Oh, nothing like that could happen to the Gallaghers of Thornback Farm. But it did.'

'I am sorry Dan, please, I thought it was for the best,' Mrs Gallagher implored.

'I do believe you did, but I have no idea why. I am not blaming you for my financial disaster, that was all my own doing, but the past crept up on me. I was that boy again, so ashamed of my failings. I can't go on anymore, thinking like that.'

'Mam, I think you better leave, I will take you home.' Tom said. He looked like he had aged within the last few minutes. He turned to his brother.

'I am sorry, bro, I wish I had known, all these years and I never knew.' His voice full of emotion.

'You couldn't have known Tom. But I am glad you do now.' Mrs Gallagher was crumbling. As she walked out the door, Dan looked away.

'I am sorry Dan,' she cried. He wanted to say it was ok but he wasn't ready to. Perhaps in time he could, but not now.

'Dan, I thought I was doing the best I could.'

'So, in some strange way, you thought you were protecting me, not allowing people to know. But times are different Mam. It's not the 1950s anymore.'

'I am sorry, Dan, I truly am. Forgive me both of you.'

'Look mam I think I will bring you home, there has been enough revelations for anyone here today.' Tom said.

'For what it's worth Dan. Your father thought I was wrong when I told everyone you had glandular fever. Don't blame him. I do like to get my way.' Dan couldn't hide a grin.

'Well we won't argue with that. Thanks for telling us.' Tom replied.

'I will be back down in the afternoon when you are discharged,' Tom added.

'Thanks, Tom.'

'Goodbye Dan, please know how much I care about you,' Mrs Gallagher said, her voice choking.

Dan nodded to his mother. It was all too raw to say anything more. Tom brought her out.

Dan felt odd about leaving. He reckoned that this is what they meant by becoming institutionalised. He had hated the hospital so much but now he almost felt afraid about leaving. He was so glad he had Tom. He felt terrible about not going to Sive, but he knew if they had any chance of being together, he had to face his demons first and come to terms with the past. He packed up his belongings and got dressed into the clothes Tom had bought for him. He had lost so much weight nothing he owned fitted him. It was strange to be in ordinary clothes, he had spent so long in bed clothes.

A few hours passed and Tom arrived back in to collect him.

'Ready to go little bro?' Tom asked with a grin.

'You bet.' Tom tried not to stare as he watched his brother's weak frame cross the room. He really was a shadow of the man he had been.

His bag was packed and the nurse saw him off. Tom could see him falter at the door of the hospital, as if leaving it and going back to the real world was just too much. His face became whiter, Tom said nothing but never left his side.

They spoke very little on the way into town. The apartment block was in a nice area in the town. Tom had left the heating on so it was warm when they arrived in. He showed Dan his room and around the apartment and set about making some tea. It was more apparent when Dan had left the hospital that he was still very weak.

'I think I will lie down for a while,' Dan said.

'Grand, I will drop a cup of tea in to you. By the way I have something for you.'

'What is it?' Tom showed him some documents.

'It's the deeds of the land. Myself and Dad bought the land you lost back in your name. It's done and dusted. I hope you don't mind.' Dan could feel the emotion building but he couldn't find the words to express it.

'It's okay, Dan. I just wish I was there for you years ago, it's killing me knowing what you were going through and me never knowing.'

'It's not your fault. I know she thought she was doing the right thing, but it was so the wrong thing. She saddled me with a life time of shame that I am now only coming to terms with. But as I said, no more.' Tom gave him a bear hug.

'Maybe I had to fall apart again to fully heal from the first time. It's like when you break a bone if it's not fixed properly it can set wrong, it almost has to be broken again, to set properly, I think my mind is a bit like that.' Tom handed him a cup of tea.

'Well, here's to no more broken bones or minds.'

Chapter 42

The Sistine Madonna
Gemaldegalerie Alte Meister, Dresden.

Beth had plans of her own today. She had the day off but she decided to drive to Dublin. She had made this journey for many years now and always alone. For eighteen years, she had driven to the cemetery her son was buried in without going in. Sometimes were worse than others but today she felt a little lighter, like the burden had healed slightly. She wanted to visit her son's grave. It was raining on the way up but when she got to Glasnevin, the sun came out. In the distance was the beginning of a rainbow. She smiled, perhaps it was a gift. She had even driven there a few months ago, but failed to go in. Today, somehow, the fear had left her. Perhaps it was the fact that she had talked about it. Bottling it all up for so long had made it more difficult to deal with.

She knew where the angels plot was from the day he was buried there. She could almost trace the steps she took on that day. It came back to her now as if it was only yesterday, the air was still now, and the sun was shining strong as it often did in spring. She could hear the sing song of the birds, as if they were singing that they were alive and well despite where they were.

He would be eighteen today, officially an adult. She wondered how he would have looked. She imagined him tall like her, with blue eyes and smiling. She would have loved him so much, he would never have felt alone in the world like she had. He could have become whatever he dreamed he wanted to be. Today she would have thrown a party and they would have laughed well into the night.

'Happy birthday sweet son, I hope you are happy wherever you are.' She could feel the hot tears down her face. But somehow, they were more of a comfort now. The pain of loss was still there, but it was less buried now, her pain could almost breathe. She sat there for a long time, her eyes closed, thinking of what might have been. The life they might have led. How wonderful it would have been to have him in her life. She had been so angry for years, angry with God for taking him, what had she done to deserve the heartache? But now she had no more anger left. She just needed some peace, peace for both. Eventually the sun had gone in and a soft mist covered the graveyard.

'I have to say good bye now pet, I have to go and live. It breaks my heart to leave you but for whatever God's reason was to leave me here and to take you, I must accept it now. And I must let you go and allow you to be in peace. You will be forever in my heart my little baby but for now, I have to live.'

She took a piece of paper out of her bag. It was a little poem she had written to help her in those first few dark days. Through her tears, she read it now and whispered it into the wind.

'Your tiny hands never to hold mine,
My kiss never to take away your pain,
Your smile never to meet mine.
I imagine you in my heart,
Your thoughts and dreams meeting mine in the night sky.
On your journey, gentle child,
The angels will illuminate your way.
Memories none were made,
Torn and stolen from us,
My tears, I feel your angel hands whisper them away.
White light shines from that same night sky,
Shining light, I beg, gather me in your arms and carry me away.'

She was a solitary figure walking back to her car, her camel coat wrapped tight around her, and her long red hair trailing over it. She got into the car and drove towards town. After a while she got a space and found herself in St. Stephen's Green. Of course she had been here before, but somehow, she could feel herself not as broken, perhaps she was mending slightly. It was good just to sit and watch the world go by. There were lots of children out in prams. So many times, the sight of a pram had almost broken her heart, but today she was fine. She knew she was stronger. Perhaps this is what they mean about letting go.

An hour passed before she got up and walked back towards the car; there was one other place she would go today. She knew Rose would be there. Rose was always there on this date, they had their own little ritual that had got Beth through the darkest of days. At times, it was the only thing that had kept her going to know she could cry and mourn her loss with her true friend.

But today she felt better than any other visit. She stopped and bought a big bunch of roses for her friend. Reds, oranges and yellows all tied together in a glorious bunch of colour. Rose welcomed her with open arms and sat her at the kitchen table. She gratefully had some home-made soup and brown bread in the cosiness of Rose's kitchen.

'Can you believe its eighteen years?' Beth asked.

'In ways, it seems like yesterday. You seem stronger than I thought you would be, I'm glad for you,' Rose replied.

They both lit a candle then, it wasn't meant to be for any religious meaning, but just watching the flicker in silence together was to signify that there was once a life. After some tea and cake, they sat by the kitchen table for two hours chatting about life and their friendship. Beth looked at Rose, she was as vibrant as she ever was, her white blonde hair piled high on her head and her signature red nails and lips. And not for the first time did she thank the heavens for bringing her to Rose's house that first night back in college. She knew she had come a long way from that frightened country girl that had nowhere to turn. Rose had been instrumental in helping her in so many ways. It was strange to think that her own mother had no idea of what had happened. In ways, she was like a stranger to her mother, just some sort of moral duty she felt that brought her down to her home place a few times a year. And as for her brother!

She had found a small house in the village for rent and Mary and the girls were arriving shortly. Mary had come up to visit the schools. It had taken a lot of bravery to leave her husband. He was begging her to come back, but Mary was determined. Maybe she had to leave for him to realise what he had to lose. But Beth felt it was too late for her brother. She hoped the girls would be okay. She would help them settle in. Her mobile rang just as she was going into her apartment, it was Dan. She wondered why on earth he was calling her.

'Hi Beth, I just wondered how Sive was doing, I hope you don't mind me ringing you, but I am worried about her.' Beth was taken aback, what could she say? She certainly did not want to become some go between with Dan and Sive.

'She's okay, Dan,' Beth said lightly.

'Thanks, Beth. I won't make a habit of ringing you, I was just worrying a lot.'

'Okay Dan, take care.' Beth hung up. She felt like asking him why didn't he ring his wife himself, but thought better of it. Still, at least he was worried about her, she knew Sive still cared deeply for Dan despite everything that had happened. Who knew where their future lay?

Chapter 43

The Artist's Studio
Jan Vermeer. Kunsthictorisches Museum, Vienna, Austria.

The ceremony was just as Jim had wished. The beautiful photograph of him and his wife that had brought Sive to him that first afternoon sat on the altar. There were readings from his favourite authors, Kipling and Yeats. A woman with a harp played a melody from the balcony that sounded like an angel. A good friend of his gave a eulogy that brought laughter and smiles to those who had known Jim the best.

'He was the most interesting man I have ever known,' was his first line and this Sive thought summed him up extremely well. It was a celebration of his life and Sive knew he would be happy. Afterwards she invited some of his friends back to the cottage where they feasted on beautiful platters of salads, salmon, cold meats and crusty breads. They toasted his life with hot punch and there was more poetry, readings and even a few songs. She had filled the house with daffodils and the stories continued into the late evening. Sive felt he would have approved.

The next day she visited the nursing home and brought up cakes and buns for the patients to have with their evening tea as she told them all about the ceremony. They shared their own stories and they finished the evening with singing one of Jim's favourite songs, *the Isle of Innisfree*. One of the patients who was always very quiet and just sat with her book looked up at Sive with a face full of concern.

'You won't forget about us now will you, now that Jim is gone, it's just that lots of people forget you when you come in here, it's as if your life is over already.' Sive could feel the sting of tears in her eyes, and she went over to the frail woman, her white silver hair held back with some clips, and took her hand.

'Of course, I won't forget you, I promise. And we have our art class tomorrow too, I am so looking forward to it.' She held her hand for a little longer until she knew she was reassured enough to know that no, she would not be forgotten.

The next day was the day of the will reading and as requested she was there. She thought she must be early as there was no one else there. The solicitor had a twinkle in his eye that brought instant youth to his face.

'Sit, sit, I have to sort out a few of these letters.' After much shuffling and searching for stuff he finally sat down and looked across at Sive over his glasses.

'Jim asked me to draw up a new will a few weeks ago. He was in sound mind and we had this written in the presence of a doctor.' Sive had barely slept the night before, worrying if the new owner of the cottage would want to keep it or would they sell it. The agreement she had with the estate agent was only while Jim was alive. If he had willed it to someone who wanted to keep it she would have to leave. Life could hardly be so cruel as to lose her second home within a year.

'Oh, but why is nobody else here, I know he had no family but surely there are other people meant to be here.' Sive had no idea what was going on.

'I am the executor of the will and his solicitor. My dear, Jim has left the cottage to you. And any contents that are in it.' Sive stared back at him. Had she misheard him? She was worried he was going to tell her she had to get out, and now he was telling her this. It took a few minutes to sink in.

'Are you sure? My God, I never expected anything from Jim.'

'Jim was a very good judge of character, I knew him a long time. He knew you never wanted anything from him and I suspect that is why he has left it to you. You brought great joy to him in these past few months.'

'I don't know what to say, my goodness.' Suddenly Sive was overcome. Jim. To think of doing this for her, she never imagined it. She wished she had known when he was alive, then she could have thanked him properly.

'He also has a few requests for you. As you know he was a great supporter of literature and Irish culture. He has left a substantial amount of money for a centre to be started in Avara promoting Irish craft, literature and art. He also owns a lovely property in the middle of town which would house it. It is quite an old building that has been renovated so it should be very suitable. He has quite a large sum of money set aside for it which should be ample. He wants you to be a director for it and to basically start a board of management to set it up. He has quite a few friends who would volunteer for the good of the community to get it up and running. He has also requested that if you wish, there should be an artist's studio for you in it.' Sive sat, aware that she must have her mouth opened, she was so shocked.

'I take it you will be happy to accept the cottage, and what about the plans he has?'

'I would be honoured to do something like that. And as for the house, you have no idea how much this means to me.'

'Very well, it is a lot to take in so perhaps we can reconvene in a few days to begin the paperwork, deeds etc.' Sive got up and shook his hand.

'Thank you. I am overwhelmed by Jim's generosity.'

'He was a good man, and I was lucky to have him as a friend for many years.'

Walking out of the solicitor's office, the irony of it wasn't lost on Sive. Not even six months ago she had walked out of another law office to be told her home was being taken from her. She never would have believed this could happen. She had almost come full circle.

Later, in the garden, sitting with a coffee in hand, it started to sink in. The garden was starting to take on the bloom of spring, buds bursting into colour. The scent of gardenia was almost seductive. There was a gentle breeze whistling through the hazel trees. Sive felt she was in her haven. And amongst the bird song and the whisper of the wind she thanked Jim from the bottom of her heart.

*

The next morning the phone woke her up. It was her dad and she realised she had told nobody about her good fortune, it was like a most precious secret that she wanted to nurture and keep safe. After the usual hellos, she told her father.

'That was so generous of him, you meant a great deal to him.'

'Oh, Dad it's so wonderful, to be honest you are the first I have told.'

'Well, I have a bit of news too love, but it's good too, well I hope you think it is.' He was hesitant on the phone at first and then he just blurted it out.

'It's me and Ruby, we are getting married.'

Sive broke into a big smile.

'Dad, I am thrilled for you, and Ruby is lovely, of course this is good news, it's fantastic news.' They chatted for a while longer and then they said their good byes. Her dad would come up shortly with Ruby and they would celebrate properly. Sive knew she was genuinely delighted for her father, of course she thought of her mother, but deep down she knew, her mother loved her father so much she would approve. She would not want him entering old age on his own. If he had the chance of happiness he should grab it with both hands. She was also aware that he had avoided any relationships when she was younger and to be fair, she probably would have handled it badly if he had remarried. She was so raw after her mother died, and for so long. Now she knew she still had healing to do about her mother's death, but at least she knew what that deep sadness she often carried around was now, it was the emptiness she felt at the loss of her mother at such a young age. She had tried to hide it, but it had been only patching it over.

There was so much to think about, the house, the centre, an art studio of her own. Her mind was racing, so she went where she knew she could settle her mind. She began a painting. It was of the garden, she wanted to capture it now in its spring beauty, so that in the quiet of winter, when only the silver birch, like the lady of the woods was clothed, she could remind herself how beautiful it would be when the winter cloak was lifted.

It was almost lunchtime and she was about to break to make something to eat when the doorbell rang. It was Beth.

'You look fantastic Beth, there is almost a glow about you,' Sive remarked.

'Really! Must be the new beauty salon I discovered, they do this amazing facial.' Sive studied her.

'Maybe. You look different, younger somehow, come in and we will have a cuppa.' Sive brought her in and put the kettle on and was about to fill her in on all the news when the doorbell rang again.

'Probably the postman, back in a jiffy.' But it wasn't the postman, it was Dan standing in the doorway, looking thin and pale with Tom standing beside him. Sive was too shocked to speak, it was so strange to be answering the door to her husband.

'Can we come in?' Tom asked. Sive was stuck for words. Beth was up beside her.

'Are you ok Sive?' Sive tried to gather herself. Part of her felt like shutting the door. She couldn't deal with any more turmoil with Dan. Her heart was worn out with him. But looking at his face, she couldn't deny how much she still cared about him. It would be so much easier if she didn't.

'Sive, can I come in?' Dan whispered. Sive opened the door to allow him in.

They stood in the small hall for a few seconds with nobody knowing what to say.

'Look Sive, I hope you don't mind us calling in on you without ringing first?' Tom said, apologising. Sive had got over the shock.

'No, it's ok, come in to the kitchen.' Sive watched as Tom walked over to stand beside Beth.

Beth began putting on her coat.

'Where are you going?' Sive asked.

'I am just popping out for something, I will be back soon, a quick run to the shops before they close.'

'Do you mind if I join you Beth, I need some…cornflakes?' Tom asked. If Beth was shocked at him asking, she didn't show it.

'No problem,' she replied and Sive was sure she caught Tom winking at Beth. Sive looked at them and was about to say something but they were gone out the door so fast she didn't get the chance. That left only her and Dan. A million different thoughts were going around her head. She went to the kitchen to fill the kettle.

'Avara is a quaint little village, it's years since I was here. We drove around for a little while trying to find the courage to come in. I can see why you love it. The sea, the old charm of the place, it's a bit of a gem,' Tom said. Sive wanted to say that she had tried to tell him that, but decided not to. What was the point? She tried to figure out why he was here. He hadn't even given her a phone call since he got out of hospital. She had enough of it all. If that was what he wanted she wouldn't fight it. What on earth would be the point? If he wanted out, he could have out of their marriage and her life. She wished it didn't tear at her heart to think of not having him. But if that was the way it was meant to be, that was just the way it would have to be. She would find out soon.

Chapter 44

In the Garden
Edouard Vuillard, Pushkin Museum of Fine Arts, Moscow.

'Look around while I make the tea.' It felt a little surreal for Dan to finally walk around the cottage he had heard so much about. It could not be more different than their former home. There were no high ceilings or sash windows, no receptions rooms or marble fireplaces. Instead the ceilings were quite low, with beams. He would have thought he would feel claustrophobic in such a small house but instead it felt cosy and homely. Everywhere in the style of the house he could see Sive's eye. The soft colours on the walls that were gentle on your mind, her beautiful art pieces discreetly displayed. The soft rugs and throws in velvets and soft wools. He walked out towards the kitchen.

'May I go into your garden?'

'Yes of course. Actually there is a really sunny spot just around the corner with some chairs and a table. If you leave your coat on we could have our tea there?' Sive replied. There was a herb garden that Sive had planted that was just coming into flower. Dan stopped to look at it. They were displayed in colourful pots with their own name tags. He could see rosemary, thyme, marjoram and a lovely scented plant labelled lemon verbena. The chairs were sheltered by a beautiful cherry blossom tree that was in full bloom with petals cascading around the area in a soft pink carpet. It truly was a heavenly little garden and Dan sat down and closed his eyes. He could feel himself relax. He had felt so anxious about coming here. Tom had wanted to ring first, but the truth was he wasn't sure he would go in. Sitting in this precious little garden now, he felt foolish for being so worried. So much had happened, he would not have blamed Sive if she didn't want to see him. He had spent so much time in the past few weeks worrying about the past, and trying to imagine his future. With the help of his therapist he was starting to try to just be in the present without spending all his time worrying about what had or could happen. Being in the present was refreshing. He had always spent so much of his life planning and thinking about the future that perhaps he had not enjoyed just being. He tried to look back to the man he was before the accident, but the truth was he hardly recognised him. For the first time in years his head was clear, he had begun to forgive himself for what had happened, and that was probably the most difficult. His mother had stopped telling people that he had a virus from the hospital or he had some bug. She had finally accepted what had happened. Dan knew that secretly it had helped him knowing his family accepted his illness for what it was, and slowly he could begin to heal. It had been a long journey and he still had a way to go but it at least he wanted to continue the road. The darkness was finally leaving him, but he was aware that he had to do lots to keep it from entering his life again.

Sive was taking forever to make the tea. Having Dan sitting in her garden was almost too much to take. Every emotion she ever had had been played out in the last year. She had been crushed when he had denied her seeing him. It had broken her heart. Watching him sink into the deep depression that he was in was so difficult to watch and not blame herself. Then for him not to want to be with her when he came out of hospital had been another blow that she had not expected. Yet here he was, sitting waiting for tea. She thought she might be angry yet she felt no anger at him. She was confused at how she felt towards him. Just to look at his physical self, it was clear he had been through so much, body and soul, that it was difficult to feel resentment towards him. It had been one of the most difficult times of her life, yet she felt stronger than she ever had. She had a clear vision of what direction her life was going in. She was so grateful for her art, it had brought her so much peace, and finding the cottage and Jim had turned her life around. Her father was happier than he had been since her mother died. She now knew that she had buried the grief of her mother for too long, and somehow through all the pain she had suffered since the accident it had given her time to think and grieve for her mother and finally be at peace with her death. Maybe that's why she had stopped hearing her mother. She had finally let her go.

Yet throughout everything she was glad Dan was here. It felt right that he should be here. With that thought she put two slices of fresh Victoria sponge cake on some old china plates belonging to her mother, and two china cups and saucers and a pot of tea on a tray. When she brought it over it brought a smile to Dan.

'Looks good Sive, even mother would approve of that cake, and china cups too,' he grinned.

'Can you remember her distaste when I gave her a mug of coffee in a chipped mug back in our first flat?'

'She almost had to be resuscitated,' Dan laughed, remembering.

'We have come a long way with our china cups,' Sive agreed, also breaking into a smile.

'You have come a long way Sive, I am so proud and glad for you, the cottage is charming and it's totally you. I love it. I feel at peace here somehow.'

'Yes, I do too, I feel like I have come home, I can't imagine not being here. If a house has a soul, this one is gentle and kind.' They sat in companionable quietness enjoying the tea and cake.

'This is delicious,' Dan said.

'Thanks. Lately when I need a break from painting, I bake.'

'Myself and Tom are going to work together. He bought the land back that I lost and gave me the deeds. We are going into organic vegetable growing.'

'Oh! what a lovely gesture, I am so glad Dan,' Sive said, genuinely delighted.

'I am going to ring your father to see if he can advise us. There is a new farmer's market starting in Avara, would you believe, so I am going to apply for a stall there for next year.'

'Watch out for the cult,' Sive grinned.

'Poor Mam, we have yet to tell her. She will surely be convinced that you put a bit of a spell on me. Tom is all for it, I think he has a lot of interest in Avara now,' he said with a wink. It took Sive a few minutes to get what he meant.

'Beth! Are they seeing each other?' Sive asked, surprised.

'I only saw them by chance having lunch in the town. They looked very cosy.'

'My goodness, Beth said nothing.'

'They probably decided not to say anything yet, under the circumstances.'

'Beth and Tom, what a wonderful couple they will make. Your mother will think I brainwashed him or something,' Sive said, smiling. 'I had a call from her recently.'

'Oh!' Dan replied.

'It's okay, it was fine. She said she just wanted to check I was okay. I was shocked but she is trying,' Sive added. They sat in silence for a while, Both lost in their own thoughts.

'Sive, if I have hurt you, I am truly sorry, you never deserved that, please forgive me.' Sive could see the strain in his face. His eyes crinkled up at the spring sunshine that was making an appearance.

'I was hurt Dan, but there is no one to blame. In a strange way, it was good for me. I had to stand on my own feet and figure out how I could go on. It took all the will power I had not to cave under and fall apart.'

'You were always strong Sive, you just never knew.'

'Maybe I was. But I depended on you too much Dan, I could never do that again with anyone. I am financially independent and I have my own path to follow. If the last year had never happened I would never have learned how valuable it is to have your own purpose without anyone else, no matter what relationship you are in.'

'You are still the love of my life Sive, you always will be.' Sive looked across at Dan. His eyes told the pain he had been through in the past year. He reached out and held her hand. Sive knew it felt right. Being here with him.

They could have talked about what they would do now, but all that did not seem important. It was just now that was important. That moment as they sat at peace together, in the pretty garden. As the breeze whispered in the wind and more petals fell like pink lace on their shoulders, Sive knew that life indeed was like lace, but with love, care and a little time life, like lace, can be mended.

Acknowlegdements

My childhood was steeped in listening to stories. They were told not from a book but from memory, stories and poems from long ago that will always remain in my heart. My late father Tommy was the most wonderful story teller I have ever known and I believe this instilled in me a love of words which were the stepping stones to my writing.

When I first told my sister Jane that I planned to write a novel, she never doubted that I would, but she also reminded me to enjoy the journey and think of who I might meet along the way. How often I have thought of her wise words. This journey into publishing was so much richer because of the kindness, friendship and comradery I have encountered

Sincere and heartfelt gratitude to all the team at Endeavour Press and especially Jasmin Kirkbride for making this book a reality and patiently answering all my mails and concerns and a special mention to the marketing department for such a gorgeous cover. My lovely agent Tracy Brennan from The Trace Literary Agency in the USA for her belief in me across the seas and who has become such a lovely friend through our constant mails. Tracy has worked so hard to help me on this road and I thank my lucky stars to have her in my life. To Carmel Harrington for being the most fabulous mentor and friend I could ever have wished for. I am in awe of the amazing generosity of your time and spirit not to mention your magic fairy dust. You are a true inspiration Carmel and I am so glad our paths have crossed. My comrades on the Wexford Literary Festival and my many writer friends throughout Ireland, I feel privileged to be amongst you. Suzanne Power and John MacKenna I am so indebted to you for giving me the seeds of hope and belief in my ability to write during my time at Maynooth Campus.

To my lovely mother Kathleen and all my family and extended family in Wexford, Wicklow, Waterford and beyond for helping in so many ways, I could not do this without you all. I am so very grateful for your support now and always.

Also to Trish, my forever friend and my other friends who have indulged me with talks about my writing. Thank you all so much for being in my life.

To my husband Shane whose support in this was immense, this novel was only possible with your unending time, patience, love and endless cups of tea. Thank you for buying me my first pink laptop and then spending an alarming amount of time trying to teach me how to use it. But you succeeded even though the odds were very much against you. Thank you so, so much for making this dream a reality.

My three children, Ben, Faye and Matthew who make me smile every day and have given me more than they will ever know. I thank you from the bottom of my heart for your constant love and support. I think too, there just may be another writer in the family in the future.

A special mention to Faye for all the chocolate pancakes.

Thank you so much for reading this book. I wrote *Mending Lace* because lace reminds me of life.

'Life like lace can get torn and broken, but it can be mended with patience, time and a little kindness.'

Sheila

Printed in Poland
by Amazon Fulfillment
Poland Sp. z o.o., Wrocław